Kasey Kiley

Skeleton Trail

Kasey Riley

DEDICATION

This book is dedicated to my fans and friends who enjoyed DESPERATE ENDURNANCE enough to request that more stories of Riverview be told. Riding in the woods last spring, I rode on an eroding trail along a creek and next to it was an old tree that had fallen over during the winter, leaving a large root hole. From that trail at Cedar Lake Equestrian Campground, this story took flight.

I hope my readers enjoy this fictional work involving both characters of my first novel and new characters whose lives center around Riverview. As you can tell, Riverview is full of possible stories and the R-B has so many likely scenarios for tales of adventure for riders and readers of all ages. I'm looking forward to finding them as I ride or hike in the woods. I want to thank all of my past and future readers for their support.

2nd Edition – 16 Feb 2015

Copyright © 2014 Kasey Riley
All rights reserved.
ISBN:1500863262
ISBN-13: 978-1500863265

Table of Contents

PROLOG 1
CHAPTER ONE 2
CHAPTER TWO 19
CHAPTER THREE 35
CHAPTER FOUR 46
CHAPTER FIVE 69
CHAPTER SIX 82
CHAPTER SEVEN 101
CHAPTER EIGHT..116
CHAPTER NINE 132
CHAPTER TEN 135
CHAPTER ELEVEN 155
CHAPTER TWELVE 166
CHAPTER THIRTEEN 174
CHAPTER FOURTEEN..187
CHAPTER FIFTEEN 205
CHAPTER SIXTEEN 223
CHAPTER SEVENTEEN..239
CHAPTER EIGHTEEN 251
CHAPTER NINETEEN 262
CHAPTER TWENTY 276
EPILOGUE 289
ABOUT THE AUTHOR 293

PROLOG

Gunnison County, CO – October 1933

Caleb added an entry to his journal. He placed it carefully into the cracker tin with the other evidence. He put the tin with its precious evidence in the hole he was using to hide it and carefully replaced the flooring. He walked out of the one room cabin, looking back to see if the hiding spot was visible before he headed to town for supplies.

Caleb never saw the gunman or felt the rifle aiming at him as he rode home later. He never heard the shot and felt no pain from the bullet that crashed through his skull causing his body to roll down the gully into the fast rushing shallow creek below.

The killer pulled Caleb out of the creek and took his wallet. He pushed the body over his saddle, walking up the trail for about a mile before he found a large round hole left by a falling tree at the edge of a wash.

He smiled like a kid on Christmas morning. This would save a lot of work. He dumped Caleb's body off the saddle into the hole, filling it with rocks and boulders. No need to put in dirt, critters wouldn't get around those rocks.

Once done, he rode back to collect Caleb's horses. He shrugged down deeper into his coat as snow began falling, signaling the end of good weather in the Rockies and the beginning of another winter.

Chapter One

Gunnison County, CO – Present Day

Megan's blue eyes grew large as she watched in growing horror the rocky bank giving way under Bethany's horse. With the horse scrambling madly, the pair slid backward out of sight. Jumping off Radar, she threw his reins in a tree as the sounds below faded into silence. On hands and knees, she cautiously approached the unstable edge, when she heard Bethany scream. "Bethany, are you okay? Are you hurt?" She cautiously lay on her belly, extending her long frame, and pushing her head and shoulders over the edge of the embankment.

Bethany had kicked free of her stirrups to dive off her horse when she felt him begin to slip backward off the edge of the wash. Coup fought the backward slide, whipping his body around to swim with the rolling dirt and boulders, slinging Bethany's five-foot-four inch frame from the saddle to land on her backside in the rocks. Landing, she felt a sharp pain, her hips digging into boulders lodged in the bank. She watched Coup stumble down the landslide and saw him come to a stop, on his feet, not thirty feet below where she landed. Automatically, she rolled onto her knees, smacking her helmet on the ground, coming eyeball to eye socket with a human skull. Her breath catching in her throat, her mouth went dry in the split second before her scream startled Coup into moving further away.

"Oh my God! Megan, there's a body down here! Ewww!" Bethany's voice, breathless, then wavering up to a shrill

shriek, rose up from the gully to reach Megan.

"What body? To hell with the body. Are *you* okay?" Megan inspected what she could see of her friend from above, looking for blood or obvious injuries. Breathing a sigh of relief, she saw Bethany looked to be only dirty with leaf matter stuck between the bill of her helmet and her forehead. She seemed more concerned with her discovery than with herself.

"I'm okay, I think. I landed where I have the most padding." Her eyes went to Coup, who was walking over to a patch of late oats to graze. Relief flooded her. He seemed to be moving okay, but she could see some blood staining his back right stocking. Knowing he wouldn't wander farther than the closest food, she looked up at Megan. "Are you going to lie there all day, or climb down here to see this?"

"Well, I don't want to start another landslide. Does the ground look solid?"

"Yeah, I think Coup's weight was the issue that caused the ground to give way. The creek's been undermining this bank for years." She looked both directions, seeing several spots where the upper ground extended over the gully by as much as five feet. "If you work your way down from where you are, on an angle toward the bottom of the gully, you should be fine," she advised. This gully was going to be a tough one to create a decent trail across because of the constant erosion. She gingerly touched the small of her back and felt the growing welt where she'd landed against a rock. She knew it was going to hurt later. Looking again at the skull, she frowned. What had this poor person ever done to wind up buried out here with no marker? Sadness welled up in her at the thought of his or her family who had never known the reason for the disappearance of their loved one.

Megan stood up, took a deep breath, and began to work her way toward Bethany. She hated heights and steep spots, no matter if she was on foot or horseback. Bethany was standing by the time she reached her. They both leaned over the wide hole to get a better look at the skeleton.

"I wonder how it got here. That hole looks like maybe a bullet hole. What do you think?" Megan pointed to the smallish round hole on the left side of the skull, and then swallowed back nausea at the mummified tissue and cloth visible beyond the skull.

"This hollow looks like an old hole created by an uprooted tree. I've seen root holes larger than this after a strong wind." Bethany pointed to bits of what looked to be tree roots along one side of the hole. "I don't think this person died here, unless they took shelter or hid in here. No way could he or she fall so perfectly into a hole. Maybe they froze here in a storm after seeking shelter." Bethany frowned in distaste and shook her head in sorrow at the thought of a wounded person trying to hide from a killer, but knew in her heart, if it was a bullet hole, the victim likely had never known what hit him or her.

"Yeah, I don't think this boulder walked up from the creek bed by itself." Megan hefted a five-pound rock located just inside the hole. "Now what're we gonna do?" She looked at the bones with desiccated tissue surrounded by rocks nestled in the shallow hole in the bank. "I think we shouldn't move anything until a forensics expert works the scene. There might be evidence in the hole with the body."

"Let's put back the rocks we know rolled out of the hole, geocache the location, tie a ton of ribbon on the trees above the bank and across the way, and start looking for the most direct route out of here to the closest road. The authorities are going to need a trail from the road to the body, preferably a short trail. We can call them when we get back to camp," Bethany suggested. She gave her friend a kind of lopsided grin. "The only good thing I can think of about all of this is now I have a name for the trail and maybe the ride I'm planning. This will be the 'Skeleton Trail Loop' and the ride can be something to do with murder and mayhem or the skeleton. Help me think of a good name?" she asked her friend. "Maybe hold it on Halloween or as a night ride and call it the 'Ghost 50'?"

"Your mind is never far from endurance, is it?" Megan shook her head and began to brush the dirt off Bethany's back. She stopped when Bethany winced, gasped, and jumped away from her hand.

"Ouch, careful. I'm going to have a nasty bruise. Why don't you go get Radar and I'll finish brushing off my butt and head down to Coup." She turned away from Megan with her hands lightly covering the injured area. "He looks like he has a cut on his back leg," she said over her shoulder while she watched her friend climb back up to her horse. Bethany stood a moment longer, gently feeling out the size and location of the growing painful welt of bruised flesh before she cautiously climbed down to inspect her horse.

Above, Radar stood happily trimming the tree where his reins hung over a branch. He looked around as Megan approached. Damn, the day had started out so well. She frowned at the thought of the complications and the fact that Bethany seemed to be in more pain than she wanted her to know. Roger would not be happy that she failed to keep his wife from injury. Not that she could have foreseen the situation, but he had specifically told her to take care of Bethany; even though Bethany seemed completely capable of taking care of herself. Crap. She untangled the reins from the tree, unclipped them from the bit, and clipped one end on the halter part of the halter bridle.

"I'm going to ribbon the tree up here before I follow you. No sense in making two trips up and down," she called to Bethany. Taking the roll of orange surveyors' tape off her saddle, she unwound several yards. She broke it up into strips and tied them all over the tree Radar was munching, making it look more like an orange Christmas tree than an aspen. Next, she led Radar to the spot where she would begin her decent and tied several strips of tape around smaller boulders before stacking them. She led her horse past the hole with the skeleton, marking a turning spot for the zigzag path down to the bottom of the gully. Looking back up the side of the wash, the orange tape screamed out of the browns of the fall and the earth tones of the rock. Yep, no one with eyes would miss this spot along the trail she surveyed with a grim smile.

Bethany waited with Coup at the edge of the dry creek. During the wet season, it would be deep, but at the end of summer, there was only one small puddle left to be seen. "I think we can make the trail go up over there. It looks like solid footing and for some reason, the wall isn't quite so steep. I expect the Trailmaster might choose a different spot, but let's start there because it's close to the overall trail." She pointed across the gully to where the ground slanted up at a less severe angle.

"Sounds good to me. Let's go, boss lady. You lead." Megan agreed and urged Bethany onward. Megan stepped her long legs and lanky frame onto the tall Appaloosa's before Bethany mounted her more petite Arab gelding. She saw Bethany wince as she settled into her endurance saddle. "Hey, do you need a pain killer? I've got everything from Advil to Tylenol-3 in my trail kit," She offered.

"I'll take a couple of Advil. The stronger stuff just makes me dizzy and nauseous. The last thing I need on horseback is dizziness." Bethany managed to smile back at Megan, but her face was paler than normal.

Digging out the packet of pills, Megan handed them over. During the past month of living at the R-M ranch, renting the house once occupied by Roger's uncle Phil, she had come to like both her new bosses and grown protective of them. Bethany worked hard creating the new pack station and guest ranch/campground, while Roger managed the cattle and horse ranch his family had owned for generations.

The R-B, which stood for Roger-Bethany, would offer wilderness trips for eco-tourists and trails for all levels of equestrians. With electric camping spots for guests hauling rigs with living quarters or regular RV's, cabins for guests arriving without horses or RV's, and horses for those without animals, it would bring new business to Riverview. They planned guided trips up the mountains and overnight or day options, along with a beautiful lodge for dinner, dancing, and gatherings. They were sinking a big chunk of money into this venture. The purchase of an additional two thousand acres at a land auction this past spring had begun the project. Then receiving permits from the Forestry to put trails for equestrians into the woods with the assistance of a certified Trailmaster had sealed the deal for the new project.

Bethany and Megan started the day at the campground, using Megan's GPS to store the trail they marked with ribbon through the woods and over hills. Bethany wanted this to be about a fifteen-mile loop that would have overlooks and stopping points, but work its way back to the main camp. For the eco-tourists, it would be a daylong ride with lunch at a meadow. For the more experienced riders and the endurance competitors, it would be a two- to five-hour trail ride. They hoped to have it marked out by sundown, but now with the need to locate the closest road, who knew how long it would be before they would be able to finish the loop. Her spirits drooped at the thought that the loop might not get finished before snowfall. Double crap.

At the top of the gully, Bethany pulled out a folded quadrant map from the USGS. The trail they had been following went off to the left. They were about seven miles from where they had started. "Did you geocache this spot? We'll need to be able to give the coordinates to the authorities."

"Yep. Got it safely stored. What does the map show?"

"Well, if we follow the trail to the left long enough, maybe three or four more miles, we should come to BLM 26. It's not much of a road, but it would allow vehicles to park within walking distance." Bethany pointed to the left, indicating the direction they should go. "Road access might also work in our favor, allowing crews or an event photographer access to this trail in a competition." Bethany thought aloud, imagining competitors needing water for themselves and their hot, hardworking horses.

Following Bethany's lead to the left, Megan stopped to put up ribbons of orange tape, while Bethany went ahead to mark further up the trail. Finding the closest road would give summer riders access to help if they needed it. Riders often overestimated the condition of their horses and then needed help getting back to base camp. Forest roads, even nasty ones, have saved many horses and riders.

"Boss, look up there. Is that a trail to the left? Maybe it goes to the road or a cabin on BLM 26?" She pointed at a faint Y in the trail marked by three stacked rocks followed by several rocks laid in a row.

"Hmmm, that's possible. Let's check it out for about

a mile. We come up with nothing in that time, we'll come back here and continue on this track. I think this might be the old trappers' trail used between the towns along the Gunnison back before the highway was built lower in the valley." Bethany put ribbon marking the junction low in a pine tree. Three ribbons marking the turn and another past the turn, almost out of sight to show the side trail. "Why don't you put the regular trail-marking ribbon on the right, where it will draw the eyes away from this junction? I don't want to divert riders, but I want to be able to find this trail again."

Megan marked the right side of the trail they had been riding, and then rode ahead on the side trail, while Bethany was tying ribbons at the junction. She put one in the evergreen tree at the top of the rise. Bethany passed her as they had been marking trail all day, going another distance up the trail before tying ribbon on the right side of the faint trail. Megan caught her and they topped a rise together to see a cabin nestled in the broad valley below.

"Look at that! There's a cabin down there." Bethany paused to admire the serenity of the scene.

"Wow! Bet we can beat you there! Maybe the owners have a decent satellite phone for us to reach the sheriff." Megan dug her heels into Radar and the gelding surged forward, carefully finding the trail down the hill into the low, lush valley before breaking into a soft gallop toward the cabin on the far side.

They were almost there when Coup caught up, put a nose in front of Radar, pinned his ears at the gelding, and flipped his tail. Radar, having a beta-type personality, immediately pulled up and let the alpha gelding take the lead.

"Coup has the best 'sneer' in this region." Bethany laughed at Megan's surprised expression. "He can make just about any horse he gets next to pull up and let him go by, just by pinning his ears and lifting his head at them," she explained, bringing him to a slow trot and then a walk when they approached the cabin. "I once won a race to the finish by that bit of horse interaction. Oh no! We won't find any phones here, sat or otherwise. Look at the door." She pointed to the cabin door. It leaned into the frame and hung by one old leather hinge.

"You're right. This place has been vacant a while, if the debris on the porch is any indicator." Megan agreed, noticing the leaves and dirt blown against the cabin wall. She dismounted from Radar and handed his reins to Bethany before she turned to walk carefully up the rough-hewn log steps to the remains of the porch.

"Be careful. I don't want you to get hurt. If it looks like it won't open, leave it, and we'll bring the boys back to investigate," Bethany warned, gingerly dismounting from Coup. "Damn, now my pants are starting to rub where they cross that bruise."

Megan laughed over her shoulder at her friend. "Guess it's going to be some time before you ride out again. We really should head home so you can get some ice on that swelling." Nevertheless, she still lifted the door to open it and peered into the dimly-lit cabin. "Wow, it looks like someone just left it yesterday, except for the dust. Looks all ready for the owner's return." Megan's voice reflected the awe she felt looking into this snapshot back in time. She could see the cot with the rumpled bedroll along one wall, the large pot hanging over the dead fire in the fireplace, the two-plank table, and split-log bench pushed against the closest wall to her, all waiting for the homeowner's return. She sneezed three times in a row, wiped her eyes and nose on the back of her glove, and said, "Yep, lots of dust, but wow, there's even still a book lying open on the table. Wonder what was being read the last time this place was occupied?"

"I don't think you should go in there. It could be dangerous. What if the floor gives way?" Bethany warned while she stood at the bottom of the steps holding the horses.

"The floor looks strong. Those planks must be at least two inches thick. I wonder if there's a name inside the book." Picking her way softly across the plank floor, she made it to the table in three careful steps. "Wow, it's a Bible. Kind of gives me goose bumps. There's a stub of a candle and a stub of a pencil here with it. Wonder what he'd been writing?" Megan touched the candle and pencil before her hand rested on the open Bible. It was open to the book of Luke in the New Testament. No telling which verse had been the last one read. Again, she got goose bumps thinking that here was something cherished by a person who had never come back to collect his things.

"Check it to see if there's a family name or inscription. Bibles have always been used to record family events." Bethany took one step up and decided to remain where she was when the tightening of the skin across her backside made her gasp.

Lifting the dusty book without removing her riding gloves, Megan mentally noted the page number before closing the volume and opening the front page. "This Bible is the property of Caleb Preston," she read aloud to Bethany. "The first part is printed inside and the name was handwritten on a vacant line." She fanned the pages to find the original spot in Luke to set the book back down where she found it. A single folded sheet of paper slipped from the center of the Old Testament to land on the floor at her feet.

"Wow, Bethany, there was a sheet of paper folded

up in the Bible." She set the book down on the table, open to the correct page before bending over to lift the sheet and shake out the folds very gently to avoid tearing the thin paper. "It looks like a letter. The handwriting is much too fine to be written by the same hand that signed the Bible." She moved a step closer to the door for better light, and then read:

October 2, 1933   Montrose, Colorado

Dear Caleb,

Thank you ever so much for the work you have been doing to find the killer of my husband. The new sheriff has been around asking questions about the "person" I've hired to investigate my husband's death. From the way he was acting, I think that not only was he unhappy with your investigation, but that he also feels threatened in some way. He told me that I needed to let go of this search and accept that the villains who shot Tuck have long since left Riverview.
 Caleb, I'm worried for your safety. If Sheriff Miller is involved in Tuck's death, he can be very dangerous. Maybe you should quit searching until next spring. By then, Miller might no longer care about your investigation. I can't stand the thought of you risking your life to bring Tuck's murderer to justice.
 Please be careful and let me know if there is anything I can do to help you. Tuck didn't leave much, but I know you must be getting short of funds. I can wire you money if you need help to get through the winter. Or, maybe you can get your old job back with the Cole spread.
 I'm doing fine and I feel the baby move often, so I know he'll be born to carry on his father's name. I just know it's a boy; he's so feisty, kicking all the time. I'll be praying for your safety and I hope to see you soon. Maybe you can get here for either Thanksgiving or Christmas. My mother and I would love to have you as a guest to show our appreciation for all of your hard work since Tuck's death.

Respectfully,

Angelica Tucker

Walking outside while she read, Megan used the bright sunlight to see the beautiful script. "Wow, I wonder if our skeleton is Caleb Preston. Maybe he got too close to finding the killer of his friend Tuck. Since the writer's name is Angelica Tucker, we should be able to assume that her husband was called 'Tuck' because it was short for Tucker." She handed the letter to Bethany. "Wonder what Tuck's first name was. I bet we can find a history in the papers of the day, since we know the man was killed within eight months or so of October in 1933." "Yeah, even in those days, babies took nine months, so if she was feeling it kick a lot, it's likely she was in her third trimester." Bethany looked over the paper in the sunlight trying to find any further information she could about the writer or the person who received it. "No envelope? Wish we could know where he received this letter. What town, post office, or maybe even at the Cole Ranch." She turned the paper over again and searched for clues.

"I could go in and search the cabin for more," Megan offered, turning back to the cabin door.

"No!" Bethany ordered. "I mean, no. That's not a good idea. If anything happened, I wouldn't be able to help you. Sorry, I didn't mean to shout. It's just scary with you in there and me out here." She apologized for her outburst. "Let's keep the letter to turn over to the authorities and head out to the road."

"Yeah, you're right. We could spend hours looking around this place for clues. Let me get this door closed." Megan suited action to words, lifting the door on its single hinge back into place, leaning against the frame. She stepped lightly down to Bethany and took Radar's reins. "Do you need a leg up?"

"I think I can still mount, but, I won't get off again until I'm home." Bethany muttered, turning to lift her left leg into Coup's stirrup. She grabbed his mane to pull herself into the saddle, settling into the seat, but keeping most of her weight on her feet to avoid resting her bruised lower back against the cantle, stifling a groan, even with all the care she took.

"You sure you can ride okay?" Megan asked.

"I can make it. I once finished a twenty-five mile race with a similar injury in the first five miles. I can ride, but I won't be able to move tomorrow," she confided, trying to keep the irritation from her voice. She knew the pain was making her snappish and didn't want to hurt Megan's feelings.

"Okay, let's get back to the main trail." Megan took the lead. At the junction of the trails, she dismounted and surveyed the placement of the ribbons to make certain riders would go straight and likely never see the side trail. "The turn is almost invisible. I doubt anyone will be up this trail before we bring back the authorities," she commented, mounting up.

After marking trail for another couple of miles, they finally heard a vehicle crunching on a dirt or gravel road almost dead ahead.

"Yippee! I knew the road had to be close. I am sooo ready to reach civilization." Bethany sighed in relief.

"Why don't I ride on ahead while you mark the spot where the trail comes out to the road? I can use my phone and call the sheriff," Megan offered. She actually planned to call Roger. They needed the trailer.

"Huh? Okay, let's get down to the road first, and

then you can ride up to the ridge crest to get the best reception." Bethany agreed, while Coup cautiously picked his way down the twenty-foot embankment to the gravel road. He automatically turned and angled down the slope, while she placed one hand on the cantle and the other on his neck to balance herself against the angle of decent.

Megan sat on Radar at the top of the embankment, watching until Bethany reached the bottom, and then let Radar pick his way down the same slope. Radar had watched Coup and followed the same path without hesitation. Once at the bottom, Megan turned to Bethany, who was tearing off strips of orange surveyors tape.

"Hold on to Coup and I'll let Radar canter up the hill," she warned, and then clucked to Radar, letting the gelding set off at his sweet rocking chair gait up the gravel road.

At the top of the hill, she was happy to see her phone showed reception at three bars. Relief flooded her while she speed dialed the R-M Ranch house phone.

"Hello, this is Shorty." Shorty's voice was music to Megan.

"It's Megan. Is Roger there?"

"Nope, he's out in the barn working with that new youngster."

"Okay. Here's what I need you to do. Go tell Roger we need him to bring the two-horse trailer. Take BLM 26 to the left just before the county line. Follow it south-southeast. We're coming out that way and will meet him. Bethany is in pain. She's toughing it out, but I think she needs a lift. Oh, and tell Roger we found a body. From the GPS markers, I think it's in the National Forest lands."

"WHAT?!" Shorty shouted into the phone, causing Megan to hold it out from her face. "A body? Bethany's hurt? You better give me something better than that or

Roger will come unglued," he warned.

"Coup stumbled and slid down a hill. Bethany dove off and landed on her butt. She has a serious bruise, but insists on riding. She landed almost eye-to-eye with an old skeleton in a hole in the embankment," Megan patiently told the man. "Think that's enough information to calm him down?" she asked.

"Well, it sounds a dang site better than 'Come out and get us because Bethany's hurt and needs you and by the way we found us a body.' Sounds," Shorty snarled. "I'm on my way out to the barn. Don't be surprised if he calls you."

"Well, I'm headed back down the hill to help her mark the trailhead, so he might not reach me. Just get him moving with the trailer, okay?" Megan's patience slipped and her voice sounded sharp with the question. "Sorry, Shorty. I'm tired and this day has been kind of crappy. Not your fault. Just tell Roger everything is fine, but we need him…with the trailer," she told the man as she closed the call. She turned Radar back toward Coup and let him long trot back down the grade. She saw Bethany had marked the boulders with spray paint and walked up the incline to tie ribbons around the trees at the top of the embankment.

"Hey, you shouldn't have dismounted. I could have done that painting," Megan called to her.

"It's okay. I want to walk for a while anyway. It might keep me from getting so stiff." Walking back down the trail in the embankment, she was pleased that the ribbon was barely visible from the road. That would keep any nosy people from following the trail back to the body. She wanted the spot to be visible "if you looked hard on the left side."

Observing Bethany's handiwork, Megan said, "Looks good. If you know where to look, you can find it."

"That's exactly what I want. Geocache this spot for me and we can be on our way." Turning, she led Coup up the road toward the ridge. "I take it you managed to reach the ranch. How upset was Roger?"

"Well, I haven't talked to him. Shorty took the message to him out in the barn. I expect one of our phones will ring the moment we get reception." Megan no sooner finished the phrase than her phone gave a half-hearted ring and went silent. "I expect that's him. He'll try again in a minute or two. Maybe by then I'll have better reception."

Bethany laughed, but it ended in a groan. "Damn, now it even hurts to laugh. That bruise must be swelling more. It sure is rubbing on my pants." She finished just as her phone gave a demanding shrill ring. "I've got to change that ring tone. By the time I can answer the phone I'm already in a foul mood from the noise," she muttered, digging out the offending item and flipping it open. "Hi, Honey. No, I'm okay, just bruised and sore. Megan said what? Well, she's exaggerating. I can too ride if I wanted to." Bethany glared at Megan while she listened to her husband. "Okay, I know the junction you're talking about and we're about a mile from there. If you're just hitching up, we should be there within about five minutes of you. Just take something to read and wait for us." She closed the phone. "I've got a bone to pick with you. You told Shorty that I couldn't ride? What were you thinking?" her voice rising with the second question.

"Well, what I told Shorty and what he told Roger are two different things, unless Roger has a tendency to blow things he hears out of proportion." Megan looked squarely at her friend. She wasn't going to justify herself any further and if Bethany wanted to be angry, maybe it would ease the discomfort she was feeling from hiking up the road. Megan got off and took Coups' reins so Bethany could move more easily.

"Okay, I forgive you. Shorty does have a problem with retelling what he hears. You might want to keep that in mind and have him write down messages. Force him to read back what he wrote," Bethany advised.

Megan snorted. "Yeah, like he would agree to that. Some people just have no good relationship with truth and unvarnished information." She shook her head and walked on ahead of Bethany, giving the woman space enough to groan, if needed, without embarrassment.

Chapter Two

Roger's hands shook after speaking with his wife. Hitting the button to settle the gooseneck trailer onto his truck, everything seemed to be moving in slow motion except his thoughts. He shuddered at his vision of Coup rolling down an embankment over the top of Bethany.

Shorty told him she was fine, except that there was so much pain, she couldn't stand to ride. Knowing it had to be something serious to force Bethany to call for the trailer, he considered calling the EMTs to meet him out where he was going to meet the girls. No, she'd kill him for over-reacting. But, damn it, the EMTs would be better equipped to judge the severity of her injury than he was.

Fuming about the stubbornness of this woman who had captured his heart, he recalled her jumping back on a horse to finish a seventy-five mile competition after surviving a kidnap attempt before their marriage. More guts than common sense he mused, checking the connections, latching the hitch, and making certain all the doors were secure. Jumping into his running truck, he spun gravel into the air as he headed out to collect his woman and her friend.

He turned right onto the highway, trying to picture where he needed to turn off the main road. Megan told Shorty it was BLM 26, just before the county line. He knew that road. There was one junction, and that was where he could turn this rig around to wait for them. Or, at least park and leave it to walk further up the road to find them. He wasn't certain he could sit and wait patiently if the girls weren't in sight when he got there.

BLM signs never lasted out here, but he saw the road he wanted on the left. Turning onto it, he took the next turn left, making it close to a U-turn. A short distance later, he turned right and headed south-southeast into the public lands. About two miles further, he spotted the junction. Knowing this road got nasty the higher it went, he would have to park here.

Slowly pulling past the turn, he backed the trailer around it until the rig rested on the side road. Turning off the truck, he drummed his fingers on the steering wheel, watching the side mirror for any signs of riders. He gave the horn a couple of long honks to announce his arrival. His patience at an end, he locked the truck and began walking up the road, watching and listening for signs of life. From the top of the first rise, he could only see another hill in front of the higher mountains. He walked down and up to the top of that hill, only to see another. Still no riders in sight. He tapped his foot, wondering if they were just beyond the next hill. He pulled out his phone, happy to see three bars before he speed-dialed his wife.

Bethany sighed when her phone let out the shrill ring tone Roger had selected. "Damn, doesn't he know we'd make better time if I didn't need to answer the phone so often?" She muttered before opening the flip phone. "Hi, Honey. We heard your horn. You must be just over the next hill."

"I just wanted to see if you heard it. Can you tell how far you are from the junction?" He heard the exasperation in her voice and knew she must be in pain. Normally she was happy to hear from him. "Do you want me to try backing the rig up the road so you won't have so far to ride?"

"Roger, I'm perfectly able to walk. We're leading the

horses because I was getting stiff riding," she soothed.

"Don't believe it, Roger! She couldn't get back up on Coup. That's why she's walking!" Megan called loud enough for Roger to pick up.

"Is that true? You couldn't get back onto Coup? That does it. I'm taking you to the clinic and you're going – no arguments." His voice sounded stern enough that Bethany knew she would have to do as he wanted.

"Yes, Dear. Just for you, I'll go to the clinic for an x-ray," she conceded quietly.

Roger hung up more worried than ever. She never allowed him to boss her. She was far too stubborn to admit to injury or illness. She must be worried. He dialed the clinic in Riverview to set up an emergency appointment for an x-ray. The receptionist agreed he could bring her in as soon as they could get there.

He sat down on a convenient boulder next to the road and again found himself drumming his fingers while he waited on the women. Staring at the top of the next hill, his eyes were watering when a couple of boulders seemed to be moving. He stood up and the higher vantage point showed the upper torsos of two women and the heads of the horses following them. Putting his fingers to his lips, he whistled and waved at them.

Megan heard the whistle and waved at Roger. She doubted he saw her because he had begun running down the hill toward them. "Damn fool man. He's going to hurt himself running on this loose gravel." No sooner was that said, than Roger's feet slid out from under him and he sat heavily in the middle of the gravel road.

"Well, at least, I won't be the only one with a sore ass," Bethany hooted, laughing at her husband.

Megan watched Roger stand up slowly before dusting himself off and continuing to walk, instead of run, down the incline. She sighed in relief. "Looks like he hurt his pride more than his butt. That's good because there's no way I could have gotten him back up the road if he broke something," she muttered.

The women met him at the bottom of the hill. Megan stood admiring the tenderness Roger showed when he gathered his wife into his arms. "Are you okay? Can you show me where it hurts? You had me worried." All the words tumbled out of his mouth while his hands roamed up and down her arms and his eyes took in the lines of stress and pain showing on her face.

Huffing in exasperation, Bethany pulled free of his arms, whipped around, and dropped her riding tights below her injury. "Both of you get a good look. It's the only chance you'll get. Now, just let me be." A black bruise ran from left to right across the top of her hipbones. It was about three inches wide from top to bottom and about six or seven inches from left to right. The entire thing was swollen above the surrounding flesh by about a half inch at the center with a defined red line across it. "Are you happy now?" Pulling her tights back over the swelling, she grimaced.

"Boy, you can really tell exactly where you hit. It must have been a flat edge piece of shale or slip rock," Megan remarked.

"Yes, you definitely need that x-rayed. You might have chipped your hipbone on either side." Roger couldn't resist pulling her back into his arms and kissing the top of her head. "Let's get you out of here. Do you want to continue walking, or would you like me to put you up on Coup? I could carry you," he offered.

"For crying out loud, both of you are treating me like I'm dying. It's only a *bruise* – get it?" Bethany pulled out of Roger's embrace. She really wanted to stay there, but knew the more she let him coddle her, the more he would worry. It wasn't like her. "Just throw me up on Coup and we'll ride back to the trailer, unsaddle, and load them while we wait for you to catch up."

Bending, Roger grabbed her calf, lifting her up so she could land gently in the saddle, smiling because her frustration and anger were more like what he expected than the quiet "yes dear" she had been offering.

"Thanks. See you at the trailer," she told him, setting off at a trot up the hill.

Scrambling onto Radar, Megan followed. She looked back only once to see Roger jogging up the road after them. Catching Bethany just as she got to the top of the hill, she said. "Okay, you can slow down now. He can't see you." She understood why Bethany had taken off, but she didn't agree with the reasoning. She knew that Bethany was proving to her husband that she was "fine."

"Was it that obvious?" Bethany slowed Coup to a walk, standing in the stirrups to relieve the pressure on her bruise.

"Only to someone who has used the same ruse," she responded. "If we keep 'em to a fast walk, we can be over the next rise before he's halfway down this hill. That way he won't see you standing in the stirrups."

They kept the horses moving so that Roger only got a glimpse of them cresting that final hill. After sitting down when he tried to run in the loose gravel, he kept his downhill pace at a brisk walk, only jogging when the angle of the grade was uphill. He knew they had slowed once he was out of sight. He trusted Megan to control the pace and she was smart enough to slow Bethany down.

Roger had a lot of faith in the common sense of his new hand. Any person, regardless of gender, who had been through what she had and kept her wits rather than give in to pain and fear, had his full respect and admiration. Uncle Sam didn't give the Silver Star for just any reason. It takes a special personality type to be able to hold terror at bay while buried in the rubble, and stay on the radio with the enemy in the same room. It was a shame her wounds had washed her out of the Army. He knew she wanted to be a career soldier and was experiencing problems returning to civilian life. Using her to help Bethany create and run the R-B was his contribution to her rehabilitation.

Topping the final rise, he saw the girls had the saddles off the horses and Bethany was leaning against the trailer while Megan put the horses into it. Her face was pale, even from a distance. One hand was against the wheel well and she wiped her mouth with the other. He guessed that she had vomited from the pain of dismounting and unsaddling, too damn stubborn to wait for assistance from either him or Megan. Frowning, he shook his head and kept walking.

Reaching her, he took her into his arms. "It's a good thing I love you, 'cause your stubbornness could test the patience of a saint." He murmured into her hair while she turned her face into his chest, resting her forehead against it.

"Yeah, I know, but you would worry more if I sat back and let you do everything." Her arms went around his waist for a quick hug before she pushed him away. "Let's get out of here. The clinic won't wait all day for us." Her smile let him know she guessed he'd called them already.

"Do you think you can sit, or would you prefer to lie across the back seat for the drive to Riverview?"

"I think I can sit." She walked to the cab of the truck.

Opening the door, he gently placed both hands around her waist, lifting her. He froze when her breath caught as she bent at the waist to put her butt into the bucket seat. "Are you certain you want to try?" He watched carefully. "There's no shame in just laying on your stomach across the back seat. I won't tell anyone and neither will Megan." He assured her, trying to get her to acknowledge that the back seat would be a better idea.

"No. I am going to sit." Gritting her teeth, she would not let Roger win this battle, even if he was right. She just wasn't going to give in to his coddling. She would stay sitting, in spite of the pain.

"Okay, okay, do it your way. I suggest that you leave your seatbelt loose and sit forward, holding onto the dash so the bumps won't force you deeper into the cushion." He conceded to her pigheaded stubbornness.

Megan came around to the truck from securing the animals and tack. "You two done figuring out which is more stubborn?" She smiled at the couple. She hadn't heard much, but the sight of them made it obvious to her that there had been a mild confrontation between Mrs. "I'm all right" and Mr. "No, you're not" that she was happy to have missed.

"Yeah, I let her win. She get's really nasty if I don't." Roger grinned.

"I guess in that case, I've got the back seat all to myself?" Opening the back door on the drivers' side, she climbed into the truck.

Climbing in, Roger automatically checked the mirrors, started the truck, and gently pulled out, headed for the highway. He watched his wife from the corner of his eye, but other than her knuckles turning white on the dash a couple of times, she seemed to be handling the rough road okay. Trying to avoid any holes he could, the truck crawled along. One section was washboard for about a quarter mile and there wasn't much he could do about it.

More color drained from Bethany's face until they reached the highway.

From there, they had only about a fifteen-minute drive to town, paved the entire way. Relaxing his grip on the wheel after making the right turn and slowly bringing the truck up to speed, he looked over at Bethany. Her knuckles were returning to normal color where she gripped the dash, her eyes were closed, and he could tell she was breathing against the pain. "We made it through the worst part. Stubborn as you are, I'm proud of you, but I would be happier if you had laid down on the back seat." She gave him a valiant attempt at her sassy grin, but with the paleness of her face, it fell short.

"I'm calling Shorty to tell him we're on our way to the clinic in Riverview. He can bring your car and take the truck and trailer back to the ranch," Megan suggested.

"Good idea. The car will be a smoother ride home for her. She could even lie down in the back." Roger glanced meaningfully at his pale wife. Waiting for Megan to finish talking to Shorty, he changed the subject. "So, Megan, tell me about the body Shorty said you found on the trail." He wanted to get her report while it was still clear in her mind and before the chaos of the clinic.

"Yes, Sir. Bethany found it, when she jumped off Coup. She screamed. I never realized someone her size could be that loud. I was off Radar fast. I made it to the edge, getting a good look at her before she told me why she screamed. Man, I was so relieved. I thought that moving had caused her pain and I was going to need the Spot 2 Messenger to get us out of there." She paused to find the water bottle she had stashed in her pocket, took a drink, and recapped it.

"May I ask why you two didn't use the Spot 2 to bring help in rather than try to ride out?" his disapproval obvious when he glared at his wife, then looked in the mirror to make eye contact with his employee.

"Don't give the girl a hard time, Honey. When all this happened, it didn't hurt much and I was mobile. No sense bringing in a helicopter and the Marines, if I could ride. It's only been since it started swelling that the pain got worse." Bethany chided him and protected Megan.

"Okay, but next time – if there ever is one – call for help," Roger ordered them. "Go on, Megan. Continue."

"Yes, Sir. Well, I got down to her level, and sure enough, there was a skull sticking out of the ground and rocks that had fallen away from it. We looked closer and could see what looked to be a bullet hole in one side and a good portion of the bone gone on the other." She shuddered at the memory. "The rocks were kind of piled around the skull, so we moved a few and found what looked to be the remainder of the body surrounded by rocks. We stopped there, didn't move any more, and carefully replaced what we'd moved. He wasn't laid out flat. I think I saw a kneecap up next to his scapula, if I remember my anatomy of the human skeleton correctly." She scratched her head, remembering how the form looked to be crumpled onto itself in the hole.

"Anyway, we put a mound of rocks over the skull so that it would be protected from critters and weather, like that would help him at this point." She snorted. "Then we marked the spot with ribbon to show the location of the grave. Bethany was moving okay, so we geocached the location and headed on up the faint trail we had found." She made eye contact with Roger in the mirror. He nodded at her, both to continue and approval of their actions.

"We figured we would be closer to a road by going forward than going back. The trail might be easier, so we could move more quickly. Our marking became secondary with ribbon being further apart, since the trail was obvious; faint, but obvious. It might have been the old main trail to Cimarron back in the day," she mused aloud. "Then we found a side trail. Not as obvious, but we thought that it might lead to a cabin or closer road, so we followed it about a half mile. All we found was an old, and I mean really old, cabin. It was still intact, but abandoned long ago by anything, but maybe mice." She paused. She knew that Roger was going to give her grief over the fact that she and Bethany had spent time investigating the cabin when Bethany was injured. "Bethany still was going strong, not looking that pale or giving any obvious signs of pain, so we rode over to the cabin and I went inside to check it out."

She kept her head down, refusing to meet Roger's glare in the mirror, and then quickly continued. "We found an old Bible on the table. The name in it was Caleb Preston and there was a letter from Angelica Tucker to him, thanking him for his effort to investigate her husband's death. We think the body is his and Tuck's killers found him in the woods and shut him up to protect themselves. Then Bethany began to show signs of pain when she remounted, so we made our way out to the road and called you without any more side trips." Using a positive voice, she hoped to deter the coming lecture. The label on her bottle had her full attention, while Roger experienced a mild melt down.

"Let me get this straight. First, my wife is injured in a fall, then she finds a skeleton. Next, you follow a side trail to an abandoned cabin that you take time to explore before you two decide it might be a good idea to get your asses out to a road while she can still ride. Is that a fair understanding of your actions?" Rogers's voice had not risen; in fact, it had become more controlled by the word, until the final question came through his clenched teeth.

"What were you two thinking?" he yelled at the women. "Never mind that question. It's obvious that neither one of you *were* thinking." Slamming his hand on the wheel, he spoke through gritted teeth, gripping the steering wheel in the same manner he wanted to grab either his wife or the woman he expected to be a good influence on her. He glared in the mirror, willing Megan to raise her eyes, silently daring her to do so. Wisely, she kept her head down.

"Roger, Honey, I'm okay. When we went to the cabin, I wasn't hurting much. I think getting off Coup got the blood flowing more to the bruise and that's why it started to be more painful. You know as well as I do that swelling causes most of the pain in a bruise." Bethany's even voice did little to settle Roger's anger, other than direct it back at her.

"Damn it, Woman. I know that I can't trust you to take care of yourself, but I expected more of Megan." His voice had lost the tightness, but gained the sound of disappointment.

"Did you really expect her to control me? I'm not only older than she is, but I'm also her boss. The most she's going to be able to do is possibly make me see a different side of what I want to do. She's not going to be able to stop or even direct me. You ought to know that." She reached one hand over to rub his white knuckles where they gripped the wheel. "Don't blame her. Blame me if you feel we acted stupidly. At the time, I felt well enough to continue riding for the remainder of the day. I knew I was going to pay for the fall later, but not as much as it actually hurts now. Otherwise, I would have stayed on the main trail and come straight out to the road." She continued to rub his knuckles until he relaxed his grip. "I love you and I'm sorry that I've scared you and caused you to worry." She smiled when he took her hand in his and lifted it to his lips.

"I'm sorry I yelled. I think I'm going to get gray hair with you around, either that or keep you under lock and key." He smiled over at her. Glancing in the mirror, he caught a smirk on Megan's face and glared back at her, forcing her to study her water bottle again. "You, I'll talk to later," he darkly promised.

Pulling up next to the clinic door, he set the truck in park before hopping out and running around to assist his wife. By the time he opened the door, Bethany had undone her seat belt. Grasping her around her waist, he lifted her carefully from the truck, taking care not to let any part of her back touch the frame as he set her on her feet. "Megan, haul the horses over to the far side of the lot, lock the truck, and meet us inside," he ordered, taking his wife's arm to assist her up the small step and in through the sliding doors.

The new office nurse met them with a wheelchair. Bethany eyed the chair and made a face that caused Roger to snort. "I'm not certain I can sit. Is it okay if I walk to the exam room?" Bethany asked.

The nurse made eye contact with Roger over Bethany's head, asking his opinion with her bright green, expressive eyes. He shrugged and nodded, knowing his wife would be uncomfortable in a wheelchair.

"Okay, Ma'am. You'll be in the first exam room. Right through this door and to the left." The petite curly-headed nurse pushed the chair ahead of her while she led the slowly-moving couple into the examination room. "Can you get up on the table?"

"I'll lift her for you." Roger picked up his wife and set her in the middle of the exam table with great care.

"Okay. Let's get your vitals while you tell me what happened and where it hurts." The nurse tightened the cuff while Bethany held the electronic thermometer in her mouth. Making notations in Bethany's chart after taking her pulse and reading the thermometer, she listened to the tale.

"I jumped from my horse as he was falling down an embankment and landed on my butt. I have a horrible bruise at the top of my hipbones. Not my seat, my hipbone." Her voice faded toward the end of the statement because the nurse had moved around and pulled her riding tights away from her body to see the bruise.

"Well, your pulse is elevated, along with your blood pressure, but your temperature is normal." Sympathy shown in her bright green eyes.

Noting the oddity of the green eye color against the warm brown hues of her skin and the extreme curl to her blue black hair, Roger wondered about her heritage.

"Hmmm, I think the doctor will want an x-ray. You're not pregnant are you?" The nurse eyed both of them, noting Roger's possessive and protective stance over his wife.

"I don't think I am, but we don't practice any birth control. I'm not due for my period for another week. Your guess is as good as mine." Bethany's chin had gone up in a challenging manner.

"Hmmm, I'll give this information to the doctor and let him make the call. You two just wait here and he'll be right in." Pushing the unneeded wheelchair out, she closed the door.

"I wonder when Doc hired her," Bethany snorted. "Kind of stern and sad, if you ask me." She leaned her head against Roger's shoulder. He had kept his arm behind her and refused to move when the nurse gave him the evil eye for getting in her way. "I'm so tired right now, I could just cry. I know it's shock from the injury, but I just want to either cry or sleep."

Hearing the strain in her voice, Roger felt his heart tighten. "It's okay, Honey. Whatever you want to do is just fine. You're injured. It's okay for you to cry." He murmured into her hair, rubbing the top of her head with his chin.

The door opened and Dr. Samuelson entered. "Well, if it isn't my favorite kidnap victim." He smiled, remembering the first time he met Bethany after she had foiled an attempt to kidnap her. "What happened this time?" he asked, looking at the notes his nurse had made. He frowned, shaking his head at their brevity, and the lack of information they provided. He looked up, noting the closeness of the couple, and smiled more broadly. They made a good-looking couple, even with her face so pale.

"I came off Coup when he fell and managed to hit myself on a boulder or something. I have a nasty bruise across the top of my hips. I guess that means I didn't exactly land on the rocks, but rather hit them when I landed," Bethany explained. She was beginning to feel that she should have the story printed to hand out.

"I'm sorry. I know you're in pain. I'll get you something for it in just a minute. Nurse Marjani noted that you could be pregnant. That's going to affect both medication and possible x-rays." He raised his eyebrows at them.

"What my wife told your nurse was that she is just past mid-cycle for her period, so we have no way of knowing if she could be pregnant of not." Roger took over for Bethany, feeling her lose strength as she leaned more heavily against him.

"Oh, I see. Well, I'd like to run a blood test. It might not be accurate at this point, but if it comes back positive, then we'll move as though you are pregnant and avoid heavy meds and x-rays." He found a tube and a syringe before gently drawing blood from Bethany. "Are you two working at starting a family?" he inquired with his back to them while he put the blood into a test tube.

Roger and Bethany exchanged looks over his bent head. "Well, we've discussed it and decided to let nature be our birth control. We want a family, but maybe not for another year, but if we conceive, then we'll have a family earlier," Roger explained, smiling when the doctor looked over at him.

"Sounds reasonable to me. I've always felt those who work too hard to have a family don't do themselves any service and create more stress than needed in a marriage. Best to let the future decide itself at this point," he agreed. "I'm going to run this over to the lab. I'll be right back." He waved at them with the test tube, as the door closed behind him.

Bethany sighed. She just wanted to lie down and sleep. She eyed the exam table, running her hand over the paper cover sheet to smooth it. She saw Roger reading her mind and smiled at him. "Think the doctor would mind if I just stretched out here for a rest? I can barely hold my eyes open."

"Here, let me help you. I'll lift your legs as you move your upper body over the table." He put actions to words and she managed to stretch out on her stomach as the door opened.

"There you are." Megan entered the exam room with Shorty hot on her heels. "What's the doctor say?"

"He wants to run some tests before they can do any x-rays, so we may be here a while," Roger told the pair. "Shorty, I know you want to stay, but it's not good to leave the horses standing in the trailer. I want you to take Megan and head home." He gave a stern look to the man who was as much a friend as he was a cook and housekeeper. "I'll call as soon as we know anything. I seriously doubt that Doc will send her to Montrose for anything, so we'll be home before the evening's done."

Shorty's face fell, but he took Megan's elbow and directed her toward the door. "Okay, Boss. I'll make something easy on the tummy for dinner and see you when you get home."

Megan paused at the door and glanced over at the couple. "I'll wait until tomorrow morning to call about the skeleton. No sense getting the town gossiping and some yahoos trying to beat the forensics people out there."

"Good idea. Nothing can be done tonight and it's not as if it's going to disappear before anyone can get back out there. Shorty, keep it quiet so no fools go out there searching at dawn, okay?" Roger's stern expression as he looked at Shorty quelled the excitement in the older man's eyes.

The door closing behind them, Roger pulled a chair closer to the exam table and sat down before picking up Bethany's delicate hand in his rough one and kissing her fingers. "I guess now we wait."

Chapter Three

Bethany felt the strength and love in Roger's grip. Closing her eyes, she squeezed his hand. "I know we haven't discussed kids much, but maybe it's time we did."

"Do you think it's time to get serious about starting a family? I thought you would want to get the new venture up and running first." He held her hand in both of his, watching her face for signs of what she was thinking. He wanted a family, more than the new pack station and campground. He also wanted her to be happy and he wasn't certain how she would feel about starting a family now.

"Silly man, of course I want a baby. It scares me to think about it, but I think we could handle raising a child. In fact, we could handle several, unless you would prefer not to," she ended uncertainly.

"I thought we decided at the Bazaar last year, before we ever married, that we wanted to have at least two." Smiling at the memory, he rubbed her hand against his cheek by lowering his head.

"Yeah, I seem to recall the subject came up that day," she chuckled, remembering the Puppy Prowl and the toddlers chasing dogs. "But, the question is when to start really working at it, rather than just not taking any precautions." Loving the feel of his cheek against the back of her hand, she let him continue to hold it.

He chuckled and squeezed her hand gently before he spoke. "I kind of thought we had been working on it – the most fun I've ever had." His face turned red and he was happy no one else was in the room.

Bethany laughed aloud. "Yeah, we've been practicing and perfecting our techniques." She blushed, too. "But there's things we can do to increase the odds in our favor; if you're serious about this."

"If the test is negative, and at the moment, I hope it is because you need the x-ray and the pain meds, then we can put some real effort into creating a family. I'm as ready as I'll ever be to have a child, so long as you are, too." Roger looked into her eyes when Bethany opened them and lifted her head. His eyes were on a level with hers and he leaned in to kiss her.

"Sounds like fun." She managed to get out before his lips sealed hers. Even though she was in pain, her body responded to his kiss. Yeah, this was going to be fun, all right.

The door opened and the sad-faced nurse entered with a syringe. "Okay, you two. This isn't your bedroom. None of that." She actually tried to smile at Roger, but only managed to make her lips straight, instead of turned down. "The tests were negative, so Doc told me to get this morphine into you." She walked over to Bethany and pulled down her riding tights to expose her left cheek before swabbing and inserting the needle.

Bethany tried not to jump, but it hurt. "Ouch! A little warning would be nice." She scowled over at the retreating nurse.

"Doc wants you in x-ray. I'll bring the wheel chair," she said, leaving the room.

"Why does that woman remind me of Nurse What's-her-name from One Flew Over the Cuckoo's Nest?" Bethany snarled.

Roger fought against laughing. "I agree. She does seem a bit sadistic," he murmured as the door opened and the nurse returned with the wheel chair.

"You're lucky this clinic has its own x-ray facilities. Saves you a painful drive to Montrose. Now, can you get into the chair on your own, or do you need assistance?" She pointed to the wheel chair. "With the morphine working, sitting shouldn't be as painful as before."

Roger assisted Bethany into the chair before the nurse could get around to the exam table. "Should I go with her?" He smiled at the nurse as he asked the question.

Unbending from her persistent frown, the woman responded to his expression. "No, I think it best if you wait here for her. I'll see that she's taken care of for you," her voice sounding less stressed.

Bethany smiled, catching the fact that Roger's innate charm was working on the woman. For her, the morphine had eliminated the pain and most of her inhibitions. "Cute, isn't he? He's the sweetest man I've ever met, but keep your hands off, okay?" She smiled up at the nurse as they started down the hall to x-ray.

The nurse laughed, knowing it was the drugs. "Trust me, I can tell he's taken. Besides, I swore off heartbreakers. I've had my fill." She patted Bethany's shoulder.

"Is that what your problem is? I wondered why you were so nasty and sad looking. You don't look like you should be so mean. What's your name?" Again, the drugs caused the words to pop out without any censure from her brain.

"My name is Kamama Marjani. My mother was Cherokee and Irish, and Daddy's family came from someplace in Africa, and it's their fault. Mom loved butterflies and wanted to honor her Cherokee heritage, so she saddled me with something I have to spell and explain. Just call me Kam," Kam explained to her drugged patient. She knew that Bethany would likely not remember anything said at this point.

"You're new in town, aren't you? I've only been here a year, but I feel like I've lived here all my life. The people here are sweet. Smile at them and you'll find yourself accepted. Try it. It might just make your day brighter, too." Bethany suddenly realized she was out of line in the questioning and the uninvited advice. "I'm sorry. I think the morphine's talking. I think I'll be quiet now." She began studying her nails, just as they turned into the lab.

One room in the clinic was set up to run blood and other tests, along with housing the x-ray machine. For MRI and other more complicated tests, the patients were sent to Montrose or Gunnison, but the doctor read his own films and Kam took the x-rays.

The table was set up. Kam assisted Bethany onto her stomach, carefully pulling her tights and underwear down to bare her butt and pushing her shirt up to just under her breasts so the entire area was free of possible interference.

"Damn, this table is cold. I'm getting goose bumps. You don't think they will show in the pictures, do you?" Bethany giggled.

"No, goose bumps don't show, but if you move once it's set up, we'll have to take more. When I tell you 'now', I want you to hold your breath, okay?" Kam positioned the head of the machine so the crosshairs shown directly on the center of the bruise after positioning Bethany so she was laying with the film situated in the holder under her hips. She moved back behind the protective screen. "Okay, I need you to hold your breath…now." She paused a split second, and then took the x-ray. "Okay, you can breathe now." She assured her patient. Moving into the room, she changed the film, positioned Bethany on her side, and repeated the procedure. She rolled Bethany onto her stomach, then the other hip, and took another shot, just to have all angles covered.

"Are you done already?" Bethany questioned. Kam took the last film from under her hip and pulled down her shirt.

"Yes, and I'm going to let you pull your pants back up because I don't want to hurt you." Kam took all the films to the slot that fed the processing room next door and put them through the slot one at a time.

"Since you're new in town, where you living? Do you have family with you?" Again, the drugs removed her natural reticence. "I stayed at the boarding house run by the Bailey sisters when I got here. At least for one night before Roger moved me out to the R-M," she confided with a smile and a snicker.

"I'm on my own and I'm staying at the boarding house. I'm looking for a place to rent where I can keep my horse, but those are rare and I'm not certain how long this job will last," Kam confided in Bethany. A lock of her curly blue-black hair escaped down to her neck when she slowly shook her head.

"It'll last longer if you smile and get a better attitude. What kind of horse? We've got room at the R-M, if you just want to board." Kam pushed Bethany up the hall toward the exam room as they were talking.

"I have an Arab mare. She's somewhat alpha, but a fun horse to ride. She adopted me a few years ago and I miss not having her close at hand." She sighed and her large green eyes clouded as she turned the chair into the examination room where Roger waited. "We used to compete in Competitive Trail, but this past year has been a mess and I don't know when we'll get a chance again."

"Honey... you'll never guess! Kam has an Arab mare and she needs a place to board. She rides Competitive

Trail. Can we find room for her at the R-M? Pleasssse?" Bethany grabbed Roger's hand to pull herself up and move to the table, her large hazel eyes pleading silently.

Roger was happy to see the sour nurse had become nicer to his wife, but wasn't too certain this was going in a direction he wanted to pursue. He noticed she hadn't let go of his hand and was wringing it, pulling on his heart and his shoulder. "I think we can make room for another horse," he conceded, knowing that he had no choice at all and making the decision to accept the inevitable, happier than ever that she was his. He loved her ability to take in strays of all kinds.

"You don't have to do that, Sir. She won't remember any of this tomorrow." Kam offered Roger a way out of the situation. "The morphine got her talking and she's kind of persistent once she begins asking questions."

Roger looked the woman over with a knowing look in his eyes. He saw her more clearly, now that Bethany was no longer in pain and being snarly. He saw a small woman, about twenty-five or so, nice shape with muscled arms that he supposed were needed in her line of work. He noticed further that her eyes were a deep green, but the expression in them was sad and she wore deep stress lines around them and the corners of her mouth. He could tell she needed a friend and he knew his wife would take that spot quickly and completely.

Bethany needed more friends closer to her own age. Riverview wasn't overflowing with women in their twenties. He could count three that he knew of: Megan, Bethany, and Marcia were about it. Steph was just over thirty and, of course, Marge was in her mid-forties, maybe older; then there was Betty at the diner and her sister. Betty was in her thirties and her sister must have turned that corner, too. He remembered she was only a grade or two behind him.

He sighed and put a smile on his face for Kam's sake. "It's not a question of what she'll remember. It's a question of what she would want. If you need a place for your mare, we have room and a lot of trails to ride. Do you need help hauling her over?" he asked. "By the way, my name is Roger, not Sir." He smiled and put his hand out for her to shake.

"Okay, Roger. Thank you for the offer. I have a trailer. A two-horse slant load. I can haul her myself." She shook his hand. "I have tomorrow off. I could bring Lady Mica over in the morning." She made eye contact with the tall man, watching to see if he was serious. "What's your number? Here's my cell number, or you can reach me at the Bailey's later tonight." She wrote a number on a notepad and passed it to him. Roger gave her the number for the ranch.

"We'll look forward to seeing you. We're normally up and working by about eight," Bethany advised her new friend. "We can't let you have the guest cabin. The contractor for the R-B is staying in it, but we do have room in the barn." She sagely nodded her head at Kam. "I think I want to sleep. Can we go home now, Honey?" Bethany's voice sounded more like a child than an adult with this last plea.

"Doc Samuelson will be right here. I can get you a blanket, if you want to stretch out on the table," Kam offered.

"That's okay, Kam. I'm here and I plan on having these two on their way home shortly." The doctor moved around his nurse as he entered the room and smiled at Bethany and Roger.

"I think you figured out the test was negative and the better news is that the x-rays don't show any fracture or chips on your spine or hip bones. I'm going to give you a prescription for some heavy pain meds for tonight and you're going to need to ice the area every hour for at least ten minutes tomorrow and the next day." He directed Bethany, but kept his eyes locked with Roger. He knew which would remember his instructions.

"She has trouble with pain meds, Doc. Most of the time, she just gets dizzy and throws them up. What do you suggest?" Roger asked.

"Well, I gave her something with the morphine to settle her stomach, but that won't last any longer than the morphine. I'll give her a prescription to help keep down the pain meds, but if she's dizzy, see that she stays in bed as much as possible." He knew Roger would do his best, but he also knew his patient was not the most co-operative. "Tomorrow evening, I want you to change from the pain meds to a dosage of three 200mg Advil and one 500mg Tylenol taken at the same time. You can do that no more than three times a day and no longer than three days. Did I make that clear?" Again, he met and held Roger's eyes. "I'm writing it down, just to be certain. She should be feeling much better after three days, but keep her down and icing the bruise for forty-eight hours."

"Excuse me, but I'm not a child and I'm sitting right here," Bethany whined at the men, causing them to smile over her head.

"It's okay, Honey. We know. Doc just knows the morphine is affecting you at the moment and he wants me clear on how you need to be treated." Roger patted her shoulder.

Just so long as this isn't a trend you two plan on developing." Bethany was proud her words had only a little slur to them. She felt her energy level draining and wanted to get home.

"Come on, let's get you home. That's all you need us for isn't it, Doc?" Roger looked up from his wife to the physician.

"Yes. I shouldn't need to see her again unless the pain increases even with icing and/or any numbness develops in her legs. Other than those issues, time will be the healer in this situation. Just don't ride again for a few weeks, okay?" Dr. Samuelson looked between Bethany and Roger, trying to get one or the other to commit to that advice.

"Don't worry, Doc. I plan on hiding her saddles," Roger told him with a smile at his wife's scowl and glare. He began moving her wheelchair toward the door, as the doctor led them out into the hall. The place was deserted and Roger glanced at his watch. Wow, almost six already. "Sorry to keep you two here after hours, but I appreciate the fact that we didn't have to drive all the way to Montrose." He smiled at both the doctor in the lead and the nurse who had followed them out into the hall. "I'll look forward to seeing you tomorrow morning, Kam."

Wheeling the chair to the small station wagon Shorty left for them, he helped Bethany to stand while he put the seats down. The all-wheel-drive diesel Jetta worked great for this country. Bethany had bought it after their marriage to get around. She kept her truck, but mostly drove the VW when not hauling horses or stock. "Okay, get in. Lay on your tummy and sleep. I'm stopping to pick up the drugs before the pharmacy closes and you're staying in the car." His tone was firm, but he was surprised when his wife followed his instructions without any argument. He wheeled the chair back to the waiting Kam.

"I called in the prescription and Paul, the pharmacist, is waiting for you. You'll have to give him the written script. The law on heavy pain meds is exact, but he'll have it ready for you," Kam told him when she took the chair.

She locked the door and watched Roger get into the Jetta and drive the car toward the only pharmacy in town. She smiled. Maybe things were looking up in Riverview. It was about time something went her way. The past year had been hell. From the moment she found the pediatrician of her last clinic with his hands on the thirteen-year-old, through the "he said - she said" charges that were filed, and the accusations the man laid against her in retaliation. Forced to leave her job, she'd had no choice. She couldn't leave him practicing where he could molest children.

Leaving the town where she grew up added one more strike against her happiness. Yes, it had been a shit year for her. The doctor swore vengeance, especially when his accusations of seduction against her failed to blacken her reputation. Only Lady Mica kept her from breaking down. Having a soft mane to cry into and a horse that only twitched an ear at her screams of frustration kept Kam from turning to drugs or some other source of relief. She knew she needed the mare close. The solace she provided kept her world brighter. There was nothing like a long ride in the wilds to work off her sadness and vent her frustrations.

"I'm going to finish writing up Bethany's chart. There's no need for you to stay once the exam room is set up for tomorrow," Dr. Samuelson said.

"Thanks, George. It has been a long day. I'll lock up, so you won't have to worry about anyone wandering into the clinic," Kam assured him. "Those two look so devoted. Are they newlyweds?"

"Well, they've been married almost a year now, but they share a lot of common interests and Bethany is the soul of Roger, and vice versa, if I'm not mistaken." Dr.

Samuelson smiled. "They went through a lot before they got married. Have Bethany tell you the story some time. It's quite interesting and everyone in town has accepted her because she brought a smile back to Roger."

George had noticed the connection Kam made with Bethany and felt it might be just what both young women needed. He knew her history. His thorough background check had revealed the entire sordid story. She had only put "to seek better employment" as a reason for leaving Des Moines, but his connections and friends there filled in all of the gaps.

George wondered if Kam knew that her report of misconduct had led to an extensive investigation that included added cameras in clinic exam rooms and film of the good doctor coercing a child not to tell her parents about his "exam" methods. After interrupting that session before it went further than verbal abuse, the doctor's home computer had been subpoenaed, and a massive amount of child pornography discovered within the encrypted files. Thanks to her courage, the doctor would lose his license and spend time behind bars. George knew Kam was homesick, but he also knew she needed a fresh start and Riverview was a good place for that.

He turned away from the nurse and walked to his office, where he picked up the chart and began writing notes. He decided to let Kam and Bethany become better friends before he told her about his discoveries about her record in Des Moines. If she had new friends here, maybe she would stay, even if her record had been cleared in the other city. He hoped so. His wife was enjoying her retirement and good nurses seldom came through Riverview looking for jobs.

Chapter Four

After seeing to Radar, Megan found herself pacing, first in the barn, then in the house, waiting for a call from Roger or Bethany with a status report. Patience was not her strongest quality. In fact, it wasn't in her repertoire at all. Since the time she had been pinned in the rubble while the enemy moved around her, she felt that every moment was important and to waste any waiting just bugged the crap out of her.

Looking at her watch, she decided to call the R-M at seven- thirty. If Shorty had no news, she was heading back to town. Bethany might need her. Since it was just six, she walked into the kitchen. Taking eggs from the fridge, she heated a pan, fried them and created a double egg sandwich. Adding a double handful of chips to her plate, she figured with the day she'd had the calories wouldn't count. Pouring herself a tall glass of tea, she sat in the overstuffed recliner to eat and plot her next move.

Her stomach still in knots, she forced down most of the sandwich and the chips. Turning to survey the kitchen, she frowned because the breakfast dishes still sat in the sink. Sighing she got up and walked to the sink to wash them. It would keep her from pacing. She pushed her long wavy blonde hair back from her face, then stopped to bring her headband down to her nose before pushing it back to hold the curls off her forehead. Her cornflower blue eyes reflected the worry that she couldn't quite push from her thoughts.

At twenty-five, she'd seen many wounds and injuries

during her tours in the Middle East, so she knew Bethany would be fine; but that didn't stop her from worrying. Friends were hard to come by and she valued having Bethany around more than she would admit to anyone, including herself. Knowing that clots would be the worst possible case for that kind of bruise, she felt reassured that a person Bethany's age shouldn't have fatty deposits to knock loose and cause blockage. So long as there was nothing broken or chipped, she should be fine with ice, pain meds and later hot packs to speed healing.

Walking back to the living room, she gathered the throw pillows from the floor and put them back on the couch. The previous occupant of the ranch house, Phil, left the most massive Siamese cat she had ever encountered behind when he went to prison. Sam came with the house and Megan enjoyed his personality and company; except for the fact that he continuously knocked the throw pillows off the couch. She'd seen him do it. He would attack one, roll with it, pull it in to his chest while using his hind feet to dig into the softness before letting go with his front feet and watching it fly to the floor. Then he would nonchalantly get back to his feet and wander down the couch to find another victim. Since there were four throw pillows that belonged on the couch, he repeated this game all day between naps.

"Sam, you keep this up and I'm going to need to recover these things. Something Kevlar might survive your claws." She smiled over at the mass currently curled up on the warm spot she'd left in the recliner when she got up to wash dishes. He opened one lazy eye to watch her putting his "enemies" back onto his couch battlefield. He yawned and made the typical Siamese maow that passed as a meow.

"Yeah, I know... it's your couch. If that's so, then why don't you move and give me back the chair?" She often asked this question of the cat who hardly slept on the couch, preferring instead to take the soft, warm, recliner; much to Megan's disgust. She could sit there too, so long as she kept twenty pounds of cat in her lap. Twenty pounds of warm cat who would dig claws into her leg any time she twitched a muscle. The room was large enough; maybe she should find another recliner for it. Hmmm, that might just be the perfect idea, something more petite than the overstuffed monster Sam loved.

    Sam slept continuously unless it was dark or feeding time. After eating his dinner, he would slink out the doggie door to hunt throughout the night. Once or twice, she'd heard him return in the wee hours, but mostly his stealth allowed him to claim a spot in her bed without waking her. If she decided to work on the computer, he would lay on her mouse pad, his eagle eyes watching her hands as they moved over the keyboard. Since she'd dumped him on the ground the one time he'd attacked her fingers, he hadn't done so again. But, he watched and made her nervous. She tried to time her keyboarding with his nightly excursions so she could work without such a vigilant audience.

    Having a house cat was new to her. Barn cats had always been around, but not one in the house. This character was proving to be both entertaining and intimidating. Her oldest brother was threatening to visit at Christmas. She couldn't wait for his opinion of Sam. She smiled at the thought of the tough Navy Seal battling the Siamese for the couch or recliner. That could make her some dollars on Americas' Funniest. She glanced around the room for a perfect spot to set up a hidden camera. It would need to show the area well. She'd work on it, rearranging the furniture if needed.

    Looking at her watch, she walked toward the telephone. She jumped when it rang. Living alone was beginning to get to her if the sound of the phone could startle her so badly.

"Hello, Megan here." She glanced at the caller ID and continued, "How's Bethany? Anything broken?"

"Easy girl. Don't worry. Bethany'll be fine," Roger told the concerned voice. "Doc says it's only a bruise, pain killers tonight and ice for the next two to three days. No riding. Looks like you're the one that will take the authorities back into the wilderness to the skeleton." Roger paused to let the information sink in, knowing that Megan's concern about her friend was first and taking a bunch of greenhorns back into the woods would be a pain but acceptable so long as her friend was okay.

"Thank goodness she's okay." Megan breathed a huge sigh of relief. "From what I can find on the map, the body looks to be inside the National Forest land. I don't recall seeing any boundary markers, but you know as well as I that those can be few and far between up in the hills. Should I call the Feds or the local sheriff?"

"Well, I would say call the sheriff first and let him know that you're calling the feds. Soothe his ego by asking him which branch would handle a cold case in the National Forest." Roger advised her. He knew the recently elected sheriff was from an old Riverview family and might be able to shed some light on the body since his family had lived in the county for generations. In fact, one of his family members had been sheriff back in the 1930's to 1980's. "If you get a chance tonight, why don't you Google the name from the cabin and the other name you have to see if anything pops up? Might be able to find present-day relatives who could possibly shed some light on the crime."

"Good idea. I'll see what I can find out on the computer." Megan was glad to have a direction to take her energy and a plan for the next day. "Tell Bethany to take it easy and I'll be over with whatever news I can find out. Expect a call from the sheriff and most likely the FBI as well. Have a good night, thanks for the taxi service today."

"Thank you for the call and the heads up that it was needed. Good night, Megan." Roger smiled at the phone when he hung up. Knowing his employee and her computer skills, he fully expected her to have all available data on the crime, possible motives and possible perpetrators by the time she headed back into the woods.

Putting down the phone, Megan headed for the computer on her dining table. Smiling to herself as she signed in, checked her email, and then began her search. First for Caleb Preston, there was very little to find. She made notes about him on the paper next to her keyboard. In the 1930 census, she found a Caleb Preston as a worker on the Cole ranch in Gunnison County but after that, nothing.

Next, she searched for Angelica Tucker and her children as well as a homicide involving a man with Tucker as a last name in 1933. She found the death of a Riverview Sheriff Michael Tucker in 1933. The newspaper story speculated that his death was due to horse thieves since the crime occurred behind the Livery in Riverview. No arrests were pending and the writer felt the murderers had since fled the county. She made more notes as a scenario began to unfold of the years of 1932-3 in Gunnison and Montrose counties. Michael Tucker had won the position in 1932 by proving his rival had ties to the local Moonshine industry.

Finding records of a son born to Angelica made her smile. Michael Tucker, Jr. had spent his life in Gunnison County, married, and records showed he had two children living in the area as recently as his funeral in 1999. James Tucker was his son and taught English at the Gunnison high school, and his daughter, Jessica, married one Samuel Cole of the 3C's Ranch. Michael's obituary listed James and Sam as his pallbearers. Now, fourteen years later, the phone book showed James with a Gunnison number, but other than the Cole Ranch, there was no mention of Jessica. From the stories of Samuel Cole that she had heard, she wasn't certain if he could have a wife, or if he was alive, dead, or divorced. It didn't sound like something feasible for the person Bethany had slapped in public over a year ago.

Angelica had re-married in 1935 to Michael McMillan, had two more children and passed away at the age of eighty. One of those two, Mary Nelson, Megan found was the librarian in Gunnison at the time of her mother's death according to the obituary.

Megan would have several avenues to offer the whomever was assigned to this cold case. James Tucker, Jessica Cole, Mary Nelson and Jonathan McMillan were all decedents Michael or Angelica Tucker. She typed her notes into a Word document, saved them to a file, printed out a copy and put the fragile letter she'd found in the cabin with the printed sheet to hand over to the investigator.

By the time she finished her research, it was after nine. She turned on the TV to hear the weather and news before she headed to take a bath. She always listened to the weather channel with interest because it could affect her plans for the next day. Her heart fell when she heard the weather was due to change. The Indian summer they were enjoying would be over by tomorrow evening. With a nasty arctic front due, snow was expected by late tomorrow. The weatherman told his viewers he expected this front to bring significant snow to the high country and possibly down as low as four thousand feet. That covered pretty much all of Gunnison County and up where the skeleton lay buried.

Crap. Maybe they would be able to get the data they needed and the skeleton out before the weather hit. Megan picked up the telephone and dialed the sheriff's office. Expecting him to have gone for the night, she would leave a message and then call the Feds. "Hi, this is Megan Holloway; I work for Roger Meadows at the R-M just outside of town. Today his wife and I found a really old skeleton in a hole next to a trail up in the National Forest." She paused for the off hours duty deputy to write down the information.

"You found a what? Where? Okay, start over, slowly for me." The operator seemed to wake up and focus.

"We found a really old skeleton up in the National Forest above Hwy 50 close to the county line. My GPS put us within the National Forest. I geocached it so we could locate the spot again. I wanted to tell the Sheriff about the find before calling the feds. Would I need the FBI, or the BLM?" She asked.

"Well, I think the sheriff would want to see the body before you call the FBI. He takes offense at them taking over investigations in Gunnison County." The operator sputtered at Megan, then sounded stern, trying to keep her from making the second call. "I think you would be wise to let him call the FBI, miss. You say you geocached the spot, what kind of equipment did you use, is it accurate?"

"I've got a hand held unit; I keep it on my saddle. Sorry, I can't wait to call the feds. There's a storm coming in late tomorrow. The FBI will need to have people out here to remove the body and gather evidence before the weather hits." she told him. "I'm just calling you as a courtesy to let you know what's happening. Got to run. Have a good night."

She quickly ended the call, heard a dial tone and entered the number she had pulled up for the Denver office of the FBI. She got a recording, but left her telephone number and a brief message about finding a skeleton in the National Forest along an unmarked trail. She mentioned the fact that within the next two days the area expected to be blanketed with snow for the winter, so they might want to have someone here immediately to get photos and evidence even if they decided not to remove the skeleton until spring.

She hung up the phone, wondering just how much they monitored the calls and if she would hear back before morning. Well, at least she'd done her part. Now it was up to the government. Her experience said it would likely be spring before anyone showed up to check out the story. At least, by then, Bethany would be able to help take the forensics team into the hills.

Tunelessly whistling, she went upstairs, drew a hot bath and climbed in. Staying for almost an hour, she let the hot water soak away the stress and work of the long day. Her shoulder muscles burned under the scar tissue, unconsciously, she massaged it while she soaked. She would never be back to full strength and the Army orthopedists told her she could expect pain if she overworked it or when the weather changed. She had a prescription for pain pills, but seldom felt the need to take them. She valued a clear head over lack of pain. If she couldn't sleep, she'd take one, but never during the day. The pain eased enough so her eyes could stop watering at every movement. She didn't call it crying, she refused to cry. She just thought of it as her eyes leaking, caused by pain.

The telephone ringing brought her awake from where she'd been dozing in the now tepid water. Damn, it was all the way downstairs. Stepping out of the tub, she grabbed her towel, rushed down the hall, and took the stairs two steps at a time. She managed to grab the receiver in middle of the fourth ring. "Hello? This is Megan, who's this?" Her voice was breathless and she had to take a deep breath to hear the person on the other end.

"Ms. Holloway? My name is Special Agent David J. Harrison. I've been assigned to investigate the body you found in the National Forest." His voice was a melodic soft bass. He paused, sensing that she needed to catch her breath. "Did I interrupt you? You sound out of breath." He hoped he hadn't called at a bad time for the lady. However, he didn't hear anything in the background, but maybe a television.

"Oh, I was upstairs in the tub. This house is old and only has one phone jack so I had to run down the stairs." Blushing, Megan admitted the reason for her breathless state. She only blushed because she knew that he would know she hadn't dressed on the way to the telephone.

"If you like, I can give you my number to call me back when you're not distracted. I don't want you catching cold standing in the hallway dripping wet." He couldn't help the chuckle that slipped out as he envisioned a woman, any woman, any age and size, dripping over a hall telephone.

"Thanks, but I'm fine. I just grabbed my jacket off the back of the sofa." Megan admitted. "How can I help you?"

"Well, you can tell me where to meet you tomorrow so that we can get back to the body. Can we hike to the spot, or do we need to ride? If we need to ride, do you have a horse for me or should I bring my own?"

"Well, it's about a four mile ride into some rough country so horses are the quickest method of travel. We can supply a horse for you if that will get you here earlier in the day to begin the ride." She told him. "Horses around here are tough, sure-footed and can maintain a pace without problems; so I suggest you let us provide the animal for you."

"Sounds like a good idea. I'll bring myself and my gear. We might need a packhorse to haul out the body once I get all the photos and collect particulate matter. Even if it's just a skeleton, riding with it on your saddle could be difficult." He smiled grimly at the thought of throwing a body bag with a skeleton over the saddle in front of him or behind. Not a pretty picture, but it could be funny.

"I take it you've looked up Riverview? About what time do you think you could be here?" She asked. In spite of throwing her jacket over her shoulders, she was beginning to shiver. She hoped her teeth weren't rattling.

"I can be at Riverview between nine and ten tomorrow. Do you have a cell number or do you want me to call this number once I get to town?" David could tell from the quiver in the woman's voice that she was getting chilled. He wanted to wrap up this call so he could get started and she could get warm. "I'll need final directions on where to meet you."

"Cell phones are kind of sporadic at best, due to the hills and mesas around here. I'll wait for your call in the morning on this line and give you the final directions. On the other hand, we could meet at Betty's Diner in town, but that might actually delay our start. Once she starts talking, it's tough to get away from Betty." Megan chuckled at the thought of Betty latching on to an FBI agent.

"I'll call you as I get close to town, no stopping for coffee at the diner, got it. Thanks for the warning." This time he let her hear his chuckle. "Now, you go get warm and I'll look forward to talking with you tomorrow." He broke the connection and slipped his cell phone back into his pocket. Here he'd thought he would have some time off. Damn it, he knew better than to tell the section head where he would be while he was on vacation.

"What's the matter, Cuz? I told you not to answer that call from your boss." David's older cousin, Nelson, laughed at the frown showing on his houseguest.

"Looks like I'm in for a three hour drive tomorrow followed by a ride into the forest and meeting up with a skeleton. Just the way I wanted to spend this week." He shrugged and shook his head. "At least my guide sounds young but with my luck; she outweighs me." He frowned again at his cousin when the man laughed out right at his summation of his day tomorrow.

"Who knows, she might just be a beauty and smart. You've met too many criminals and not enough nice girls. I was going to introduce you to some of the sexy women around here – but now I can tell you're off on another of your adventures. Good hunting, cousin. Let's call it a night." He punched his cousin in the shoulder and tried to take the beer he was drinking from him.

"You don't remember I carry a gun, do you? Touch the beer and I think I can legally shoot you for abusing an agent of the FBI. I'll finish this and call it a night. I'll let you know when I can head back this direction. Thanks for the room; sorry I'll be missing the weekend with you." David stood up, hugged his cousin and headed for the back bedroom. Once there, he finished his beer, did a quick background check on Megan Holloway, whistled when her picture appeared and shook his head as he read her file from her days in the military. Thick, long blonde hair that curled over her shoulders, blue eyes, sun-bronzed complexion; yowsa, a looker, with a brain and a silver star. This could be fun.

After hanging up the phone, Megan ran back to the bathroom jumped into the barely warm water to ease her shivering. Drying herself slowly after she got out of the tub, she slipped into her warm robe. Downstairs, she heated water for a hot cup of chocolate while she did a quick search for Agent David Harrison.

Okay, David Joseph Harrison, to be exact. Native decent, raised by his mothers' family in the Dakotas. Nice photo, strong features, excellent background, finished well both in college and at the FBI training facility. She smiled at the photo. She wasn't looking for romance, but he was very easy on the eyes. He should be able to handle himself in the woods from his background. Well, maybe this babysitting gig wouldn't be so bad.

She spent extra time rubbing liniment into her aching shoulder, wishing, not for the first time, that it didn't look so damn ugly. The scaring would fade over time, but the loss of tissue created its own ridges and valleys, bothering her the most. Well, if she ever found a man, he would just have to deal with her deformity. At least she came by it honorably. Shaking off the momentary melancholia, she quickly slipped into her warm flannel pajamas and slid under the covers of her pre-warmed bed. She once more silently praised the person who came up with the heated mattress pad idea. Better than a warm dog for a comfortable sleep, she mused.

In her dream, Radar was screaming. Then Megan came full awake to the sound, it wasn't a dream. She made it down the stairs, grabbing her coat and slipping on her boots before the coat even settled over her shoulders. She opened the door to a sight from hell. For a second, she relived the explosion that pinned her under her desk over a year ago. She fought the urge to dive for cover. But no, the barn was burning. Radar wasn't locked in a stall, but his pen was only twenty feet deep and that was too close to a fire this hot.

Running out the door, she used all of her speed to get to the far gate on his run. She opened it, letting him loose to run, knowing he could be captured later. Then she did the same for the other two horses that belonged to Phil. Running back into the house she dialed 911, gave the details, then was back outside grabbing the hose from the house to wet down the roof. The barn looked to be a loss, but she could keep the fire from spreading.

Damn! Her tack was in the barn. Everything she had taken off Radar this afternoon, including the GPS in the front pouch on the saddle. Crap. Good thing she and Bethany marked the trail with ribbon. Otherwise, they'd never locate the trail or the skeleton. She wondered if her insurance would cover this while she wet down the side of the house and the ground between it and the barn. At least she'd parked her trailer safely across the yard and none of the horses had suffered serious injury. A distant wail told her the fire trucks were coming. The Volunteer department took a few minutes to gather, but those boys tended to move quickly when a barn was burning.

She saw the first vehicle; it was a truck full of R-M hands. Shorty was driving, Roger and Aaron were in the front with him and she could see three more in the back seat. She noted all this while continuing to hose the fire. It wouldn't do much, but it allowed her to feel useful in a hopeless situation.

"Megan! Are you okay? What started this fire?" Megan handed the hose to Shorty so she could face Roger and give him what answers she knew.

"I'm okay. I woke up to Radar screaming and got out here in time to turn the horses loose. None of them're hurt to my knowledge. I wet down the house to keep it safe, called the fire department and that's about where we stand. I have no idea what could have started the fire." She told him. "All of the tack I used today is lost. I was going to need it in the morning, so I left it on the saddle rack across from the stall," she explained. "I think my insurance will cover it, but that GPS had the spot of the skeleton cached as well as several other spots along our ride today." Megan frowned at the thought. "Thank goodness I have my old back up saddle in the trailer. It doesn't fit Radar as well, but we can get by with it."

"Stuff is replaceable, even horses if it comes down to it. I'm just thankful you didn't try to get into the building and rescue your tack." Roger noticed the stress in Megan's eyes while she watched the fire being attended by the newly arrived tanker truck. "Too many memories in the fire? Are you okay?" He asked her, reaching out to put a comforting hand on her shoulder.

"Yeah, I've seen too many fires and lost too many friends. I'm okay, there was only a second or two when I was suddenly back under the rubble." She confessed, warmed by the gentleness of his concern. Damn, her friend Bethany was so lucky to have him. She ducked her head and started for the house. The night was retreating and the false dawn brought shadows other than those cast by the fire. "I'll make a pot of coffee."

Aaron walked over to Roger and noticed the concern on his boss's face while the man studied her departure. "Everything okay, boss?" He asked. He liked Megan and if the boss was concerned over her, he wanted to know if he could help.

"Yeah, I think so. This fire brought back some nasty memories for her that she won't admit. I wish Bethany could come over and spend some time. Megan needs to vent some of this out before it eats her alive." Roger looked over at his foreman. "Why don't you go help her make coffee? She might talk to you, but don't push her; just let her know we care," he suggested. He sensed his foreman wanted to get closer to Megan; maybe this would draw them together. Since his marriage, he wanted the happiness he was living for all of his friends and Aaron had been a friend for many years. As Rangers, they had served together in Iraq and saved each other's ass more than once. He would understand Megan's emotional state.

"My pleasure, Boss." Aaron could not help but smile at the obvious maneuvering of his friend and employer. He headed into the house. He found Megan staring vacantly at the coffeepot while it overflowed in the sink. He moved carefully up behind her. "Megan, it's okay. You did fine tonight. All the stock is safe and anything else can be replaced," he murmured to her, putting one hand on her shoulder and reaching over the other to turn off the water.

Blindly, she spun in his arms and buried her head in his shoulder, her body beginning to shake from the sobs. "All I saw when the door opened was the wall that trapped me under the desk falling all over again. I came so close to diving under the nearest chair. Am I ever going to get past seeing that moment?" She felt the arms around her close behind her back. The chest against her cheek smelled of horses, sweat, smoke, and man. She tried to stop crying, but it got worse and her knees began to shake.

Knowing she didn't even know who was holding her, Aaron wondered at how right she felt in his arms. He ran his hands up and down her back until he felt her start to sag. He backed up and sat on the closest chair, pulling her onto his lap so she could cry herself out, knowing that she needed this, and likely had needed it since the trauma occurred.

Long moments later, Megan began to be aware of her surroundings. Trying to control the sobs that were shaking her entire body, she found her face pressed against a chest covered by a shirt wet with her tears. Hands held on to her, a chin rested against her hair, lips murmuring senseless calming phrases. "Oh, God; I'm so embarrassed. I've never cried like this." She muttered, finally regaining her self-control. Her voice was scratchy and soft. She wanted to hide, she didn't know who was holding her, but she hoped it was someone she didn't know so she'd never have to face him again.

"Hush, no need to be embarrassed. You needed this; you deserved to cry over what happened. You think you're the only soldier who ever had a melt down after being in combat? Woman, I could tell you stories… all of us have come apart at one time or another. Nothing to be embarrassed about." He stroked her hair, loving the sensuous feel of it under his palm. Soft, thick, the curls wrapping around his fingers at the ends. "You'll be okay, this will pass and you're going to feel so much better for letting go. Trust me, I know; okay?" He hugged her again as her tears began to flow once more.

She recognized his full, masculine voice. "Oh, Aaron. Look what I've done to your shirt. It's a mess. I owe you one. I'm so sorry that I fell apart. One minute I was running water the next I was reliving that last battle and then you were there and I was crying. Friends, fellow soldiers, my military career, all of it gone." She sniffled, looking for a tissue or towel. She became aware that she was sitting in his lap and blushed. "I've worked so hard not to feel sorry for myself and look how far it's gotten me. I'm a mess." She wailed, the tears flowing harder.

"You've come a long way from that day and I've never seen you show any remorse for what you lost. You're allowed to grieve… it's in the rulebook, grieving is okay. That way you can put it all behind you and start fresh. Until you've grieved over your loss, the wound is still open and festering. Now you've let it out; you should be able to pick up and move on. Here, dry your face." He handed her a dishtowel he managed to snag from his stool at the counter.

"Th… thanks. I know you're right, but I'm still embarrassed. I've never used, literally, a shoulder to cry on before. A pillow on occasion, but not a real live human." Wiping her cheeks and eyes with the soft cloth, she tried to smile at him. "Not only your shoulder, but it looks like I'm sitting in your lap and I don't even know how I got here." This time she did giggle at the position in which she found herself.

"Well, I'm proud to have been the shoulder and lap that were available for service." He smiled at her, thinking that even with her face flushed and eyes almost swollen shut she still had an inner beauty. He felt his groin tighten, he wanted nothing less than to hold her and comfort her for hours, but he could tell that she was recovering her composure and would soon want out of his arms.

"I still need to make coffee for the firefighters." Megan said. She knew she needed to get out of Aaron's lap, but she was experiencing a strange inner reluctance to move. It just felt too damn good to be held like a child. It was a long time since a man had held her; even if he thought she was some sort of weakling to fall apart because of a little barn fire. She sighed, wiggled to get her legs to the ground and noticed a lump under her right cheek. She ducked her head so he wouldn't see she had noticed his predicament but could not prevent the smile on her lips.

"Oh, so you think it's funny?" His voice turned lightly teasing. He knew that she had felt his erection and saw the blush as well as the smile. "Come here." He pulled her back against his chest, lifted her chin with his free hand and gently kissed her. His kiss deepened when he felt her surprise turn to acceptance and her lips open to his. He heard the back door and lifted his face to see who would come in without knocking. He glared at Roger.

"Let me up, I need to get that coffee made." Megan jumped up and moved to the sink, keeping her back to Roger. She didn't want him to know she'd been wailing like a baby just moments before he came into the house.

Roger took in Aaron's wet shirt and the towel on the table, raised his eyebrow at the man but refrained from commenting when Aaron shook his head and tilted it toward Megan's back. "Hey, how's the coffee coming?" He asked instead of the questions that he wanted answered.

"I'll bring it out shortly. Aaron, could you check on Radar for me? Put all three in the round corral with a water trough, if you would?" She asked still keeping her back to the men.

"Sure, I can do that. I think one of the volunteers managed to get a halter on Phil's mare before I came in to help you with the coffee." He said standing up and moving toward the door. "Boss, is the fire almost out?" He asked jerking his head toward the door for Roger to follow him. "I'll let you know when all the horses are in the pen." He led his boss out the door.

"What was that little scene? Did I interrupt something?" Roger asked, watching Aaron close his jacket over his wet shirt.

"You were right. She was ready to come apart at the seams. She had a small melt down. I think it's the first cry she's had since her injury." Aaron shook his head at the thought. "I just held her until she got it all out. She was getting up when she noticed the effect she had on me. Damn, a man would have to be dead not to react to that armful and I'm far from dead. She ducked her head and was about to giggle so I gave her a kiss to salvage my pride." He smiled at Roger, feeling his own cheeks burn.

"Well, take it slow. I think she's not ready for serious emotional involvement yet. Bethany would take a whip to both of us if Megan got hurt," he told his friend with a smile. "Good luck. She's a fine woman."

"Changing the subject… Have you found anything that points to a source of this fire?" Aaron asked.

"Well, I need to speak to Megan, but if she didn't store a diesel can and spare tire in the back corner of the building; we may have an arson fire. We found a burning tire with the smell of burning diesel almost overpowering the burning rubber. It takes a lot to get a tire going, but they burn hot and long once they start."

Roger scowled at the thought of someone burning a perfectly good barn for any reason. "We walked the property, especially around the house and found nothing suspicious close by. However, we found a trail behind the barn and there was some spilled fuel there, like the can sloshed." He sighed. "I'm having Shorty set up surveillance equipment. I don't want Megan to be in danger. I don't know what's going on and that bothers me most of all. What brought on this barn burning and what does it mean? A warning? An attempt to scare Megan off the property or even out of town? I just can't picture anything she would be into that would warrant this kind of thing."

"Well, if you need someone to watch over Megan, I volunteer." Aaron suggested.

"Not yet. She should be in the company of law enforcement over the next couple of days, getting the body out of the woods. That should keep her safe, at least during the day." Roger rubbed his forehead just under the brim of his hat. "I'll warn her to keep her gun handy for the night and we'll keep cameras on the outside in case the arsonist returns."

"Okay, but I'm not certain she shouldn't have one of us stationed in the second bedroom to keep guard at night." Aaron argued.

"Yeah, like I could trust you to stay in the second bedroom." Roger grinned at his friend with a knowing look in his eyes. "Give it a day or two. Let's see if we can ferret out the cause behind this first." He turned, hearing the door open and seeing Megan with her arms full of cups and the coffee pot. She lined cups along the rail of the porch and poured coffee. "Come and get coffee, you guys. Good job on the fire. Now take a break." She set the pot down and went inside, returning quickly with sugar and coffee creamer.

The crew stopped putting away hoses and came over for a hot cup of coffee. It was dawn and soon the sun would warm the day but at this moment, hot coffee would warm them.

Megan passed out some doughnuts she'd found in the freezer. She had cooked them in the microwave while the coffee finished and the men just about took her hands in snatching them from the plate. She knew they had to be hungry and this was the most she had to offer. "Thanks for getting here so quickly. Any idea what caused the fire?"

All eyes turned to Roger for the answer. Megan knew he was involved with the volunteers, but she hadn't realized he was in charge. Only the sheriff would take over and then only if Roger called him.

"You didn't have a can of diesel fuel in the barn, did you?" He asked.

"Lord no, I've more sense than to store flammables in with animals or wooden structures." Megan huffed at his suggestion that she could be so stupid.

"No offense. Just had to confirm it. In that case, it was arson. We found an empty five-gallon can of diesel fuel and a burning tire in the back right corner of the barn," he told her. "Someone wanted a long, hot fire and used them to create it. Did you have a can of diesel on the property?"

"I don't think so. I haven't done an inventory, but there's nothing here that uses diesel, unless the previous tenant had a diesel truck or tractor. Can't think of any other reason to keep the stuff around," Megan said.

"We'll get the sheriff's office to check for prints, but doubt if any will be found." Roger drank his coffee, looking around the group. "Keep your ears open. If anyone hears of any reason why this barn was torched, I want to hear about it. I'm having my crew set up surveillance cameras. If he comes back, we'll know it." Roger made the warning clear to all of them. He hoped it would get back to the arsonist. He didn't want this to happen again, especially not with Megan in the house.

"I'll keep my eyes open too." Megan said. "Can I borrow the stock trailer today? Do you think Bethany would let me take Harley? I need a second riding horse to take the FBI agent up the hill to collect the skeleton. Do you think one of Phil's horses would work for a pack animal to haul it out?"

Aaron stood up frowning at the thought of Megan going into the woods with a stranger.

"I've got a good pack horse for you; and so long as you ride him, Bethany likely won't mind you taking Harley." Roger filled in before Aaron could object. He pinned his foreman with a glare that kept him quiet.

Megan completely missed the looks exchanged over her head. "Good. I'm expecting him by ten and I want to haul in to where you picked us up yesterday. The skeleton is less than five miles from there and that's the easiest way in. We'll get to it by noon or so and be back at the trailer by three if all goes according to plan." She smiled at the group, missing the concerned looks exchanged amongst the men.

"Miss, maybe one of us should go with you; just to keep you safe." A quiet voice stated from the back of the crowd.

"I've got my pistol, my rifle, my knife and three years of military service with two deployments behind me. I think I can take care of myself, but thanks for the thought." Megan stated, using her fingers to tick off her experience and weapons.

A light laugh came from the group and a different voice called. "Maybe one of us should come along to protect the agent from you." This caused louder laughter and Megan blushed.

"Okay fellas, let's call it a day. We all have chores at home and the day is already starting. Thanks for the response. Joe you'll drive the truck back to the station, right?" Roger began sending the men home and directing traffic out of the ranch yard.

"I'll be over in a while to get the trailer, Harley, and the pack horse." Megan called after the departing men. She began to move into the house when Aaron stepped in front of her.

"Are you certain you're okay? I could likely find the trail and lead this guy in, if you don't think you're up to it," he offered.

"Thanks, I appreciate the offer. That cry did wear me out; but I feel much lighter and even with this disaster, my outlook seems brighter. Thank you for the shoulder. You're right. I needed to let all of that out. I'm not well yet, but I'm further along the road to recovery than I have been since it happened." She smiled shyly up into his eyes with the admission.

"You're going to make it through this and when you do, I'll be here waiting for you. I want you to know that."

Aaron kissed her forehead, stepped off the porch and trotted to the waiting pickup.

Megan waved, watching that last truck leave before entering the house, and then closing and locking the door.

Chapter Five

As the sun rose in the east, Agent David Harrison happily drove west-by-southwest to get to Riverview. Even so, the sun periodically blinded him in his rearview mirror. If he'd been driving directly west or, worse yet, east, his eyes would be watering in spite of his Ray-bans.

While filling his tank in Gunnison, he called Megan. It was just after eight; but he hoped she would be getting ready to meet him. He wanted to get on the trail, locate the corpse, gather all available trace evidence and get back to civilization before dark. The aching in his left ankle warned him of the weather changing. The only benefit of the break during his football years in school was a weather-predicting ankle. He smiled as the pump clicked off. At least he wasn't handicapped.

He heard ringing at the other end of his call and Megan's breathless voice. She really should set up a second telephone in that house. That, or get into better shape.

"Hello, Megan Holloway here. Is that you Agent Harrison?" Megan panted. This time she'd been in the bathroom brushing her teeth. The man had horrible timing.

"Yes, Ma'am. I'm in Gunnison. Just finished filling the tank. Want to give me directions on where to meet you?" David asked.

"Can you hold just a second; I need to spit out the toothpaste. You're going to need a pen and paper." Megan set down the phone and walked the four steps to the kitchen where she rinsed her mouth and returned. "There, I should sound clearer, talking without a mouth full of toothpaste."

"I've got a pen and paper. Am I coming to your place, or meeting you at the trailhead?" he asked.

"Well, the parking is crap at the spot the trail hits the road, so I thought it would be best to bring you here. I'll have the truck and trailer all set up so we can head out as soon as you transfer your gear." Bringing him to her place would be easiest of the options she'd considered. She'd get the ranch truck, stock trailer with Harley and the packhorse, and wait here. If he were just leaving Gunnison, she would have about half to three quarters of an hour.

"Sounds good. I don't want to have my Durango damaged in an out of the way parking area," David responded.

Megan shook her head; she wasn't going to waste time telling him they wouldn't be parking at a public trailhead. He'd see when they got there. "Okay, once you leave Riverview heading toward Montrose, drive about six miles until you come to NF867. Turn left and be ready to make another left turn, almost a u-turn within five hundred feet of the turn off the highway. Follow that road about three quarters of a mile and you'll come to a pretty sharp right curve. Just beyond that, you will see an old farmhouse with a burnt out barn. Pull into the drive and park anywhere in the yard that doesn't block my rig's access to the drive."

"Do you have the GPS coordinates for your location?" David asked. He didn't think he could get lost; but they would help him feel more comfortable about back roads and sharp turns.

"Sorry. My GPS burned in the fire last night and I don't recall the exact location for this spread." Megan frowned. She didn't expect to miss her Garmin so soon.

"Excuse me. Did you say 'fire last night'?" David

asked.

"Yeah, I'll fill you in when you get here. Right now, I need to go get the rig and extra stock from the main ranch. If I don't get started, I won't be here when you arrive." Megan patiently explained to the agent. "I'll see you when you get here. Call if you have problems finding this place." Not waiting for him to answer, she hung up the phone.

Grabbing her jacket, hat and keys she headed for her truck. She automatically pulled her hair through the back of her hat. She had it tied at the nape of her neck and hated how it felt under the edge of a ball cap. Once at her truck, she checked all the tires just to make certain nothing had gone flat over night. With the condition of the road to the house and the holes in the drive, nothing would surprise her. She drove cautiously up the pot-holed drive to the gravel road, turned left to head out to the highway.

At the ranch, she found one of the ranch trucks hitched up to the gooseneck stock trailer. Aaron was busy loading the pack gear into the tack area along with Harley's saddle. "Thanks, but I could have done this myself."

"Roger wanted me to get this all together and loaded for you. He says to make certain you lock the truck and the tack part of the trailer. Should be safe, but there are some yahoos who heavily use that road to get back into the woods. No sense tempting them with an unlocked truck." Aaron smiled over at her. Considering last night, she looked pretty good; her eyes had lost the swelling and looked clear and lovely. "Why don't you run up to the house to visit with Bethany before you leave? I'm almost done here; I'll load the horses next."

Megan walked up to the main house. "Hi! Is Bethany awake? How's she feeling this morning?"

"Yep. Come on in, she'll be happy to see you." Roger motioned her inside and pointed toward the living room. "She's in there, all comfy on the couch."

Megan saw Bethany seated on the couch with an ice pack at the base of her spine. "That looks cold."

"You got that right. But it numbs the pain quicker than the pain meds." Bethany smiled. "You're the one riding Harley, right?" She confirmed.

"Yes, I wouldn't put anyone on your horse. I'd rather that a stranger ride Radar. He's bombproof." Megan said.

"Good. In that case, use the hackamore." Bethany told her. "I wouldn't want a stranger to use that bit on him... he tends to test but I know you can handle it." She said. "I've seen you ride and you're enough like me that he won't mind."

"Okay, I'd better get going, the agent called after he left Gunnison and I need to get back to my place before he beats me there." Moving toward the door, she smiled at her friend. "You feel better soon and don't try to do too much before that bruise is healed." Megan waved to Roger as she let herself out. "See you two later."

Walking back to the barn, she found Aaron loading Harley. Hearing an approaching vehicle, she looked up to see a truck with a two-horse trailer stop in front of the house. They saw the driver go into the house.

"Yeah, I gave you old Millie for your pack animal. She's tough and she can keep up with the pace you'll want to go." He pointed to a paint mare in the trailer next to Harley. "I brought her up this morning and fed both her and Harley. A horse can't maintain a decent energy level without a good meal." He moved past her and grabbed a closeable bag that he proceeded to fill with oats from the feed storage bin. "Take this in case you need it. You can tie it on the back of the saddle"

"Thanks! I appreciate you getting both horses fed

and helping me load the trailer. I've been talking to the FBI agent and he should be here within a half hour." Megan took the bag of feed and threw it into the tack compartment. "Feels like you gave us enough for a week," she teased.

Aaron smiled at her. "Do you want me to send out a search party if you don't call before say, seven?" He teased back, ignoring her jibe.

"Hi, sorry to interrupt, but Roger told me I needed to see Aaron about where to put my mare, Lady Mica." Neither Aaron nor Megan noticed the approach of the truck and trailer or the petite, dark-haired woman who drove it. "My name is Kam." She smiled at the pair working at the trailer. "I can leave my tack in the trailer if you have a place to park it."

"I'm Aaron and this is Megan. She works for the new spread, the R-B Campground. She and Bethany were marking trail when the wreck happened yesterday. I understand you're Dr. Samuelson's nurse?" Aaron smiled at the small, dark-skinned woman, struck by the green of her eyes. He put out his hand in greeting.

"Glad to meet you both. I brought Mica over and was hoping to get a trail ride in today since it's my day off. Once you point me to a pen, I'll need directions to the closest trail. I have all day so any length will do." Kam shook Aaron's hand and nodded to Megan.

Before Aaron could speak, Megan cut in. She had a great idea, no sense her riding out alone with the agent, maybe she could talk Kam into joining them. "I'm heading out for a ride that should take up most of the day. I'm meeting up with another rider, and we're covering some of the same trail Bethany and I rode yesterday. Would you like to come along? Does your mare have shoes, the ground is pretty rocky." She smiled at Kam. "We're headed back to locate the skeleton and the other rider is an agent who is authorized to move it and bring it back for further investigation. Should be a fun time." She laughed at the uncertain expression on Kam's face.

"You have a strange notion of fun; but it does sound like an interesting ride. Mica can go twenty-five in a day without worries, possibly further," Kam assured Megan. "She's shod, but no pads. Think that will be enough?

"We seldom use pads unless we're competing over rough country. Regular conditioning or trail riding, we use regular shoes all year." Megan informed her. "Let's throw your mare and tack into this trailer. We'll leave from my place. The third rider should be arriving soon." Megan turned back to Aaron. "In answer to your earlier question about communications; I'm not certain if the agent has a sat. phone, but if he does I'll make certain to let you or Roger know when we start heading back. There's a cabin up there that Bethany and I found; he might want to check it out while we're up there."

"Well, just be certain to keep your Spot2 handy in case of any emergencies. This time use it, and if we don't hear from you by seven, I'll bring a group of the boys up looking for you." Aaron patted her back as he looked into the trailer at the two horses that filled the front section. Megan's big appaloosa and Kam's mare would fit in the back section of the trailer.

"See you later, Aaron. Kam, let's get loaded." She grabbed Kam's tack to store while Kam unloaded, brought her mare over, and loaded her into the stock trailer. Getting into the truck, they headed down the drive with the load of horses and gear.

Driving back to her place, Megan let herself think about Aaron. Of all the men she had met, he most fit her idea of a "good man." In the month she had been working for Roger and Bethany, she had seen him in many lights. She had witnessed him being a boss over the hands, best friend of Roger, concerned citizen and now he was a concerned friend of hers. Aaron accomplished all those different roles well. In fact, she had yet to see him floundering over anything. He even handled a sobbing woman well when most men would vacate the area at the first sign of female tears.

She sighed. He was nice on the eyes, too. Just the perfect height for her to rest her head on his chest, strongly built without any flab, his arms felt well muscled and his thighs under her seat felt strong and thick. She grinned. The lump in his pants hadn't felt too shabby, either. His lips were generous, but partially hidden by his soft, curly beard that shaped along his strong jaw. His eyes were green, flecked with gold, suiting his tanned face surrounded by curly, reddish-blonde hair a shade or two lighter than his beard. His kiss had been tender, then moved into hot and knowing. She felt her face flush at the memory and felt a need to try that again, only this time without interruptions. Whoa, she shook her head and frowned. Now was not the time for her hormones to awaken. She knew she wasn't emotionally ready to find romance and casual sex had never been her style.

"Shit." She almost missed her turn, She needed to quit daydreaming. Megan made the sharp left onto the road that led back to the ranch she rented. Movement in her mirror caught her eye and she saw a Durango take the turn behind her. It was likely one of the crew working at the R-B, but it could be the agent. She hadn't had a call from him, but then she hadn't been in the house to receive a call either. She followed the road past the sharp right curve, pulled into the ranch yard, and parked by the round pen. The Durango followed her. Cautiously, she leaned over and pulled the pistol from her glove box. "Don't get excited, a Durango just followed us from the highway. I'm expecting an FBI agent, but since someone burned my barn last night, I don't want to jump to conclusions," assuring Kam when the woman eyeballed the pistol. She'd put it there because of nerves over the fire, now she was happy she had. She slipped it into her jacket pocket before casually opening the door and climbing out of the truck. Her hand rested in her pocket, never leaving the pistol, she flipped off the safety.

"Ms. Holloway? I'm FBI Agent David Harrison," the man said, extending his hand in greeting.

The approaching man matched the photo she'd seen online so she took her right hand off the pistol and reached out to shake his extended hand. "Nice to meet you. Call me Megan. This is Kam Marjani. She's decided to join us today." Taking back her hand, she casually put it into her pocket to flip the safety back on the pistol as she made the introductions.

"Call me David. Would you like to see my creds?" David offered, reaching for them in his hip pocket. He smiled at her thinking her photo had not done her justice.

"Fine, David it is. No, you look just like your photo on the net; creds can be duplicated; faces take a lot more time and effort." She smiled at him, taking in his average height, his barrel-chested build, longer black hair tied at his nape, warm cinnamon toned skin and dark brown eyes. This man got all his looks and size from his Native heritage. Between him and Aaron, she liked Aaron's shape and coloring more than the stouter man in front of her. She frowned. Why should she compare the two men?

"Well, your photo must be older, it makes you look tougher, more like the soldier you were." David admitted researching her as she had obviously checked on him. "I like the new look better. It's more feminine." His eyes made contact but it was a simple cursory glance. His eyes narrowed when he looked over at the newcomer. Her size seemed to belie her physical strength. He could see muscles in her biceps and even her thighs bunching when she gracefully moved forward to shake his hand. Her touch to his hand was firm and dry, but warmed him all the way up his arm.

"Hi, my name is Kam" Her voice matched her size, soft, sweet, and easy on his ears.

"It's easier to let your hair grow when you know you'll be home at night to wash it." Megan said, missing the interaction behind her. In her mind, that was the main difference between her military life and her current life. She wasn't aware that the military photo showed a stern face of command where, especially after last night, her current expression was more tired, and a bit sad. "Let me get Radar loaded along with his saddle. David, you can put your gear into the back seat of the truck or the bed, whichever suits your needs." She told them, moving toward the round pen.

For the three horses, there was only one halter hanging on the gate and she didn't recognize it. One of the volunteers must have grabbed a halter from their own truck to use on the loose stock this morning during the fire. She would have to get Radar a new halter and swipe a couple from Roger for the other two horses. His uncle Phil couldn't exactly provide new halters for his stock from prison. Each horse needed an easily accessible halter; last night was proof of that, even if there hadn't been time to halter the horses before turning them loose.

Fortunately, the halter fit, on the last hole; but it would work today. She led the horse to the trailer, opened the back gate, tied the rope over his neck and allowed him to enter. Megan then took her saddle from her trailer, threw it into the tack compartment managing to fit it in around all the other tack. She circled the rig checking and securing all the latches and wiring. She turned to David and Kam. "You ready to rock and roll?"

Both nodded. Megan climbed into the driver's seat, waiting and watching as Kam and David seemed to jockey for the shotgun position. This truck had no back seat, so one of them would be in the middle on the bench and she didn't care which lost the coin toss. Using the electronic button on her armrest, she rolled down the passenger window. "Okay, quit fussing. I had a bath so one of you get in here next to me. I don't bite, either." She called to them.

David opened the door. "I carry a weapon and need to be able to exit the truck quickly. Kam thinks she should have the window. You've seen combat; explain the facts of danger to this woman." He pleaded with Megan.

"I hate to admit it, but the man has a point. On a daily basis, he would always take the window to protect others in the vehicle. We're not in danger, but old habits die hard, so Kam; unless you want to see the agent scowl the entire five minute drive, let him have the window." Megan explained to the other woman with a sigh.

"Fine, I'm just used to seating people in the old 'girl, boy, girl' configuration. I didn't mean to interfere with FBI regulations or male protective hormones." Kam couldn't help but laugh at the satisfied smirk on the agent's face while she climbed into the cab next to Megan.

"How'd you join this venture into the wilds, Kam?" David inquired. He liked being next to the petite woman but managed to keep his arm at his side rather than run it behind her as he wanted.

"Oh, I was the nurse who attended Bethany yesterday after the ladies got down off the mountain. Bethany offered me a place to stable my mare. I got there to find Megan loading Harley and the packhorse. I said I wanted to ride out today. Megan told me about this trail ride and asked me to come along." Kam managed a sideways glance at the agent and blushed when she met his direct, measuring stare. "I didn't realize there was a body involved until this morning. Bethany only told us about her fall, not what she found on the ground."

"Interesting. Any reason why the finding of a skeleton would have been held back, Megan?" He looked over at the driver with raised eyebrows. Forced to lean forward, his arm brushed Kam as he turned. His skin tingled at the contact with soft female shoulder.

"Yeah, we thought it best not to let out the information because Riverview is a hotbed of gossip and we wanted the authorities to get to the skeleton before the locals messed up the scene. You have no idea, what these people around here could do to a nice orderly crime scene." She laughed, turning onto the highway.

"Well, thanks for the thought. Now, what happened to your barn last night? Was it arson, or was there a lightning strike without a storm?" David kept his eyes on Megan but noticed out of the corner of his eyes the surprise on Kam's face.

"What fire? Megan, I saw the burnt barn but figured it must have happened a while ago. Gossip hasn't reached the Bailey's yet about any fire." She told Megan and David.

"Well, all we know is that it was arson. We still don't know why or who but Roger is setting up surveillance for the property and an intruder alarm system for the house. The fire took out the saddle and tack that I used yesterday, including the Garmin where we geocached the location of the skeleton." Megan told them, turning onto BLM 26 from the highway. "Bethany and I marked the trail so we should have no trouble finding it; but it bugs me that I lost all our work from yesterday."

"Would anyone be able to use your Garmin to find the skeleton?" David asked.

"I think so, but they most likely would have to start where we did at the campground rather than start where we came out. Why do you ask?" Megan glanced over at the agent.

"Who knew about the skeleton? Exactly who did you tell?" He asked.

"Well, Shorty took the call. He told Aaron and Roger. It's possible he told the other hands over dinner." Megan paused and thought a minute. "I left word about it with the dispatcher for the sheriff, so that's at least two more people, and could be that whole office by now, and then I left word for your office," Megan concluded. "It was about nine when I called the sheriff's office. I did that just before I called your office." She shook her head. "Honestly, with the gossip mill in this area, just telling Shorty yesterday afternoon could have spread the word across the county. I never told him not to mention it, so who knows how far it spread."

"So who knew you used the Garmin to mark the location and are you certain it was burned up in the fire? Did you see the case?" Frowning, David pressed the question.

"The R-B crew would know because Roger has mentioned that anyone working on the R-B should carry a GPS to geocache specific points that might interest our future guests." Megan explained. "I didn't see anything in the barn, because I haven't been back in there to check. It was depressing and I've been busy this morning getting ready for this ride."

"You think that maybe someone took Megan's GPS and then started a barn on fire to cover its theft? That's a bit extreme for a gadget that costs less than a few hundred dollars, isn't it?" Kam's face mirrored doubt as she asked.

"You have a point, but what if the fire was to deter Megan along with getting to the skeleton before us?" David asked, his suspicious mind mulling over all the possible reasons.

"That's a possibility, but there's a crew working at the grounds of the R-B and anyone following the GPS trail would be visible at the trail head." Megan reasoned.

"What about one of the workers? Or could a rider or hiker find the trail from a different location?" he inquired

Megan thought over the terrain and location of the trailhead. "Well, a person on foot will be spending a long time getting to the skeleton from the campground. It's about seven miles in from there and the ground isn't easy walking." Megan told him. "If they found a spot to park and work their way up the hill to find the trail on horseback without going through the campground; it could be done, but they'd have to really know these woods. I can think of a spot or two where they might be able to park a rig; but it wouldn't speed them to the skeleton. Here we are folks. End of the line." Megan said as she maneuvered the rig into the same spot Roger had waited the day before. "We can unload and saddle here, but it's another half-mile up this road to where the trail comes out. Let's get moving or we're going to be out here all day."

David got out and aided the petite Kam to the ground from the tall truck. She smiled up at him, but moved off quickly, not staying long enough in his arms to even bring a blush to her face. He grinned after her departing back. Yep, this was going to be an interesting day.

Chapter Six

With little conversation, the group saddled up. David saddled Radar with Megan directing tack usage. Ready to ride before the others, Kam spent a few moments checking the water bottle holder, adding her cell phone to the pouch and strapping her Garmin 305 to her wrist. She might not be able to geocache, but she'd be able to track the ride later. She noticed a full rifle scabbard on Radar's saddle. "Expecting trouble?" she questioned, pointing to it.

"You know the adage in the woods – 'few riders have ever complained about having a rifle, but not having one can mean your life'." Megan and David repeated the oft-used phrase almost in unison.

"Okay, y'all ready to ride?" Megan mounted Harley and looked around at the other two. "David, pass me that lead line for the packhorse. Thanks." She took the line from the agent, waited while both riders mounted and headed south on the gravel road. "We've got less than a mile along here before we turn onto the trail. We'll move out on the up hills and walk the down. This gravel can be slippery over the hard packed road." Megan urged Harley to a trot.

Grabbing Radar's mane it took David a second to get in harmony with the easy movement of the large Appy. He hadn't expected Megan to take off at a trot. "Easy, Boy," he murmured to the gelding.

Kam giggled at the surprised look on the agent's face. It was clear he could ride, but obvious that he wasn't used to this kind of pace for any length of time. Her mare moved into her long trot going up the hill before shifting into a lope, using the power of her hindquarters to propel them up the moderate incline. "Come on, David. Let him move." She urged, passing him.

He felt his eyebrows go up and knew he had to catch the minx. He laughed and urged the long legged gelding into a good gallop and overtook both riders at the top of the hill.

As they shifted down to a walk, David's face was all smiles. "Wow, that was fun. I haven't been on a horse in ages. I like this guy. He's smooth and willing to move out."

"Yeah, Radar can keep up with any horse and he can go all day. Last time I competed on him, year before last, we finished a decent fifty in less than seven hours. Not bad. We came in tenth. Even got a great vet score, but had too much time to make up to win Best Condition," Megan bragged on her gelding.

"You ride endurance, I ride competitive trail but have been thinking about trying the faster sport. Cool, now I have someone to train with." Kam's eyes lit up at the thought of having a riding partner.

"Excuse me. What are you girls talking about?" David's face looked puzzled. The three continued downhill abreast at a walk.

"Endurance is a distance race for horses with vet checks and criteria such as amount of time you can take and breaks for the horse. Competitive Trail is a distance sport, but there are limits on how fast you can go and obstacles or tests to pass during the ride. It's more controlled and judged than endurance and the distances are shorter." Kam explained to the agent.

"What kind of distances are we talking here?"

"Well, endurance events are fifty miles and up, but they also offer a category called Limited Distance that ranges from twenty-five miles up to fifty," Megan explained her sport.

"Competitive trail never goes beyond thirty-five miles and offers different levels for those who want less time in the saddle. Judging starts from the time you sign in at a competitive trail ride. Everything from how your horse is tied to the trailer to how you present the animal to the vet for inspection. It's a lot more complicated that Endurance." Kam gave him an overview of her sport.

"These horses compete in distance races? All of them?" He glanced over at the two helmeted riders. "That why you wear the head gear?"

"I was told that 'If you have a brain to protect, you wear a helmet; otherwise you don't need one…' to quote my mentor of many years ago." Megan said.

"I've ridden since I was six without a helmet, come off lots of times, broken bones, but never felt the need of a helmet." David proudly bragged.

"It only takes once. Sooner or later, it will catch up with you." Megan warned then decided to let the matter drop. Helmets weren't mandatory to ride a horse, motorcycle, or even a bicycle; but they made sense to her.

At the bottom of the hill, the horses shifted into a trot then a gallop as they headed up the next long hill. The riders moved into the horses, catching manes in fingers while leaning into the speed. They crested the hill with Kam in the lead on the Arab mare, Radar just behind because of his long legs and Harley bringing up the rear; irritated that the old packhorse held him back.

"That is so not fair. Harley could have beaten both of you, if not for Millie. She sees no sense in racing. Almost pulled my arm from the socket." Megan rubbed her shoulder. Of course, it was the left. She knew better than to use that arm, but some habits just died hard. She would pay tomorrow for this action today.

"Okay, no more racing. But it was fun." David said. "How much further to the trail, Megan?"

"See that orange ribbon about half way down this hill on the left? That's where we turn into the woods and begin following the trail Bethany and I marked yesterday. I'll lead." She pointed to the ribbon flowing in the breeze up on the side of the road.

"Wow, if you hadn't told me where to look, I would have missed it." Kam said. "I take it you didn't want it to be completely visible to every truck driving this way?"

"You catch on quick." Megan let Harley walk out, the mare keeping pace with his faster walk without objection. Apparently, she only disagreed with trotting and galloping uphill.

"Let me lead the mare, we'll make better time if she's following all of us." David offered.

"No, Radar wouldn't tolerate the lead slapping on his flanks. How's your mare with ponying a packhorse?" She asked Kam.

"She's kind of alpha, but with a long lead rope; she won't kick out. I can take Millie." Kam rode up to Megan and took the lead from her extended left arm. She noticed the wince when Megan stretched out to hand it over. "Are you okay, did Millie pull hard enough to hurt you?"

"I'll be fine, old battle wound; only acts up before weather and if I overextend my arm. Today, I'm guilty of one and nature the other. I took an Advil and I'll be fine until tomorrow." She smiled at the other two riders before turning to head up the faint trail in the embankment.

Kam frowned at her back and glanced at David who shrugged before he followed Megan up the bank and into the woods.

"Bethany really wanted to have this trail marked

before snowfall. Now, I'm not certain it'll be finished until spring. We're due weather by tonight." Megan frowned, thinking of how badly Bethany wanted this first trail set up for use by the time snow melted.

"What needs to be finished, I thought this was the trail head." David commented.

"Well, we planned on making a loop. We started at the R-B Campground, went higher on the hill and wanted to bring the riders back there by a lower trail." Megan responded. "This spot could be used by either a rider's crew or by guest support to bring in picnic supplies to riders."

"Hmmm, can you mark the trail back to the campground without any help?" Kam asked. Riding at a walk in the woods allowed them to continue their discussion.

"Sure, I always carry surveyors ribbon on my saddle. I can use it to mark the trail. The color isn't the same, but that's not an issue. Why?" Megan turned to look at Kam.

"Once we reach the skeleton, the trail back to the road is well marked. You give me the truck keys then use my compass and GPS to find your way back down the mountain to the campground, marking trail all the way." Kam suggested to Megan over David's shoulder. "David, you don't need her help with the skeleton, do you? You trust me to get us back to the truck?"

"I don't know, is it safe for Megan to ride through the woods alone?" He frowned at first one then the other of the riders. "I wouldn't want anything to happen to you, Megan. I don't like the idea of you going off alone in an area without any trail."

"Oh, come on. We condition alone all the time. You two will know where I'm headed and if I get turned around, I'll just go downhill until I reach the highway. Also, my Spot2 didn't burn up and it's in my pocket if I need help." Megan smiled at the idea of being able to finish this trail for Bethany. "It's only seven miles. I'd be done by two at the latest. I've got Bethany's rifle on this saddle. Roger put scabbards on all her saddles." She argued.

"Well, I still don't like it; but I'm outnumbered. Just remember that I voted against this idea." David conceded defeat in his attempt to keep them together.

"Yippee! Bethany will be so happy that we got the trail marked and ready for finishing in the spring!" Megan whooped.

Kam smiled at her, knowing she was right and hoping Megan would be safe. There was really no reason to worry, but David did have a point about splitting up not being a great idea. "I've got my cell phone, but it might have problems with reception in the woods. David, do you have a cell or satellite phone?"

"Government doesn't issue sat phones; but my cousin gave me his when he found out I was going 'back country' on this investigation." David pointed to the phone strapped to his waist. "Cell phones are pretty useless once you're in the mountains."

"Good. We each have a way of contacting help, if needed. I think this should work great," Kam assured her riding companions.

The trail narrowed, became rocky and conversation ceased while the horses navigated down into a wash. Dappled sunlight lit their way where the trees allowed it to penetrate. The horses picked their way across rough ground while foraging animals were heard in the leaf matter along the trail. A young buck bound away up the hill and the riders soothed the startled horses while they enjoyed its smooth movement.

"Oh, look. See the three ribbons on this aspen? They

mark the turn to the cabin." Megan pointed to a tree with three ribbons tied around the base. "We didn't want to confuse riders into thinking it was a definite turn in the trail, so we put a high ribbon on the right to draw the eyes and only put the ribbons down low to tell us this is the spot for the cabin trail."

"Great idea, I've been watching upper ribbons, I never would have thought to look down." Kam told her. "How far up that trail is the cabin?"

"It's not far. We began marking that trail just over the rise from this one. If you look, you can see rocks leading you up the hill…" She pointed to five or six small boulders in a row. "Once you get high enough to see over the rise, you'll be able to see the ribbon on a tree to follow the trail to the cabin."

"Wow, how clever." Kam smiled. She liked the way Megan and Bethany marked a trail any rider or competitor could follow.

"I'm real happy you ladies know what you're talking about. All I know is to look for the next ribbon or follow the hoof prints on the trail." David said. Pointing at a ribbon ahead of them, he took the lead at a faster walk. "Come on boy, we don't have all day." He grumbled.

Megan and Kam laughed before following, but Kam made a mental note of the cabin trail. It might be fun to come back here in the spring and take it.

"I think I found the wash. Is that the spot over there where the rocks are painted orange just below the edge of the gully?" David called back to the riders behind him. "I'm dismounting and leading Radar down, I don't like the looks of the ground around here."

Megan and Kam rode up in time to see Radar's ass going over the edge into the gully. "I think walking is better than riding around here, especially after what happened to

Bethany yesterday." Megan dismounted from Harley, waiting for Kam to get off Lady Mica. She started down into the wash, finding the trail she and Bethany marked the day before.

"Wow. I see why you're concerned. Look across the wash, that overhang is dangerous." Kam pointed straight across to the overhang above the skeleton.

"That's the spot where Coup caused a slide; see the rocks and debris forming that vee to the left of the skeleton's grave?" Megan pointed while leading Harley down the zigzag trail.

Dropping Radar's reins, David had gotten up to the skeleton, not by the trail so carefully marked, but by climbing straight up the side of the wash. Megan shook her head; she led Harley over to the patch of wild oats, hobbled him, and removed the reins while Kam did the same for Lady Mica and the packhorse. She walked over to Radar, hobbled him and removed his headstall so he could graze with the others. The horses would graze but not leave the wide gully while the riders worked above.

"We put the rocks we moved back over the skull, but originally, the skull was exposed." Megan walked up the trail marked the day before to join Kam and David at the skeleton.

Photographing the scene, David moved up the bank to the top of the gully to get angles showing the site from the upper ground level. Next, he came back down to get the hole at eye level; he had already photographed it from below. Once he had shots from all angles, he carefully approached and began to move boulders out of the way, taking care not to disturb the hole or its gruesome contents.

"We think that this hole is from a tree that fell over. You find round holes all over in the woods around here.

The ground isn't tight and old trees fall due to wind or an ice storm, leaving large holes where their roots once held them up." Megan explained. She wasn't certain how much the agent knew of forestry and mountains. She expected him to know, but thought it wise to mention the conclusions she and Bethany reached.

"Yeah, I've noticed them as we rode here and wondered why so many trees seemed to just fall over without signs of an avalanche. You're right about the ground. It's all rocks and loose. It wouldn't take much to topple a tree when the roots are shallow and the ground loose like this." He paused to examine the land around the gully before carefully choosing another boulder to remove.

"What do you want me to do? I can help you with the rock removal, or perhaps work as a gofer when you need something from your packed equipment." Kam offered.

"Well, as I get further into this hole, it would help if I simply pass rocks to you rather than have to lean out to toss them down into the wash. We need to set up a tarp to hold any that seem to have evidence on them and a second one for any clothing or personal items." David began directing Kam and Megan while still carefully lifting out rocks.

"I'll bring up a couple of tarps for you and spread them out. Megan can find your plastic evidence bags in the pack for small things and such." Kam walked back down into the gully, quietly approaching the packhorse. "Easy, Girl. Just me," she murmured, touching the mare's back before looking into the closest pack for the tarps she remembered Aaron storing.

"Good girl. I'm over here." Megan spoke softly to the mare before opening the pack on the other side to take out the clear bags with "Evidence" stenciled on them.

Using available rocks, Kam created a dish in the side of the gully, and spread a tarp across and into it before securing it with boulders. She did a second one next to the first before climbing back up the wash to David.

"Here you go, where do ya want me to set these Evidence baggies?" Megan climbed up the gully wall to avoid the tarps so carefully set out by Kam.

"Oh, let me have them, I'll put them above the hole to the left so they're handy when I come across special items." David reached back without looking taking the proffered bags and setting them under a smaller rock to his left. "Wow, look. That's his patella next to the scapula. Since humanity seems to feel that a corpse needs to lay full out for burial, I think this was either a body dump or a hole crawled into for protection. Against what, maybe we can find some clues. He's crumpled up on himself." Pausing in his rock moving, David took a close-up of the bones mentioned. "Wait, there's a break in the femur, his pants are torn, either from it or from the age of the fabric." He pointed to the grim appearance of a white bone jutting away from the angle of the others in the hole and ragged denim exposing it. "There's no blood residue on the fabric. Very likely this bone was broken and the pants torn after the victim's death."

"You can actually tell that? Amazing, but gross." Megan gave a delicate shudder and stepped back from the worksite. "I guess the body was bound to be exposed eventually. This gully has widened over the years and now you can likely expose the entire hole from the side rather than having to dig down from the top." Changing the subject, Megan looked over the ground where the creek had eaten away the side of the gully. This past spring had been very wet with rain on the snowpack causing major run off problems back in May.

"I remember this past spring being so wet, but I thought that was just in the Midwest." Kam looked over at Megan, and then waved at the gully. "This gully looks like it had a lot of high water this past year." Debris had been deposited above where they currently stood in a couple of spots.

"It was bad, over the road in places that are just small run off creeks." Megan assured her. "Looks like you two are set up. Here are the keys to the truck." Megan handed Kam the keys in trade for Kam's Garmin. "I'm out of here; I'll see you two back at the ranch. I'm going back the way we came for about a mile before I turn downhill. You'll likely hear me when I work my way back across this wash later." She turned, reattached Harley's reins, removed the hobbles, mounted and rode up the trail they had so carefully walked down earlier. Strange how uphill trails always feel so much safer than downhill trails.

Kam waved at her before turning to take a boulder from David. "Looks like we're on our own. Trust me to get us back to the truck?" she teased.

David looked around in surprise. He'd been so involved with removing the stones without compromising the corpse that he hadn't noticed or heard Megan leave. "Huh? We are? Okay, we can handle this. Here, take the camera and get a few shots of the hole with me next to it for scale and location," he ordered Kam, looking around when she just stood there, not taking his camera from him. "What?" His confusion made her smile, but she only tapped her foot. "Oh, I'm sorry. Would you please take the camera and get some shots for me? Thank you." He finished when she stepped forward and took his camera. "I didn't mean to be rude; I just get into my work and forget you don't work for me. But, you're right, even if you did, I can still remember to ask and say thanks." He smiled before turning back to the hole and once more being oblivious to his surroundings. "Damn woman." He muttered to the long dead body.

Kam snickered, moving to different locations to take photographs of the agent with the hole. She knew his kind of concentration. Her father had been a paleontologist and once entranced by a dig site, nobody could get his attention without actually touching him. She also heard his mutter, but ignored it, knowing he would always express frustration in this manner. She'd once caught her father in a detailed conversation with some bones in a hole about how her mother expected him to remember to show up for dinner. She smiled at the memory, took one last shot and moved back to begin accepting rocks from David and throwing them either down into the gully or over onto the tarp.

"I will say this is the first time I've found a hole so easy to access." David actually turned and made eye contact with Kam. Her smirk startled him. "What? Do I have rocks in my hair? You're smirking."

She laughed at him. "No. You're fine. I was only remembering another man who could be so involved with bones in a hole that a volcano could explode and he wouldn't notice."

"Hmmm. Lover or relative?" He his curiosity forced him to ask.

"Not that it's any of your business, but it was my late father. Mom met him on a dig in South Africa. We traveled with him until his death and I spent a lot of time at dig sites, being told to be careful not to disturb the bones." Her eyes misted with the memory. "I was ten when he died. We moved back to the US and mom began teaching. After that, I spent my summers with my mother's people in Oklahoma." She felt her face warm. She hadn't meant to reveal so much to him.

David saw the warm hue. He smiled at her, hoping to ease her discomfort. "I was raised in the Dakotas by my maternal grandparents. I learned white man's history in school and Lakota ways from my grandfather and uncles. I like to think I'm well rounded, but sometimes wonder what I'm doing so far from my people. I never met my father or his family. He died when I was only a year old and my mother died before I was six. Now, we're even. I know about your heritage and you know about mine. Pass me the camera, please." He held out his hand.

They worked in silence except for exchanges about the rocks or bones until the entire body was exposed and the shape of the hole defined. After taking more photos, David pulled out a tape recorder to document the actual removal of the body. He handed Kam a pair of latex gloves and a facemask before donning his own.

Watching him intently, Kam remained silent. His hands were exceptionally gentle and respectful once they began to handle the remains.

"Body appears to be a male of undetermined age. Tissue is desiccated rather than decomposed. Lack of air, moisture and possibly the cold of this altitude possibly retarded decomposition for an extended period of time." He handed the skull to Kam who laid it gently on the clean tarp.

"Body folded in on itself, roots from tree tangled with arms and feet. Tree shows lack of decomposition as well. Length of tibia and fibula lead me to assume victim about six feet tall. Only trauma evident on remains other than apparent bullet hole in skull is the broken femur protruding through torn leg of jeans." He next passed her the main torso, dried muscle and connective tissue held it together as one part down to the base of the spine.

Kam handled it mostly by the heavy shirt fabric,

which remained in surprisingly good condition. The odor of decay was mild compared to what she expected. There was dried brain tissue splattered over the shoulders and back of the shirt along with dried blood. Good thing she'd never been the squeamish type; she thought.

"It appears that the body has been well protected by the rocks and lack of soil in the hole. Very little deterioration to clothing or boots. Boots look to be from some time in the first quarter of the twentieth century. Pockets of victim turned inside out. Possible motive for the murder could be robbery." David attempted to lift the hips and legs of the body as one unit but the weight of the boots caused the body to separate at one knee where bent joint for so many years weakened it and at the broken spot of the one femur. "Oops. Well, I knew I wouldn't be able to pull it out in one piece, but I'd hoped for fewer than three." David sighed.

Kam took the hips, one femur whole, one femur partial and workpants from him by the belt and laid them next to the torso. David picked up the left boot with the tibia, fibula and foot still within it. He carefully passed it to Kam who set it next to the other remains.

David next passed Kam the broken right leg and boot before turning back for the arms. "Unless they were stolen, there appears to be no rings or jewelry with the corpse. Hands are desiccated and partially curled from the dehydration process. Rings should still be on the fingers if any had been buried with the body." He passed the left arm over to her. "Try to keep it in that position, at least until we get it photographed."

Taking the arm, Kam made a face at the mummified tissue holding it together. She laid it down, shuddered, took the camera and photographed it from the angle of the shoulder and again from the hand end to get a good representation of the shape of the hand and overall position of the arm.

    David reached into the hole, carefully lifted the right arm, passed it over to her, watching as she set it down, and photographed it. Reaching into his hip pocket, he pulled out his personal flashlight and leaning into the hole began to carefully inspect it for any further body parts or evidence. Quartering the space mentally, he moved the light slowly within the quarter before moving it to the next. "Aha! Here's a button with a piece of cloth. Must have gotten stuck on the body." He pulled out the small item and slid it into a baggie before passing it to Kam.

    The next two quadrants were clean of anything other than rocks, but in the last section, where the torso had been leaning, he hit the jackpot. "Well, lookee here." He breathed out the phrase softly to himself. "This looks like the front concho of a saddle, with the saddle strings still on it. Bet the killer didn't know he left this behind."

    David had to step into the hole to reach across and pull the saddle strings from between two rocks bringing the leather rosette and the silver concho with them. "Looks like there's a brand engraved on the concho, but I'm going to need a magnifying glass to see it. It's pretty dinged up." He showed the concho to Kam, but didn't let her touch it before he slid it into a fresh baggie of its own. He took a larger baggie and began to scrape the loose rocks and gravel into it from the bottom of the hole in case there might be any small trace he'd missed. Then he did the same three more times, one for each remaining section of the hole. Each baggie weighed about four pounds when he finished loading them. He sealed each evidence bag, labeled it, and then climbed out of the hole to examine his amassed find.

    "I know it's not exactly what you might want, but it's after one – can I interest you in some lunch?" Kam interrupted his train of thought.

"Wow, that late already? How time flies. What's on the menu?" He smiled over at her.

"Well we have bottled water, jerky, granola bars, cookies, Heath bars, and yogurt covered raisins. What's your pleasure?" She asked moving over to the horses while removing her gloves and mask.

"Let me see... Think I'll try a piece of jerky, a granola bar and a Heath along with a bottle of water. Please." He followed her, removing his own gloves and mask.

He found a large boulder in the sun. "I think this 'table' has been reserved for us. Don't you?" He turned to accept the food she carried over to the sunny spot he selected upwind from the remains.

"Excellent choice of table. I think this boulder has my name on it." She laughed, sitting down on a medium-large rock.

David spread out the food so that they could help themselves before he passed her a bottle of water and sat down on a taller rock next to her. "I'm glad Megan didn't stay, this is kind of a light meal."

"Well, I was wishing she had stayed. She forgot she had the sandwiches." Kam laughed. "I think I heard her cross the wash while you were still pulling rocks out. If I'd remembered then, I would have called her to bring back the food."

"Well, it's not like we plan on camping out for days. This will get us through until dinner. If not, I've got a pistol and I see a rifle on your saddle. Know how to use it?"

"You don't grow up in Oklahoma without learning to hunt, especially not in Cherokee country. My grandfather was pure Cherokee and he believed in us grandkids respecting and learning the old ways. I'm damn good with a bow too. I can even make one if I have the materials." She smiled at his expression. "We aren't that different, you and I. You're Lakota and I'm Cherokee mixed with an Irish African paleontologist, both raised, at least in part, by extended family who believed in the old ways and traditions."

"Any mystics in your family?" David asked. His great-grandmother had contact with "the ancestors" and spent many hours telling stories of the "time before whites". David wasn't certain he believed where her stories came from; but they entranced him as a child.

Nodding, Kam took a bite of candy bar. "My mother's father's father was a medicine man. Much respected and feared by the tribe. I only met him once, just before his passing. He put his hand on my head and told my grandfather that he should trust my sight because I could see what should be remembered." She shook her head. "He died the next day and I've never understood his statement. But my grandfather used to ask me my feelings and opinions at odd moments until his passing when I was eighteen."

"Hmmm, sounds intriguing. Ever have visions?" David looked her in the eyes.

"You're serious, aren't you?" Kam shook her head. "I've had some strange dreams over the years, but never any I would call 'visions'."

"My heritage allows me to be more open-minded than most whites can allow themselves to admit. The mystic is part of my culture. It doesn't frighten me to work around the dead because I'm trying to aid in finding them peace. I don't expect a corpse to talk to me, but I doubt if I would run screaming if I had a clear dream about a murder I was investigating. Can anyone be certain that the dead can't give us help in solving the mysteries of how they died or who might have been involved?"

Kam studied his face as he spoke. She knew he believed in what he said, but her experience had yet to show her anything mystical. If, on occasion, she knew the name of a person before she heard it or knew where the late husband put his will, that was just intuition and common sense. Nothing mystical.

"Well if you're done eating, we better figure out how you plan on getting Caleb out of here. I think the weather will be shifting before dark." Kam stood up before she looked over at David.

"Why did you call him Caleb?" he quietly asked.

"Huh? What? Did I say Caleb? Is it? Maybe Bethany or Megan mentioned it." She blushed in front of his narrowed eyes.

David saw the fear in her eyes. She knew the name, but not how she knew it and he could see that this worried her. He smiled. "I don't know his name, but if it is Caleb, you likely did hear it from one of the girls." He gently patted her back before he turned to walk back to the body.

Kam let out a shuddering breath. The name had just come into her mind and rolled off her tongue. She even had a mental image his appearance in those clothes. Whoa, her imagination was way too active.

David managed to wrap the boots into the small tarp, followed by the torso, topped by the hip section and the arms, and gently slide the tarp into the body bag he'd brought. Zipping the bag tightly he led the packhorse over closer to where they worked.

Kam loaded the other evidence into the pack bags on the mare then helped David gently place the body bag across the top of the pack and tie it down securely. Finally, they secured the shovel and David put the camera back into his pocket. Looking at her watch, she realized they had spent over two hours packing and loading up for the trip back. It was almost three-thirty. Clouds were sweeping in from the north and west. Looking at the clouds, Kam worried at the density and speed of their movement. She hoped Megan had gotten down off the mountain; the weather would be closing in soon and her senses felt it was going to be a serious storm.

Mounting, they headed back toward the truck at a slow pace. Kam felt the passing of the projectile at the same moment when she heard the report of a rifle.

"Damn! Get moving and keep down!" David yelled from behind her.

Chapter Seven

Following the trail she and Bethany marked, Megan rode about three quarters of a mile past that left turn to the cabin before turning downhill to the right. She needed the upper trail to be out of sight before turning again to start the trek back to the R-B Campground. This would make the loop just over sixteen miles from start to finish; but they would need to bring a good GPS out when cutting the trail to get an accurate distance measurement.

Humming, she zigzagged down the hill for half an hour, marking each rollback turn. When the Trailmaster brought the crew through, he or she might have a different idea of how to get down the hill without causing erosion, but for Megan the zigzag and water bars would keep soil and boulders from moving down the hill over time with trail usage.

She stopped Harley to look up the hill. She followed the ribbons left then right until she lost sight of them over a rise. Good, she couldn't see the original turn off the main trail. Now for the turn back toward the campground. Tying three ribbons on the aspen next to where she stopped, she walked Harley to the next tree and hung a ribbon from it, then rode about a hundred yards before putting out another ribbon. Secure that riders could follow the trail, she rode until the ribbon behind was almost out of sight and tied another. She would need to continue with line of sight ribbons because there wasn't any trail to follow otherwise. At least on the upper trail, there had been a faint trail to keep riders going straight. Here, it would be ribbon only until the crew brought out the paint to mark the trees permanently.

After another half hour, she came to a wide wash. Looking up it, she paused to listen. Ahhh, the sound of voices and rolling rocks. This must be the wash with the skeleton uphill. Megan smiled and checked her watch. Just over an hour from the time she left them. Not too bad; but, if it continued to take this long, she might have to space ribbons farther apart to save time or she would not be back at home before five. Planning her time, she would continue marking until about three, and then she would decide how much further she was from camp. She checked the GPS before she left them and again now. It was seven miles from camp to the body on the upper trail. That shouldn't take more than three hours to mark. It was almost one, she calculated; she should be in camp by about three or four.

Dismounting before she got to the edge, she didn't want a repeat of Bethany's accident, she looked carefully downhill. Not a bad slope, but she put out ribbon on the tree and rocks before beginning to angle down. Halfway to the bottom, she put out more ribbon to signal the turn and angled back across the slope until she reached the bottom. Does a trail need to point upstream or downstream? Upstream might wash out more quickly, or it might get washed out from water trying to join the creek. Again, something the Trailmaster would know.

Crossing the wash, she angled the trail upstream on that side, marked a turn halfway up and finished off the uphill trail facing downstream. She used lots of ribbon on a tree and in the boulders at the start of the downhill trail for those who might arrive from camp on the lower trail. After marking the spot, she mounted Harley and rode along through the woods. The trail cut across the downgrade of the mountain, but the grade was minor so riders would feel comfortable. She'd ridden trails where the mountain fell away so sharply it made a rider nervous about the possibility of a horse falling down the mountain. This trail, with proper water bars and widening, should endure many seasons of erosion and rider use.

She stopped to look uphill, enjoying the peace of the mountains and woods. She saw movement, quite a distance uphill. Must be a deer or bear foraging before the arrival of the coming weather. Harley's ears twitched uphill, his head snapping around while he scented the wind. Exhaling a long snort, he sounded a loud whinny. "What, Boy? You think that's a horse?" She asked him, patting his neck. Far away, uphill she heard a response to his call. "Radar heard you, I guess we aren't as far from them as I thought." She laughed. "Come on, before you call again, let's keep moving. Before moving on, she thought she heard horseshoes on the trail above. Must be just the echoes of the boulders Kam and David were throwing in the gully.

The afternoon slipped by while she and Harley tied ribbon within sight of ribbon for what seemed to be forever. She paused to grab a snack allowing Harley to graze on late oats when she realized her saddlebags had all the sandwiches. "I hope they didn't get too hungry." She snickered. Then she discovered she only had one bottle of water on her saddle. They had the rest of the water and the candy. Damn.

Well, she had candy at home and didn't need extra water. One bottle should work fine. She drank most of the water to wash down the peanut-butter-and-jelly sandwich before pressing on with her chore, enjoying the thought of the riders in the future who would travel the trail she set today. Marking trail always gave her the satisfaction of knowing she would leave behind something for others to enjoy. The only thing more satisfying would be coming back with the trail building crew and the Trailmaster.

"Come on, Boy. I think we should be getting close to camp." She put a ribbon on the tree next to the oats and urged Harley to move on. In the distance, she heard what sounded to be an air brake to her left. Must be getting close to the highway, she smiled. Won't be long now. Fifteen minutes later, she heard a chainsaw buzzing and the scraping sound of a road grader. Smiling hugely, she knew the sounds were the construction of the campground for the R-B.

"We're almost out of the woods boy. Yeah!" She looked at her watch. It was past three-thirty. Far in the distance, she heard the report of a high-powered rifle followed by a second. Stopping, she swung her head to listen and see if she could tell the direction of the shooting. In the mountains, someone was always hunting something; she just worried that a careless hunter might hurt someone out on horseback or even hiking. There was one more shot, then silence. She shook her head, impossible to tell, but it sounded like the shots came from above and behind her or maybe just off the road where the truck was parked. "Let's get done and out of the woods." She marked the tree and before she got out of sight of that ribbon, she was at the edge of the campground. Using the ribbon she had left, she flagged the last tree with about ten different strips.

"Whew! Let's get you home, baby." She turned Harley and let him move out to his fast trot then a lope across the campground. He knew the way home, Bethany rode him over to the construction site a lot and all Megan needed to do was hold on and enjoy the ride. She waved to the crew who waved and hooted at the galloping pinto.

Once into the narrow strip of woods between the highway and the campground, Megan pulled Harley down to a reasonable long trot then a walk as they popped out of the woods on the side of the highway. Looking both directions, she saw one of the local sheriff's cruisers parked in the pullout about a quarter mile up the road. She waved, crossed the quiet highway and was back into the woods in less than ten yards. Harley picked up his long trot, dodging trees along the trail, ears forward, calling to the ranch horses in the pasture ahead.

"Guess you're as glad as I am that we're down from the mountain." Megan petted him and laughed. "I enjoyed your company too." In the distance, she heard the sound of galloping hooves. "Sounds like you have a welcoming committee boy."

The trail opened to the ranch drive at the corner of the home pasture. It surprised Megan that no horses were charging the fence in welcome. Instead, she saw four cowboys headed down the road toward her. Stopping Harley, she waited for them.

"Hi! What's happening?" She asked as the group slid to a stop. Roger in the lead with Aaron, John who managed the stud barn and Nick who managed the bulls faced her with concerned expressions.

"Did you see Coup? He's missing, along with his saddle." Roger explained, his face lined with worry. If anything happened to that horse, his wife would come unglued.

"Well, he didn't saddle himself. Anyone been around who might take him out for a ride? Wait. Harley called when we were on the mountain, but that was over an hour ago. I thought he got a response from Radar, but maybe it was Coup. Why would anyone take him up the mountain?" Megan got a cold chill at her next thought. "Roger, someone was shooting up the mountain, not half an hour ago. Shit, Kam and David could still be up there." She turned Harley around and took the lead back up the trail.

She looked up at the sky; when had the sun disappeared behind those ugly clouds?

Roger noticed her looking up. "We don't have too long to find him. If it starts to snow, we'll have to turn around and know he'll come home if he gets loose." He was directly behind Megan with Aaron behind him. "Aaron, tell Nick to drop back and wait at the ranch. Call the sheriff and report the theft, but wait here at the barn in case he's loose." He pressed his horse to catch back up with Harley.

At the highway, Megan urged Harley for more speed. She barely paused to check traffic before letting the gelding trot across the road and pick up the gallop on the far side. She saw the patrol car still parked in the pull off. Snickering, she thought the deputy must be talking with his girlfriend, eating his lunch, or catching a nap. County tax dollars at work. Yep, it happens. They broke into the campground clearing. Megan looked around at the scattered workers. She dropped Harley back to Roger.

"Maybe these guys saw Coup go across and can describe the rider." She suggested.

"John, stay here and question them. I want to know how long they've been here and what horse traffic they've seen today." He pointed at John, and then motioned toward the workers. Roger let Megan take the lead; she had already been on the trail.

Harley took off across the clearing, Megan spotted the original spot she and Bethany had marked as the trailhead and aimed him for it. Thankful she was riding a well-conditioned horse she let him continue his long trot through the trees. His experience with wooded mountains let him dodge trees at a pace that would cause a flatland horse problems.

After several miles, Megan heard the wind above the

sound of hoof beats. Looking up, she pointed into the trees forcing Roger and Aaron to look up. The pines were swaying where the wind hadn't reached ground level yet.

"That's not a good sign." Aaron yelled above the sound. They slowed, watching what clouds they could see between the pines and the increasing movement of the trees. "Not good at all." The light was failing, but it was at least a couple of hours to sunset. They felt the storm closing in.

Harley skidded to a halt, the other horses bumping him from behind on the narrow trail. He screamed into the wind, eyes and ears pointed directly ahead along the trail. In the distance, there came an answering call, the sound of hooves on rocks at a fast pace reaching the riders as the first flakes of snow hit them.

"Hold up! Listen. Sounds like a rider coming." Megan held up her hand to stay the riders behind. Beneath her, Harley tensed and called again. The approaching horse called, louder and closer now. The snow began to fall heavily, blinding them. "Riders on the trail!" Megan yelled to alert the approaching rider to slow. The horse came into view, without a rider. "Whoa! Coup! Easy boy! Easy. Whoa!" Megan put out her hand to the panicked gelding.

Roger, behind her, grabbed his lariat and managed to get a quick loop over the head of the gelding as he pushed past the horses on the trail. As soon as he felt the rope tighten, Coup stopped. "Easy, Boy, easy. You know us. Here's your buddy, Harley." Roger spoke to the spooked animal, reaching out to pet his sweaty neck. "There, see, nothing's going to get you." He continued to murmur.

Megan turned Harley to bring him next to Coup on the far side. This made a three horse wide trail out of one that might fit two small ones. She petted him and murmured while Harley snuffled and nuzzled his buddy.

Coup stood trembling, quivering and snorting, his eyes wild while he searched his back trail. Something had set him off; Megan listened to see if she could hear anything. With the snow, she couldn't see more than twenty feet away. "Let's head back. If this keeps up, we're going to get lost just making it to the clearing, much less the ranch."

Aaron reversed his mare and using a loose rein, let her lead the group. She could find her way better than he could direct her. He urged her on at a faster pace than she might choose, but he knew the longer they spent out here, the tougher it would get. "Come on girl, find us the way home."

At the clearing, John joined them. "Glad to see you guys. I was about to head back and get a search party. This is no weather to be on horseback in the woods," he nodded at his boss.

Now it was four riders and five horses. Megan brought up the rear with Harley to settle Coup about whatever monsters he thought were up that trail. She had never heard any stories of the red gelding spooking so she worried about two things. What happened to his rider and *who was* his rider today? Who had the nerve to steal Coup from his stall? Did they know he was the fastest horse with the most stamina of any on the R-M?

Even with the increasing snowfall, the group arrived back at the R-M before five, to the relief of all four riders and those waiting word. "Aaron, take Coup, use gloves and remove his tack carefully. I want you to put it on a rack by itself on a tarp. I plan to have a forensic specialist go over that saddle top to bottom for prints or any trace that might be on it. Put the rack in the barn office and lock the door." Roger handed Coup's reins to Aaron along with those of his horse. He needed to get up to the house to calm his wife. "John, I want you, Nick, and Aaron up at the house as soon as the horses are cared for. Megan, you, too. We have a spare room for you; I don't want you driving in this mess." His tone allowed for no discussion; he turned and strode for the house, keeping his head down against the weather.

"Aaron, which stall is Harley's?" Megan led the gelding into the barn behind Aaron who led three.

"The first five stalls on the left are empty. We knew we'd want to stall the riding horses for the night and Roger had them prepared when we found Coup missing." Aaron jerked the top of his head to the left, pointing out the stalls. "Give Harley the first, Coup can take the second, then my mare and Roger's gelding with John's mare next to Nick's filly on the end." He had already eyeballed the distance from the second stall across to the office door. He remembered a new tarp they bought a while ago. Still in the package, it would be perfect for what Roger wanted. Finding a freestanding saddle rack might be more difficult, but he could use the chair at the desk in a pinch. All ranch saddles fit on wall racks in the tack room, the last time he'd seen the folding rack; it had been going into Bethany's trailer. The office chair would have to work.

Leading the horses, he stopped first to send Rogers' gelding into a stall, then his own. Holding Coup he looked around, Megan had Harleys' saddle and bridle in her arms and was headed into the tack room. "When you drop that saddle on a rack, could you come back and to hold Coup while I set up the tarp to take his gear? Hard to hold him and unfold the tarp. Thanks."

"I didn't quite hear Roger's instructions. Why are you putting Coup's saddle over a tarp in the office?" Seemed extreme to her, but he was the boss and not to be questioned.

"Roger thinks there could be trace evidence

belonging to the person who stole Coup on the saddle. I'm not certain how, but it's possible. With the saddle locked away and over a tarp, anything that falls off will be found and no one can mess with it to confuse matters." Aaron shrugged. He thought this was overkill, but Roger was really pissed about the theft of his wife's favorite horse. The last time Rogers' face had been that tight was the day someone stabbed her in a kidnap attempt.

"I think he's been watching too much CSI." Megan snickered while holding Coup's reins. "Hope my 'trace' is acceptable. Might not be, Roger doesn't really know me that well."

"I think, since you were with us when the horse came running down the trail, you're not a suspect. But, I don't think I want to be whoever took this horse right about now. If he's lucky, he'll freeze on the mountain, he'll wish he had if Roger catches him."

"It is kind of a nasty day to be hiking back down that trail. I almost feel sorry for the guy." John shivered in sympathy for the thief. He finished unsaddling his mare and rubbed her down with a dry rag. The barn was toasty so she'd be plenty warm, even with the wind howling outside and the snow making visibility limited.

"Where'd you find that rag? I need to rub Harley down too." Megan headed back for the tack room when John pointed that direction. Harley deserved a good rubdown, he'd worked hard today. Also, it was warm and friendly here in the barn; she wasn't certain she wanted to face the upcoming scene with Roger in the house. Maybe, Nick had heard from the sheriff or John had news from the construction workers.

John finished his mare and moved into the stall with Roger's gelding. He unsaddled the horse, put the saddle in the tack room and began rubbing down the tired horse.

The riders had been through all the home pastures searching for Coup before they headed toward the trail to the R-B where they found Megan. These ranch horses were in good shape, but not used to galloping willy-nilly around the property, then up a mountain. He shook his head. None was stressed, but all would need a day of rest to recuperate. From the looks of the snowfall, they wouldn't be working tomorrow.

After locking up the office with all of Coup's tack centered on the tarp in the middle of the room, Aaron unsaddled his own mare. He grabbed another of the dry towels kept to wipe down wet horses and began to rub her down, talking as he massaged her body. "Good girl. You did fine. Those old geldings have nothing on you." Just silly words to soothe her and show his appreciation of her efforts. He often was guilty of talking to his animals. At least, they never argued or talked back. "John, when you finish there, check the water and feeders in all these stalls. We were interrupted while we were setting the barn up. I just want to make certain everything got finished and the horses are good for the night."

Megan heard John moving around while she continued to rub Harley. He wasn't that tired, but he was damp. Like Aaron, she talked to him while she worked. "What a beautiful, strong boy you are. So brave, going back up the mountain to find your buddy. You tried to tell me he was up there, didn't you?" She remembered him calling and a horse answering. It must have been Coup and the thief. "Aaron, I'm worried about Kam and David. I wonder if they got off the mountain before the snow started. I really hope the gunfire was only another hunter up on the mountain. Let's get done here and check to see if Roger's heard anything."

"Yep, John's got the horses all fed and watered and

I've rubbed down Coup and Nonnie. I think we're just about finished. Let's turn out the lights and make a run for the house. I hope Shorty has dinner ready." Aaron walked out of Coup's stall taking his rag into the tack room where he pitched it into the laundry box with the others. Walking back out he checked stall doors to make certain they were secure before taking Megan's arm and heading for the barn door. John had already headed for the bunkhouse to collect Nick. "Watch your step. It shouldn't be icy under the snow, but the snow itself could be slick." He kept a hold on Megan's arm to assist her through the drifting snow as they half-trotted toward the house in the gathering dark and blinding snow.

Roger paced the living room, he checked out the window for the fifth or sixth time. What were they doing down there, taking a coffee break? The snow created a veil between the house and the barn, but he caught movement as a muted figure headed for the bunkhouse, then a larger shadow looked to be heading for the house. He went to the door, cracking it and saw the shadow split into two figures; one mostly behind the other. He pulled the door open as they climbed the front steps. "About damn time. I expect the horses well groomed for the amount of time you took." Roger grumbled at the pair, closing the door.

"John should be here any minute with Nick. Have you heard anything from Kam and the FBI agent?" Aaron brushed the snow off his hat before taking Megan's coat and hanging it next to the door. She smiled her thanks at him. He put his coat and hat on the rack next to hers.

"I'll tell the story as soon as John and Nick arrive. They can add whatever information they have to it." Roger moved toward the teakettle that was just starting to whistle. "Chocolate, spiced cider, tea, coffee, hot buttered rum, peppermint patty? Anyone want something warm to drink?" He pulled a cup down, added a package of spiced cider mix and topped it with rum before adding the hot water.

Megan followed him to the kitchen after automatically removing her boots. "I'll take chocolate with peppermint schnapps; I've always been a sucker for peppermint patties. How's Bethany?" She mixed her drink, looked at the huge stew pot on the stove, lifted the lid and inhaled the mouthwatering fragrance of Shorty's chili. "Wow, Shorty; I think I love you. Chili is perfect for the weather outside and my innards will appreciate it almost as much as my hands and mouth appreciate this cup of chocolate." She smiled and bowed toward the older man at the back of the kitchen.

"Shorty makes one of three things when snow is predicted. Chili, stew, or chicken noodle soup. We having nachos with the chili, or is there cornbread in the oven?" Aaron moved between Roger and Megan, grabbing a mug and pouring coffee into it. "You don't have any of that Irish Cream left do you?" He looked over at his boss. Roger pointed under the sink.

"Bethany hoards that stuff, so whatever you do; don't use the last of it." He warned his friend with a smile. "You do not want to be here if she finds that bottle empty. Not that she drinks it that often, but I learned last winter that running out was against the rules, according to my wife." Laughter rang around the kitchen.

At the sound of boots at the front door, the group turned to see John and Nick enter. Each brushed the snow off their hats before shedding coats and hanging them on the rack. "Bethany says all boots off. What do you want to drink?" Roger called to them.

"Coffee and some of Bethany's secret Irish cream." The men responded in unison, each taking turns using the bootjack before heading toward the kitchen. "Until she got here, we never had such good tasting coffee." John laughed. "I'm buying the next bottle of that stuff."

"Are you boys drinking my liquor?" Bethany shook a finger at the group as she painfully and slowly walked toward the dinner table. The loose skirt she wore lapping at her calves with each stuttering step.

Roger jumped to help her, pulling out her chair and taking her elbow to lower her down to the seat. "You didn't have to get up. I would have brought you dinner. Are you feeling up to this?"

She smiled up at his hovering form. "I was going crazy and I think I've slept enough for a week. I heard you take a call, now tell us what's going on." She then frowned up at him. "And for God's sake sit down, you're making me nervous."

"She's right, dinner's ready, everyone pick a seat so we can eat." Shorty pointed to the table and the others gathered, each choosing a seat close to or across from Roger and Bethany.

Aaron sat on Roger's right with Megan on the bench next to him. He smiled at her as he passed down the napkin wrapped silverware Shorty handed out. Since the others were across the table, she put the silverware down and the napkin on her lap. Next came the plates followed by the linen wrapped cornbread bowl. She passed the bowl across to John after taking two squares of steaming cornbread.

Shorty spooned the chili from the large pot into the stoneware bowls, sending one to his left then one to his right until everyone at the table had steaming bowls of chili. He served himself and sat down. "Who wants to lead the evening prayer?" He looked around, not surprised when Roger stood up to lead them.

"Lord, thank you for this food and thank you for keeping my wife from being seriously hurt yesterday. I would like to ask You to please watch over those out in this storm and see that they make it home safely, if it is Thy will. Amen."

"Amen," affirmed all those seated at the table.

"Roger, you don't think you can eat without telling us what's going on?" Bethany questioned her husband while she buttered their cornbread.

"Okay, this is what I've learned so far: …

Chapter Eight

Digging her heels into her mare, Kam laid her body low against Mica's neck and sent her flying up the trail; pulling hard on the packhorse to follow. She heard a second report; it came from behind them. David grunted and she saw red blossoming against the sleeve of his tan shirt when the appaloosa passed her at a wild gallop. "Turn to the left!" She yelled after him.

David's right arm was numb and the gelding took off; galloping past Kam. He held on to mane and reins, without much control. He heard Kam yell, but couldn't tell what she'd said; at the same moment, the appy ducked to the left, heading up the side trail they had seen earlier. Wrapping his fingers deeper into Radar's mane, he managed to stay centered in spite of the sharp turn. The gelding seemed to know the way while Lady Mica and the packhorse tried to keep up. The three horses moved at a dead run with Radar leading. Uphill, downhill, made no difference. The trail narrowed, and Radar slowed.

After the left turn, there had been only one more shot fired. They must have gotten out of range, but the shooter could soon catch up. They needed to get to safety. Somewhere that would afford them some cover. His thoughts veered to the cabin Megan mentioned. If they could get there, maybe they would be able to mount some sort of return fire with the pistol and the rifle in Kam's scabbard. David hoped they could hold off this shooter and silently prayed there was only one.

The trail opened up to a broad, shallow valley, and

Kam saw the cabin on the far side. She kicked her mare, sending her past David and Radar. She heard a squeal, looked over her shoulder in time to see Radar bite the pack mare on her butt to encourage a faster pace. Together they charged across the valley. Skidding her mare to a stop at the cabin, Kam grabbed her saddlebag and scabbard before sending her mare on and grabbing David off Radar who herded his mares to safety behind the cabin. David stumbled going up the steps, but made it to the door. Kam had to lift the door open because of its broken hinge, but got David inside before his legs gave out. She managed to close the door before taking her rifle to the window to peering outside while keeping her head down and close to the corner.

Across the valley, she saw movement and a glint of sunlight against metal. Aiming carefully, pretending it was a deer in her mind's eye, she squeezed the trigger and felt the familiar buck of the rifle against her shoulder. The sound in the cabin was deafening, but the rider coming out of the woods pulled his horse sideways before heading back into the trees.

Kam prayed that if she'd hit something it was the shooter and not his horse. A bullet embedded itself into the frame of the window before she heard the report of the rifle. Well, she hadn't done much damage; he was still able to shoot. Keeping her head down she moved to the other front window, trying to see if she could spot him.

Radar called and the rider's horse answered. Maybe that meant she hadn't hit it either. Kam hated the pain or death of anything. She gave up hunting at thirteen and took up target and skeet shooting instead to satisfy her grandfather because she mourned for any living thing she killed.

Nothing moved in the trees and no more bullets hit

the cabin. Maybe he gave up. Kam tried something she hadn't done since the year she gave up hunting. Closing her eyes, she rested the rifle barrel on the windowsill. Silently praying to her ancestors to guide her aim, she let the barrel move gently in her hands while she squeezed off another round.

A scream followed by a rifle report, but no bullet hitting the cabin. Had she managed to hit the shooter? She remembered the last deer she had shot in much the same manner, only that time she had prayed for a miss. Again, all grew quiet.

She crawled over to David. He was holding his bunched up shirt against the wound in his arm, trying to tie off a makeshift pressure bandage. "Here, let me see." She pushed his hand away and lifted the tan shirt from the wound. It was bleeding seriously, but not with any pulsing, so no arteries hit. She tenderly felt the arm and could feel no broken bone. Could be fractured, but at least not a compound fracture. The bleeding was slowing, even as she inspected it. "Hold this while I locate my knife. I need to make a bandage from the shirt. Can't tear it without a cut edge."

"My knife's in my pocket. It's closest. Right front." David smiled at her, watching her reach gently for the knife. "Careful what you grab in there," he teased.

"Must not be hurt too bad, your sense of humor is still working." Kam reached further into his pocket without any more hesitation. Using his knife, she cut strips from his shirt and cut off the other sleeve to use for packing. Wrapping his arm with the doubled sleeve reaching both entry and exit wounds, she then tied it off with the strips. Carefully, she made certain it was tight, but not so tight as to restrict blood flow. "It looks to be a clean through and through with nothing broken. You've lost some blood, but not enough to cause serious problems."

"You better get back to the window. Where're our horses?" David managed to prop himself up against the bed in the far corner.

"I think they went around back. Unless Radar took off after he called the shooter's horse. If he did, he likely took the mares with him." She looked at him against the bed and made a decision. "Think you can crawl over to the window and keep an eye out? If so, I'll slip out the back window and hobble the horses. We need them here."

"I don't want you to go out there, but we don't have any choice. I'll make it over there, just stay down." David began to crawl across the cabin.

A bullet smashed into the door followed by the report of the rifle just as a second and third hit around the window. The reports echoed around the valley. There were at least three, possibly four shots. Then silence again.

David hit his belly at the first shot and Kam landed beside him. She carefully sat up, peered out the corner of the window across from her rifle. No movement, all quiet.

"Wonder if he saw you move?" Kam mused.

Time passed. Kam looked at her watch. It was after four. This had all started after three. How long should they wait? She still needed to get the horses hobbled, but she'd rather get out of there. Hopes of escaping fell when she heard the wind rising and noticed the snow falling heavily. She knew they wouldn't make it down to the truck unless they left right now, but if they tried, they'd be sitting ducks. It just wasn't worth the risk.

David made it to the rifle, Kam slipped out the back window, happy to see the horses standing in a lean-to attached to the cabin. Removing bridles, she hobbled them and grabbed both David's and the packhorse's saddlebags. She also grabbed the heavy bag from behind the packsaddle. She remembered watching Aaron fill it with grain. Food for the horses and themselves. It pained her, but the horses would need to stay saddled and hobbled for the night. She hoped they would forgive her and David eating their gain. She reached into the bag, and fed each horse a double handful of oats. She pushed the remainder along with the bottles of water in the saddlebags over the window ledge into the cabin. While she hoped they had enough food left over from lunch, she knew they didn't. Oatmeal made with horse oats couldn't be that bad, could it?

Keeping the horses between her and the woods, she tossed in the saddlebags before moving back to Radar to grab David's jacket from the back of the saddle. Next, she unlatched the wooden shutters and climbed back through the low window. She pulled the shutters closed against the possibility of prying eyes, gunshots, and cold wind.

"Too bad I can't reach the front shutters. I'd feel a lot safer if I didn't feel like a bug under a microscope in here." She told him.

"Well at least you got the back ones closed. Seems to me their aim isn't the best under any circumstances. But, that could change, or they could get lucky again." David smiled and all Kam could see were his white teeth in the darkening cabin. "I can't tell if there's more than one, but I don't think there is. All the shots have come from the front so far."

"I noticed. When Radar called, only one horse answered, but that doesn't really tell us much." Kam crawled over to the other window, peering out along the edge about waist height. "I'm just thankful these logs are solid and thick. I don't think anything short of armor piercing bullets could get through them."

"I hope they don't decide to burn us out or have

smoke grenades. We're safe in here; but out there we would be easy pickings." David reached for his satellite phone. "It's time to call in the cavalry, don't you think?"

"Good idea. Maybe they can get to us but the wind is picking up out there, hear it?" Kam paused to listen, and then frowned. "Damn, from the roaring in the trees, we might be too late for any helicopter to get here."

"Is that the wind? My God, it sounds like a jet engine." David listened to the roar of the approaching gale in the trees. "Well, I'm calling anyway. We need to let them know what's happening." He dialed his section office.

Kam listened while he gave an approximate location and cussed the fact she'd given Megan her GPS, then smiled at the thought his sat phone would pinpoint them for the rescue. Looking around the side of the window once more, she saw the light was fading very fast with the thickening clouds and blowing snow. Oh, crap, just what they needed. Even if the shooter was gone, they were going to be stuck here for the night. Shit.

"Snow's falling and the wind is going to drift it quickly. Maybe it will drive the shooter from the mountain. We have the shelter; he, or they, don't." Kam pointed out the window. A few flakes were blowing in the opening.

"When it picks up, maybe we can get the shutters closed in the dark. Once visibility is gone, we should be safe to move around." David said, hanging up from his call. "Got anyone you need to reach?" He handed the phone to her.

Kam pulled Roger's number from her pocket, thankful she had been carrying it in case she had problems finding the ranch. In the half-light, she had to bend the paper several ways until she could see all the numbers. She dialed the R-M. "Hello? Roger? We have a bit of a problem. You need to make certain Megan got back down the mountain before this snow gets much worse. David and I are stuck in the old cabin. We had to take shelter, first from a gunman and now from the storm." She paused and listened to him cuss and mutter. "Megan left to mark the trail. The ranch truck and trailer are still sitting on the road waiting for us where you parked yesterday." She listened for a second. "Well, we have some food, but not much. I'm planning on making oatmeal for us for tonight using the horse oats. If we're lucky, we'll get out of here tomorrow. The FBI knows where we are and about our situation. I think I winged the shooter, so tell Dr. Samuelson to be on the lookout for anyone with a hole in them. Also, tell him I might not make work on Monday. Got to hang up, need to conserve batteries." She ended the call and passed the unit back to David.

"Well, looks like we're here for the night. Think you can get the front shutters closed now? That wind is cold." David smiled at her as he took his phone.

"I'll get them closed. I saw a few loose boards on the porch; maybe we can use them for firewood. Got matches?" Kam cautiously ducked going under the window then lifted the front door to get it open enough to slip her body out. She unlatched the first shutter then paused to pitch a couple of pieces of the porch railing in before closing the shutters of that window. She felt and found more railing she could tear off, threw the pieces in the door as she worked her way across to the other window. The railing wood was old and would burn fast, but at least it would be heat; if the chimney was clear.

At the far end of the porch, she managed to get up some of the floorboards. Thankful that they didn't extend through the wall of the cabin, she pulled up each one she could before she unlatched the shutters. She continued throwing wood in the door, hoping David was able to move most of it over to the fireplace with his good hand. Even if the old wood burned fast, they should have enough to get through the night.

"Did you leave any boards on the porch?" David asked watching Kam enter the cabin, lift the door closed and latch the shutters on both windows.

"Let's say if any bad guys think to attack through a window they're going to have problems reaching them without a porch to stand on." Kam looked for a bar that worked on the door, found it against the wall and barred the door. "Okay, now we can get some lights and a fire going. There's a stub of a candle on the table. Find your matches?"

"No, but I have an emergency kit in my saddlebags. I keep it for moments like this. No matches, but there's a self-striking flare. We can use that to light the wood," he offered.

"Great idea, but where would we put the flare once we get the fire started? I don't think it's advised to burn the entire thing in a fireplace and I don't want to toss it out into the wind. Let's save it. I've got a striker in my saddlebag. Not as nice as a match, but it works." Kam walked over to her saddlebags and dug out the kit she kept for lighting fires in the wilds. Sticking it in her hip pocket, she began to assemble wood in the large fireplace after swinging the old black pot out of the way. Once the smaller pieces were loosely angled, she opened her kit and removed the folded paper sheets, tore one into several pieces and stuck them under the kindling.

Saying a prayer that no critters had nested in the chimney and the old stones had not fallen in on themselves over the years, she began striking her flint against the papers. Holding her breath when one side began to burn, she moved to the other and repeated the process until the papers around the kindling were burning hotly and the kindling began to smolder.

"Wow! Woman makes fire and good field bandages. Now, if you can find us a meal and cook it, I may have to marry you." David gave Kam a leering look that was offset by his smiling eyes as he teased her.

"Huh. Once upon a time, us spending a night together like this and you would have had to marry me… if I could cook or not." She laughed back at him.

"Are you an old-fashioned girl? Does my grandfather need to bring ponies to your grandfather in payment?" Smiling he watched her eyes at the half-serious question.

"I don't believe in selling women and I can take care of my own negotiations; thank you very much." Kam rose to the bait, realized his intentions and threw a piece of wood at his good shoulder.

"Oww! Not fair. I can't duck."

"Then, don't provoke me and sit there grinning about it." Getting up, Kam walked over to retrieve the wood. She offered David her hand to help him get up from his seat on the floor.

"You didn't answer the first part of the question. Are you an old-fashioned girl?" He asked as he came to his feet directly in front of her and not letting go of her hand.

Kam felt her face warm and breath leave her body at his closeness. She took a step back and frowned when he wouldn't let go of her hand. She looked down; suddenly shy. "Depends on you definition of old-fashioned and which culture you're asking about."

Taking a half step into her space to recover the step she had taken, David turned loose her hand, instead, lifting her chin to see her eyes. "Any culture where you feel comfortable." He leaned in, watching her eyes as his lips brushed hers. He inhaled the scent of her before slanting his lips over hers more passionately. She smelled like wood smoke, horses and lavender. He liked the combination.

Kam felt frozen in place like a rabbit in tall grass hiding from a hawk. His mouth was warm, he smelled of sweat, musk, and the blood from his wound. Unsettling. His kiss deepened, his tongue pushing into her mouth and tasting her as she tasted him. She stiffened, breaking the contact. "No! We are so not going there. This has to stop right here." She pulled away from him, spinning around, putting her hand to her mouth to wipe off his kiss.

"What's wrong? You taste sweet." He stepped back, giving her space. "It's okay. You're safe with me." He put his hand out, but withdrew it when she quickly walked to the fire. Her arms folded across her chest and her hands rubbed them as if to warm or erase the feel of his closeness. He frowned. Someone had either forced her or hurt her; that was obvious.

"I'm not interested in sex or a relationship." Kam couldn't keep the quiver from her voice or the shiver from her small frame.

"Okay, just friends and co-workers. But, I'm interested. You're quite a woman. Capable, caring, and able to defend herself. I like that combination. You also smell good and taste amazing." He couldn't help but tell her, smiling at her back.

Kam glanced back over her shoulder, seeing the laughter and an undercurrent of desire in his eyes. "Well, I think your sense of smell must be off. It's been a long day and I doubt I smell of much besides horses and smoke." She managed to smile back at him. "Now, let's see what I can find for dinner. Sit down." She pointed to the log bench next to the table. It was only a kiss, her reaction had been more than it deserved. "Sorry, I didn't mean to react so poorly, I just wasn't expecting you to kiss me."

"I didn't quite plan it; I just couldn't resist the temptation." David admitted, walking to the bench and sitting down carefully using his left hand to brace himself. He turned to face the table and discovered the Bible still resting where Megan had replaced it. "Look, there's a book here. I hadn't noticed it during all the excitement earlier." He pointed out.

Kam looked up from checking the pot hanging on the hook to see if it had dried food in it. "Wonder how long it's been sitting there." She paused, closed her eyes, hummed a second and smiled at David. "Caleb read his Bible every morning while he ate his breakfast." Then she shivered. "How do I know that?" She asked him. "I also know this was his cabin, or at least he was living here before he was shot."

"Your heritage is showing. Spirits are out there; some people are just more open to them." He tried to soothe her. "I expect his spirit might still be around. Maybe with his body being found, he will be able to find peace."

"Yeah, maybe. Looks like he kept a clean kitchen. This pot is ready to use. I'm going to put some oats and water in to boil. Flavor it with the last of the candy and we have dinner. We still have some jerky, but I won't put it in the pot; that would be nasty." She measured out two handfuls of oats, added water to cover, threw in another small handful and added the candy in small pieces. "Here, keep this half, we might need it to get the flavor of this oatmeal out of our mouths." She passed him half the candy bar, not certain if chocolate covered toffee was going to make the oats more or less edible. At least, the dish would be filling.

"Other than my pocket knife; do we have any utensils for eating? Is there a plate or anything around to put food on?" David looked around the sparsely furnished cabin.

"We can eat out of the pot with our fingers if necessary, once it cools. That will also let it thicken more." Kam replied, doing a mental inventory of items in her saddlebag. "My first aid kit might have a tongue depressor; but I doubt it. Personally, about the time this cools, I'm going to be hungry enough not to care how it's served." She laughed.

"I expect to get out of here tomorrow, but should we save back some rations in case we don't? I hope the snow is done early and it starts to melt." He looked toward the window.

"Funny, other than noticing the prediction of the storm's arrival, I don't remember seeing the predictions for duration and amount of snow. Do you?"

"No, and if my ankle is to be taken seriously, we are in for a spell of wet weather." David rubbed his sore ankle with his good hand.

"Weather prediction by body ache. You're kind of young for that, aren't you?"

"Damage done in high school. Been predicting weather for years with it." He smiled at her, watching her stir the mush with his pocket knife.

"This is thickening up nicely. I might even add a little more water to keep it from getting too nasty. I hate gummy mush, no matter what it tastes like." She confided.

He laughed, remembering his early attempts to make oatmeal and how impossible it had been to swallow. "You have a point there. Better oatmeal soup than gummy, nasty, lumpy stuff."

Kam took the pot off the heat of the hearth, turning it out to the room to cool. Stirring it with the knife, she watched it dribble off the blade. Should be okay, it didn't look too nasty at this point. Proof would be when it was cool enough to eat. She pulled two strips of jerky from the saddlebag and handed him one. "This will keep us until that cools. I'm going to check the bed. I doubt it's usable after all these years, but it might surprise."

She walked to the other side of the small cabin to inspect the narrow cot built into the far wall on the left side of the cabin. It was out of line of the weather that would have come in the door; but age had to have affected it. Lifting up the bedroll she inspected it for bugs, not certain she wanted to shake it out.

"Wait. Don't open that blanket roll. Perfect spot for scorpions to nest. Just pitch it outside." David started up to take it from her, but instead opened the door with his left arm.

"You have a point there. They'd love all the folds and crevices. I'd love to have some sort of blanket, but we'll be fine close to the fire." She carefully held the roll out from her body and gently walked to the door where she threw the offending item out of the cabin. "Glad you thought about that. I forgot all about those critters."

She helped David get the door closed; the storm wasn't slowing. "I am so glad you got the shutters closed when you did." He told her, leaning against the door for her to bar it.

Thinking about sleeping, Kam walked back to the fire. Using the cot might not be the best idea. Built into the far wall, it would be cold so far from the fireplace. She shook her head, sleeping next to David was almost the last thing she wanted, but neither did she want to freeze. What could happen, they were both going to be dressed and it would be cold by morning. She'd used his shirt for a bandage, but he now wore the jacket from the back of his saddle. She had her sweatshirt over her t-shirt but hadn't brought a jacket. Having a warm body next to her wouldn't be as unpleasant as not having one.

David stepped beside Kam, watching her check the consistency of the oatmeal. It looked edible; he stuck a finger in it. "Ouch, that's still pretty warm."

She slapped his hand. "The least you can do is rinse your hands with some of the water. I don't mind eating with fingers, but I'd like to think they're somewhat clean."

He laughed and grabbed a water bottle. "Would you pour some over my hand, seems my right is still refusing to work."

"Okay, then you can do the same for me." Kam poured a little over his left hand, watched him rub his fingers together then wipe them on his jeans. She passed him the open water bottle and held out both her hands to him.

"Here, is that enough? Don't want to waste drinking water." He dribbled water over her hands carefully.

Rubbing her hands together, she then rubbed them against her belly, the cleanest part of her shirt. She glared at David when she saw the gleam in his eyes as they followed the motions of her hands.

"What? Just because I want to wipe my hands there too? I'm injured, not dead." He laughed at her glare.

"Let's try to eat before this stuff gets cold, gummy and nasty." Kam ignored his comment and used her shirttail to protect her hands when she moved the pan over to the table. "Better to singe our fingers and get full bellies than end up not being able to swallow the stuff."

"You have a point there." David reached again into the pot with his left index and second digit, scraping the top of the mush and getting enough for a mouthful before cautiously bringing his fingers to his mouth.

Kam watched his reaction to her attempt at making

dinner. He swallowed it, took the water bottle and a large swig before reaching for another bite. "Well, you aren't choking, so I guess I'll try some."

"Were you waiting to see if this caused me damage before trying it? I thought you tasted it while cooking; like most cooks do." He teased.

"I normally do, but I didn't want to eat from a knife edge so this is my first taste." She followed his example, using two fingers to skim the top to get a mouthful. Taking from the top kept them from burning their fingers. "Not bad. I'm not going to say I've had worse; but it's better than going hungry." She managed to swallow then took the water bottle from him for a swig.

"Okay, I won't take back the proposal; but there will be no wedding until you have a chance to cook a real meal for me." He laughed at her expression.

"I don't know why it is you think that A: I would accept, or B: I owe you a meal. Maybe, I need you to cook me a meal before I consider a proposal." She teased back.

Each managed to eat enough to satisfy the need for food, but as the mush cooled and thickened the bites became less frequent and smaller.

"My God, that stuff is horrible cool." Kam barely managed to swallow the last bite she put into her mouth. "Give me that half candy bar. If I don't get this flavor out of my mouth, I might not keep down the meal." She grabbed for the candy bar sitting next to David.

Oh, no. It's mine first." David snatched it and bit the end off before letting her have the remainder.

Kam slowly chewed her half of the candy, relishing the flavor, even sucking on the toffee center; letting it sit on her tongue. Sighing at the pleasure of the flavors washing away the mush she looked over at David. His eyes were dark with desire. "What, you've never seen anyone appreciate chocolate before?"

"Not like that. Makes me want to see how you appreciate other pleasurable flavors and sensations."

Kam felt her face warm at the husky timbre of his voice. "Well, just put your mind back on where we are." She jumped up and walked over to the fire, adding more wood to stoke it for the night. "We don't have blankets or pillows, but I suggest we sleep back to back here close to the fire. I'll put more wood on during the night." She lay down about two feet from the fire, facing it; laid her head on her arm and closed her eyes.

David sighed, such an unusual mixture of strong and vulnerable. He got up, walked over and lay down with his back to her, resting his head on his left arm.

Chapter Nine

Standing at the dinner table, Roger began to tell the group what he'd found out. "The FBI agent and Kam were attacked up on the mountain; sniper, but not a great shot. They made it to that old cabin, but the agent was wounded. Not seriously." He interrupted the questions that several of them began. "They're safe inside, out of the storm. Not much food, but enough for tonight. The horses are in a lean-to off the back. The FBI office has been called. I'm not certain what the plan is for tomorrow, but for tonight seems that we're just waiting out the weather." He looked around the table. "The shooting stopped about the time the snow began to fall. Kam thinks she might have hit one of the shooters. Now, John did the construction workers have much to add about Coups' adventure? Did they see him go by with a rider, if so when?" All eyes turned to the ranch hand.

"Well boss, one of the men saw the red horse with a rider at about one or so heading toward the back of the construction area. All he saw was the back of the rider, but the person wore a cowboy hat. Since Bethany rides through the area a lot, no one really looked close. He said he thought it odd that the rider wasn't wearing the helmet he's used to seeing." John scratched his head. "I asked him if he could tell if the rider was large or small, and he said it was clear across the field from where they were working, so he couldn't really get a feel for size."

"Did you think to ask if all his people were accounted for today? We're still trying to figure out who might have taken the horse, and those workers are close to the ranch." Roger questioned.

"Didn't think to ask him about that. I guess we'll have to question the supervisor tomorrow. I didn't see Mike, but he tends to leave early to check on things ordered and other details as the contractor. Sorry, boss." John ducked his head, embarrassed that he neglected that line of questions.

"That's okay, I only just thought about that possibility myself. I expect the FBI will do most of the questioning from here on in. Anyone have anything more to add?" He looked around the table before sitting down to eat his chili.

"If I had thought anything about the shots I heard, that someone might be shooting at Kam and David, I would have turned Harley around and gone back to help," Megan said in self-disgust.

"Yeah, and likely gotten yourself shot. You're not to blame for any part of this. In fact, being able to tell us about what you heard and saw may come in handy when the FBI start piecing the events together." Aaron covered her left hand with his right. "I just wonder what happened to the rider. It was starting to snow, where could he have gone?" He wondered aloud.

"All I know is that when I find out who took Coup, I just might take a crop to him. Nobody steals my horse." Bethany's eyes narrowed as she looked around the table.

"Well, best case scenario is the shooter was alone, took a bullet, and hiked out safely. If he goes to any medical facility, the wound will be reported and we'll have him. Then, we'll find out why he stole Coup and wanted to shoot the people recovering the body." Roger spoke around a mouthful of spicy chili before taking a long swig of water. "If the shooter dies on the mountain, we'll never know his reasoning. I just hope he gets good and cold before he finds help."

The remainder of the meal passed in normal conversation and at its end Aaron, John, and Nick left for the bunkhouse.

"Megan, there's a spare room straight down the hall. It has its own bath and there's an extra toothbrush for you there. Go soak away the day and we'll see you in the morning." Roger ordered. He stood next to Bethany's chair, ready to help her to stand and lend her an arm to make it back to their room for the night.

"Thanks. I appreciate your hospitality. Good night. Hope you feel better tomorrow." She waved to the couple, took her hot drink, and headed for the back of the house. Her mind buzzing on all the happenings of the day, sleep was a long time coming, but once she managed it, she slept solid until morning.

Chapter Ten

Kam knew she was dreaming, but could not force herself awake. She watched in terror as a bullet smashed into the skull of a man on horseback, sending blood and gore spattering onto his clothes. Silently screaming while his body rolled off his horse and down into a creek, she felt tears burning in her throat. Next scene she seemed to be looking out of a hole and up into the killer's face while rocks rained down into the hole around her. She fought to wake up, but it did no good. Thrashing around on the floor in front of the fire in the small cabin, she disturbed David.

"Huh? You okay?" He murmured without actually waking before he sank once more into his own dreams.

Still in the grasp of the nightmare, she next saw the cabin, but it was different. The door had two good leather hinges and when she looked around the room, it was tidy, and a fire smoldered low in the fireplace. Looking down, she saw a tin box in the hands of a man. He walked across the room and lifted a floorboard from under the bed shelf built into the wall. He slid the box into the small hole, and secured the board with a wooden peg before spreading some dirt into the grooves around it. Then he left the cabin after looking back from the door to see if he could spot the loose board. Next, she was seeing the rider again same as before. She jerked herself awake before the replay of the murder and lay there trembling, breathing hard. She lifted her hand to put more wood in the fire, but found it shaking so badly she couldn't close her fingers around the firewood.

"David! David! Wake up." She rolled over toward

him, gently stroking his back before pinching the back of his neck. She didn't want to hurt his sore arm by jerking him by it.

"Oww! I'm awake. What's wrong?" He rolled onto his back and looked up at her face. In the firelight, her normally warm skin tone seemed ashen.

"You remember when you asked if I'd had any 'visions'?" Sitting up, she looked down at him, still trembling and trying to get control by pulling her knees up to her chest and holding them tightly. "Well, I think I just might have had one. It definitely was a bad dream and it might have been more," she confided.

"What did you 'see'?"

"I think I saw the murder, the killer, and a hidey hole used by the victim here in this cabin. If what I saw was a true vision, there should be a hole below a loose board under the bed. We can check it at daylight." She pointed across at the bed shelf along the wall.

David found himself rubbing her back; he could feel the tremors chasing each other up and down her spine. "Put some more wood on the fire and move to my good side." He ordered. Maybe the commonplace chore would give her a chance to get beyond the fear gripping her.

Kam shook out her hands and tried again to pick up some firewood. This time she managed to hold onto two boards and kneeling set them into the fireplace, on top of the smoking coals. "I'll be okay, it was just so real." She said over her shoulder. "In all my life, I've never seen any dream that clear. The spooky thing was I knew it was a dream but couldn't wake myself up." Adrenaline kept her talking even as she moved to the other side of David and lay back down facing him. "Have you had anything like this? Why me? I don't have any physic powers. At least I never thought I did."

David extended his good arm and Kam settled her head on his shoulder so she lay within the comfort and possible safety of his strength. "I think it's called 'lucid dreaming' but I'm not certain. I've never had any unwanted or unexpected visions. In the sweat lodge, I saw my ancestors but that was likely the smoke and heat bringing out what I expected to see." He found himself stroking her arm and quickly stilled his hand.

The tremors were going away and she seemed to be relaxing against him. "We both have ties to people of power. The spirit of this man wants us to find his killer, tonight. You were more open to him than I was, maybe because my wound focused me on myself, instead of him. If I'd fallen asleep thinking about the crime, he might have come to me. What was your last thought before you slept?" He could feel her slowly melting toward him as the rigors of the day began to drive her again toward sleep.

"I felt sorry for the man and wondered what happened that last day. Hmmm, you're shoulder is a great pillow." Her voice trailed off as she fell asleep.

David lay there holding her and thinking about her revelations. He wished he had paper and pen to write down a good description of the killer. If she saw him, the vision might fade by morning. Well, he'd just have to hope it stayed fresh enough to give him details when she woke. He didn't have the heart to wake her now that she was back asleep. Besides, this felt too damn good to interrupt. It'd been awhile since he'd had this soft and cuddly of a bed partner. Most of the time, either he or his partner would leave after they were satisfied. Sleeping together indicated commitment and he'd not been in a serious relationship for a few years now. Her warm body woke parts of him that needed release, but even with that discomfort, he was happy to lay there and hold her. Eventually, he fell asleep with his arm around her protectively.

Kam felt warmth under her hand and head. The rest of her was really cold. Muted daylight filtered in the shutters. Her eyes adjusted while she tried to focus. Oh, crap. She was nestled against David, her hand on his chest with his hand covering it. She noted sleepily that the hand on his wounded arm not only held hers, but that it was warm. She could feel his other hand resting on her hip, making her feel warmer and amazingly safe here in this deserted cabin. The hand she rested on his chest twitched so she moved it up to run her fingers through her curls as she brought her body into a sitting position.

"Hey, Sleepyhead. Feel better?" His voice was low and soft. His eyes watched her as she moved out of his arms and over onto her knees. His groin tightened, damn, that was a fine sight. He smiled.

"I'm awake and still wondering what happened last night." She sat back on her heels before reaching across him for more wood to throw into the fire. The movement took her belly and chest across his before she realized the view this provided him. She jumped back and up in one swift move, glaring down at his laugh.

"Don't glare at me. You're the one who provided the view." He smiled and teased.

"A gentleman would have closed his eyes."

"A gentleman would have made you think he closed his eyes; but trust me, no straight man would have been able to resist the urge to watch that movement." He did have the grace to blush. He watched her ass as she walked away, smiling again.

"I guess I'm lucky you're injured. But, don't blame anything on a 'fever' because you don't have one." She turned back to laugh at him. She reached the back window and opened the shutters. Three horses looked back at her, two nickered a greeting. Beyond them, she saw only white and shadows of trees. "It's still snowing."

Rolling over onto his knees, David managed to stand using his good arm on the bench next to the nearby table. Leaning over the table, he cracked open the shutters for the front of the cabin. A cold breeze blew in, and the snow was sticking to the shutter. Beyond that, he got the impression of a field of white across the valley floor. The fine flakes came down lightly, daylight trying to filter through the clouds. "Looks like we got a few inches, and it's not done yet. Wonder what the radar shows?" he mused. Until the weather cleared some, they would be stuck here. The only good news was the shooter likely had left with arrival of the snow and darkness.

"We need to make something edible from the left over mush. I have to give the horses the grain. They can't graze in this weather. Wonder if I can find something to melt water for them to drink?" Kam looked around inside and came up with nothing. She grabbed the bag of oats and climbed out the window. She fed each a double handful and looked around in the lean-to. "Ah-ha! There's an old bucket out here." She called back over her shoulder as she bent to pick it up from the corner where it lay in the dirt. Filling it with snow, she set it inside the cabin before following it through the window holding the almost empty grain bag.

"You melt the snow. I'll work on making some oatcakes. Can't fry them because we've no grease. Maybe I can bake them, turn the pot upside down to create an oven effect. That should dry them out, maybe even make them crunchy." He explained while she put the bucket over the fire. He scooped out a handful of the gloppy oatmeal from dinner and made a patty, and then he scooped out another until he had four patties lined up on the table. He watched

Kam take the bucket of melted snow water back to the window. He took one of the smaller wood boards, lined up the patties on it and set it down at the edge of the fireplace. Next, he turned the pot over to cover them and used his knife to shuffle coals around the pot to create heat in the makeshift oven.

"You're a regular Davy Crockett. If you were 'MacGyver' you would have turned one of the horses into a snowmobile and gotten us home last night." Coming back into the cabin with a fresh bucket of snow, she laughed at his oven at the edge of the fire.

"Well, we have to eat something. We couldn't afford to toss out that stuff and it might poison the horses, so making oatcakes was the only way I could picture eating it." He watched her put the second bucket over the fire. "Wash water, or are you going to boil it for drinking?"

"Well, there's lots of snow out there and we have two bottles of water left so I thought we could wash up a bit with this. I know I'll feel better with a clean face and you'll smell better if we can manage to bathe a little." She pushed at his good shoulder.

"Sounds like a good idea, but you've got to promise me you won't ogle my naked chest while I wash up. We can both use my tattered shirt to wash with. At least to dry ourselves since we have no spare cloth." He smirked at her.

"I'm a nurse and I've already seen your 'naked chest'; but I'm too polite to mention it." She grinned back. "Let me check that wound. I'm not going to unwrap it, I just need to look for swelling, redness, or streaks up you arm." She walked over to where he'd sat down on the bench.

Using great care, David shrugged out of his jacket, exposing his arm and his chest for her inspection. When she took his arm in her hands, he leered at her and watched her face grow darker. "I knew it! You like seeing my naked chest, don't you?" he teased.

"You forget. I've got hold of a part of you that I can hurt very easily. You'd better be nice to me," she warned, inspecting the bandaged arm carefully. "Looks very good. Very little bruising or redness. I think you heal fast. Must be the Native blood or good living." She managed to tease back at him.

"Did you know your face turns the most amazing light pecan color when you blush? I've never noticed that color on anyone before." He smiled into her eyes for a second before she dropped them and his arm. "Changing the subject. I need you to give me a description of the killer from your vision last night. We don't have paper to write it down, but if we both have the information, maybe we can make a drawing when we get back to civilization."

"I don't think I can ever forget that face. I think, I'll know him if I see a photo. It was 1933 so I doubt if he's still alive." Kam shuddered. Closing her eyes, she began to describe the killer to David. "He's tall for that era, I think about six feet. Dark hair with dark eyes, but the eyes are small and the nose pronounced with several old breaks. He's got a serious scar on the underside of his chin, about dead center running toward his throat, but stops before it gets to his very large Adam's apple. His skin is weathered, but white. Flabby and wrinkled both. Broad shoulders, but has a gut and overall looks to have a soft rather than a hard body. His jacket had insignia on it, but I can't see anything other than those things that run from shoulder to neck 'epaulets?' They're anchored by some kind of pin or button. I can only see the side of it. The jacket he's wearing in dark brown, his shirt is tan, there seems to be a strap of some sort from the left shoulder across to his right hip where it ends in a holster. His hat looks like a uniform type, but the angle doesn't let me see any insignia." Opening her eyes, she looked over at David. "Did you get all of that?"

"Very good. Close your eyes again and look only at what clothing you can see. Does it remind you of any specific branch of the military or occupation? Take your time." He watched her close her eyes, her face serious. She frowned.

"Now that you mention it, he could be either in the Army or some sort of law enforcement. Those uniforms seemed almost interchangeable. I can't get enough of a view to see any badge or insignia." She repeated her one disappointment in this view of the killer.

"Okay, from now until we get out of here, I need you to refresh your memory as often as you can. Either you can tell it to me again or you can repeat the description to yourself. I think the broken nose and the scar might be important, but so's his clothing." He stood and walked over to the makeshift oven. Pulling the board away from the heat of the fire, he carefully tipped the pot from over the oatcakes.

"Well, they don't smell too bad and the texture has to be more palatable than that nasty oatmeal. Toss me one." Kam inhaled the fragrance of baking oats and chocolate.

"Here you go. Do you have a bottle of water for us to split?" He looked around as he pitched a warm oatcake her direction.

"Come on up here to the table. Might as well eat in a civilized manner. Also makes sharing the water easier." She directed him back to the bench beside her. She pulled out a bottle of water and two strips of jerky. "There's only two more pieces of meat left. We better save them in case we can't get out of here today."

"I really hope the weather clears enough for the chopper to get here. Shit, they can't take the horses. I don't want to turn them loose; they might or might not make it home." David frowned at the thought.

"Okay, the chopper can take you and Caleb out and leave me more food. I'll bring the stock out as soon as the snow clears enough to ride out to the truck; it's less than four miles." Kam finished her oatcake and walked back to the front window to look out across the valley. The light looked brighter and the snow didn't seem to be falling as thickly. She sighed. "I hope that ass got caught in this. Serve him right. What did he think he was going to change by shooting us?"

"My guess is he wanted to reach the body before us and missed that chance. His next goal would be to keep us from getting the body back to the lab. At least, if I wanted a murder to stay unsolved, those would be my goals." David took a swig of the water and passed her the bottle when she circled back his direction in her pacing. He smiled at her pacing, she was like a caged creature; full of energy and not able to use any of it.

"What's so funny?" Grabbing the bucket of melted snow water from next to the fire, Kam set it in the middle of the table.

"Human nature. Here we are stuck in a cabin in a snowstorm. I'm wounded, yet watching you pace is warming me up nicely." He wiggled his eyebrows and laughed at her expression.

"Since the cabin is cold, you can use the sensation; but don't get any smartass ideas." She mildly glared at him.

Each reached one hand into the bucket, splashed water on their faces and then finished by rubbing their hands together before wiping them on their pants. Each seemed synchronized with the other.

Grabbing his jacket, he managed to get his sore arm into the sleeve without assistance then finished sliding his good arm into the warm fabric. Taking his hat from the table, he walked to the door. "I'm going to find a convenient bush, then you can do the same." He closed the door behind himself, but not before catching a glimpse of Kam unbuttoning her shirt to wash herself more. Damn, he wondered how much she planned on washing, watching would have been very nice indeed.

He gingerly stepped down the log steps, hardly remembering the mad dash they'd made up them not a full day ago. Walking around the cabin, he found the horses nestled under the protection of the old lean-to roof. He checked the saddles and the pack and apologized to them that he couldn't remove the tack. With no place to set the saddles or the corpse the only safe place for all of it was still on the horses. He scratched ears and rubbed noses before continuing his circle around the cabin. On the far side, he found a pile of rotted firewood, none of it useable after eighty years out in the Colorado weather. There was an old ax leaning against the pile. He wouldn't trust the handle, but the cutting edge looked good.

"David! Where are you? The sat phone is making noise. Want me to answer it?" Kam looked out the front of the cabin and saw tracks heading to the right. She paused, waiting to see if he would come from that direction.

"I'm coming." His voice sounded from the left, surprising her.

"What'd you do, walk all the way around? Find anything useful?" She was hoping he'd discovered a locker full of food for them and the horses.

"Just an ax. Where's that damn phone?" He cleared the three steps in one bound, passing her on the way. "Yeah, this is David. I kind of worried about that. What's the prediction for later today? We can make it another night if we have to, but food for us and the horses is getting scarce." He paused to listen, nodding his head then frowning. "That's weird. Okay, let us know later about the helicopter. We'll stay here until we get word that the storm is breaking up."

"What? Are we going to be stuck here tonight too?" Kam asked.

"Well, they don't know at this point. The back side of the front is less than fifty miles away, but it's moving more south than east so they can't tell exactly when it will clear this area." David watched her face fall. "Come on now, I'm not that bad of company, am I?"

"No, it's just going to get hungry around here. We'll walk the horses into the woods later so they can munch on trees. Any other news about the guy shooting at us?"

"That's the strange part of this story. Seems someone stole Bethany's gelding from the R-M and used him to get up to where we were working. Megan heard a horse respond to Harley, but thought it was Radar. That was about half an hour before she heard the gunfire." He frowned. "I'm glad she didn't realize the shots were at us; she might have ridden into the gunman. Any rate, the owner of the R-M had mounted a search for his wife's horse, Megan joined it, but the animal came out of the woods without a rider." He scratched his head. "They think the gunman rode him back, and then turned him loose before heading down the mountain on foot. Of course, by that time the snow was falling, so they abandoned the search. They'll never find any trace once the snow melts. Guess the guy will get away unless you did manage to wound him." His expression was grim but his mouth turned up at the corners at the thought of a wounded gunman.

"Wow, someone really doesn't want us to document this murder. How can an old murder affect people so far removed from the crime? I just don't see any reason to kill over it at this point." Kam shook her head, trying to reason out the actions surrounding the attempt to stop them from recovering the body.

"What about the second part of your vision? Maybe there's something hidden in the cabin that would make sense out of this." Eyes narrowing; David looked around the room. "Where did you see him put that box?"

Kam closed her eyes and visualized the dream. Opening them, she walked over to the built-in bed and dropped to her knees. "There's a hidden hole under one of these boards." She began to feel for either looseness or perhaps a board higher than the others without any luck. "Damn, I can't feel anything different about any of this wood under here." Frowning, she closed her eyes and brought the vision back to the front of her memory. "Ahhh, now I see it." Her hands moved to a board next to the wall, it seemed to be a hair higher than those surrounding it. "Give me your pocket knife." She put her hand back to David.

David passed her the knife, but kept quiet, watching her concentrate on her find. Her hands moved over the board, and then around it, finally she used the knife to pry out a wooden peg and work the board loose.

"Got it." She passed back his knife and lifted the board completely out of the floor. "Wish I could see what I'm reaching into." Almost reverently, she reached into the unseen hole and ran her hands over a metal box. "Really hope no spiders live in this hole." She ran her fingers under the box and lifted one end out before running her other hand under the box to grasp it and drag it clear of the overhanging bed. Rocking back onto her feet from her knees, she carried what looked to be an old cracker tin tied with string over to the table and set it down.

"I haven't seen a tin like this other than in a museum depicting frontier life. It must have been old when Caleb filled it and buried it." Dave spoke softly, as though a loud noise would cause the tin to disintegrate.

Running her hands over the painted tin, Kam admired the old logo and the wonderful condition of the metal after so many years in the ground. "This tin is mine. Whatever is in it might be evidence, but I claim the container." She told him before gently beginning to untie the string and work off the lid.

"Fine by me, but we might have problems with the forensics team about that idea. If they know about the container, it'll never see the light of day again. Evidence is evidence no matter if it has bearing on the case or not."

With the string untied, the lid worked free with the scrape of tin on tin. Kam looked inside the box with David's chin resting on her shoulder. On top of some wax paper wrapped items was a note written on paper clearly of a different era. "I think someone found this between the time that Caleb buried it and now." Kam reached for the paper.

"Wait!" Grabbing his riding gloves, David put them on. "Let me. There could be prints on the paper, if it's from this day and age, they could be traced." He gently lifted the paper and shook out the crease in the middle. He read it aloud to Kam:

"June 22, 1983

To whom it may concern,

If someone other than me is discovering this box, then my plan hasn't worked out and either I'm dead, or I've disappeared. Either way, I hope this information will aid in solving the death of Caleb

Preston and possibly the recovery of the lands belonging to Jacob and Michelle Hendrix.

I plan to approach Samuel Cole about this matter. His grandfather is guilty of coercing the Hendrix family into signing over the H/J ranch and lands to the Cole Ranch in 1933. All the evidence is in this box. I hope that Samuel will see that he can rectify the deeds of his ancestor by giving that land back to the decedents of Jacob and Michelle.

If he refuses, I have no choice, but take this evidence to either the sheriff or a state prosecutor in hopes of getting the ranch back for the Hendrix family. Samuel owns half of the county and part of New Mexico, letting loose of a thousand acres should not be that much of an issue for him.

If whoever finds this box will carry through with my plan, I appreciate it. I know the Hendrix family will appreciate it, as well. Just remember that I went to Samuel Cole and the sheriff. If I had no luck, you may want to seek out a state or federal agency with this evidence. I told my brother-in-law, Phil Dunkin, I found this evidence, but nothing about where it's hidden. He's too young to get involved in this, but I felt someone needed to know. God speed and please say a prayer for me.

The letter is signed 'Richard Meadows'. I wonder if he's any relation to Roger Meadows of the R-M?"

"Well, I know the name of Samuel Cole. He's a patient of my boss. It gives me chills to think that he might have caused this Richard Meadows to disappear back in 1983," she shuddered.

David put down the sheet on the upturned metal lid then reached it to withdraw the items wrapped in the waxed paper. Everything was dry and looked as though it could have been secreted away yesterday; not eighty years ago. The tin box served its purpose well and along with the dry conditions of the high desert, the ground had not damaged the box or its contents.

Gently put the wax paper wrapped bundle on the table, David sighed. "Wish we had more light." Kam ran over to open the shutters in the back and next to the door; giving the room what little natural light there was on a cloudy, snowy morning.

He waited for her to sit down before unfolding the stiff paper that protected the original items of the tin. On top was a small, thin book. David opened it to find a daily log that began in mid May of 1933. Gently thumbing through the book, he found the last entry was October 13, 1933. Looking at Kam he commented, "Wonder if that was the day he died?"

"Possibly, in my dream he left the cabin after he put the box into the hole. It might mean it was his last time to see his home."

He set the journal on top of the letter from Richard in the lid of the tin before looking down at the remaining items. The first was a photograph showing a sheriff with a man and a woman in handcuffs in front of what looked to be a still. Kind of a typical photo of the era, arrest of moonshiners by elected official. But, the photo below it showed the exact same scene; but it included a lot more background. This photo was the same except that on the other side of the still was a well-dressed man standing in front of petroglyphs on the rock wall behind him. Without captions, they would need a local historian to detail them. David felt Kam's fingers dig into his shoulder. He glanced at her to find her eyes wide and staring and her face had turned a muddy shade. "What's wrong? Are you okay?"

Knowing she sounded like an idiot, Kam lifted a shaky hand and pointed at the close-up photograph. "That's him! The guy with the gun. That's the killer. David. The sheriff killed Caleb! Oh my God!" She buried her face in his shoulder, unable to stop the tears that began to pour out. That poor man, killed by someone he should have been able to trust. She felt David run his arm around her waist as he tried to soothe her.

"Easy, Honey. It was a long time ago. You're safe. That man probably met his maker years ago." He gently stroked her trembling back while she cried.

"The other man looks like Samuel Cole, but he wasn't even born in 1933, much less an adult. It has to be either his father or grandfather." Kam looked closer at the wide-angle photo. "This must be what Richard Meadows meant. I'll bet Cole's grandfather blackmailed that couple into signing over their property to keep from being prosecuted for running booze. I wonder where those petroglyphs are located." She looked into David's eyes as she brushed the tears away and moved away from his protective arm. "I'm sorry I fell apart. After last night, seeing that face scared the crap out of me." She admitted.

"I don't blame you. It must have been like seeing the person who will kill you. Even knowing it was all in the past doesn't make it any easier to accept." He carefully put both photographs with the journal and Meadows' letter before turning back to see the final item still in the wrapping. "Look, another journal." This book was thicker than the other was and the first entry was the name and date of the person who owned it.

"November 15, 1931
Personal Journal of Joseph Tucker
Newly elected Sheriff of Riverview and Gunnison County, CO
This is the first of what I hope will be many log books detailing my life as a Sheriff of Riverview."

David stopped reading. He expected the journal would end before the other began a year and a half later. He thumbed through the pages of the thick book. Most had only a few lines per day, but some days covered a page or more in his bold hand. "Look, here in May of 1932: *A man approached me today. He offered me money to stop my investigation into local moonshine operations. He said that his employer could make my life more dangerous if I refused to accept this 'token of appreciation'. I declined, and told the man to relay to his employer that I work for the town, not for any specific landowner. I think I know who sent him, but I have no proof.*" He thumbed his way further through the book. He paused and read the final entry: "*Cole has grown bolder; I've sent Angelica to her mother in Montrose. He told me if I refused his offer of a thousand dollars a year to ignore his 'private business' he would kill me and my family. I don't know who to call for help in this. I wrote to the ATF and the FBI, but neither has responded. My days may be numbered, so I'm giving this book to Caleb today with instructions to hide it. It may be only hearsay evidence of Cole's involvement, but if anything happens to me; it could help the next sheriff. Sad to say, I'm afraid Miller will take my job and he's in tight with Cole.*"

David closed the book after making certain there were no more entries. The last was dated May 1 in 1933. "We need to check the records of that time to find out what happened to Sheriff Tucker." He looked over to see that Kam had recovered some warm tone to her complexion. "You okay?"

"Yes, this all begins to make sense. Between moonshine and land grabbing Cole was dirty from head to toe. Throw in a couple of murders and it paints a lovely picture of those days." She pointed from the journal in David's hands to the photos and the smaller book on the table. "We know the current head of the Cole family is involved in this mess, but he's about seventy and I can't quite picture him stealing a horse and trying to take the body from us. Either he hired someone, or there's more going on than we know."

"You've got a point there." He looked around the cabin; it looked lighter than it had when they opened the box. "Look, I think the sun's breaking through the clouds." He pointed at the light shining on the floor in front of them. "Maybe we can get out of here today after all."

"Let's get this packed back into the box. Wait, what's that in the wax paper?" Kam pointed to a large, flat item still lying on the paper.

"Looks like a fancy button. Maybe from a uniform? That looks like dried blood on it." David held up a metal button with an insignia embossed into it that had a brown stain on one edge. "Let's put it away with the rest of the items, we'll get a chance to read the journals later and they'll probably explain it." He placed it back into the box then layered the items in the same order that Caleb had placed them so long ago. None of the villains were alive to atone for their deeds, but Samuel Cole would be questioned and so would the Hendrix family; if they could be found. Once all the items were in the box, he wrapped the string back around it as it had been found. "I'm glad we didn't have to cut the string, I feel safer about the tin with the lid tied on."

"I'm going out to the horses. You pass me stuff through the window and I'll get it put on them so we can get the hell out of here." Kam walked over to the back window and climbed out. It was easier than walking around the cabin in the snow. "I think once we get to the trees on the far side of the valley, there will be less snow. They shelter the trail from the wind and keep the drifts from forming. If we can get out of here in the next hour or so we should be able to make it to the trailer before four, even at a walk. It's only noon now." She glanced at her watch. Outside with the horses, she moved from one to the other, checking saddle position, tightening cinches, removing hobbles and putting on bridles.

David filled the large black pot with water; maybe someone would be back here soon to clean it, but he didn't have time. Swinging it over the glowing embers of the fire, he began collecting their few items. He added Caleb's Bible to the stash before he began passing saddlebags through the window to Kam. He was amazed his arm moved so well. He fisted the hand and bent his elbow, hardly any pain at all. Riding should be easy, he hoped. "I put Caleb's Bible in your saddlebag and the tin in mine." He walked over to the front window where the rifle leaned against the closed shutters; his pistol lay on the floor next to it. He didn't remember taking it out of his shoulder holster; Kam must have done that when she worked on his arm. Gingerly he put his holster on the outside of his jacket and put his pistol back into its sheath, next he then passed the rifle over to Kam.

"Do you think we should call your office and let them know we're out of here?" She asked.

"Good idea. I'll take care of that while you bring the horses around." He walked over to the satellite phone, to call the office, but paused when he heard the distant whoop-whoop of an approaching helicopter. Damn. Well, they could take the body back to the forensics team. He wasn't letting go of the box until he had a chance to read at least the small journal. He finished dialing and heard a voice answer. "Hi, I can hear the chopper approaching. Thanks for the response to our predicament." He chuckled, and then continued. "We're riding out of here, to get the horses off the mountain, but the helicopter can take the body for us. Also, I hope they brought us something to eat. I'm starved." He listened to the voice on the other end protesting his ideas. "I'm fine, my arm is barely sore. I'll get the local MD to check it over. There's more to this case than we thought, and I want to work on it. I don't have time to be on the injured list for this scratch." He hung up the phone before his boss could order him back to the office.

Kam watched the helicopter land in the soft snow and was pleased to see it only sank about a foot. Riding shouldn't be too bad if the snow in the open was that shallow. Along the trail, it should be even easier than in the open. The horses shuffled around her; spooked by the sound of the helicopter. Once it settled and the engine died; the horses ignored it. She watched four people pile out of the large machine.

Chapter Eleven

Before even opening her eyes, Megan knew she wasn't in her own bed. There were people moving about and the smell of coffee and bacon floated around her head as she sat up. Looking around the nicely furnished guest bedroom, she remembered Roger and Bethany insisting she spend the night. One glance at the clock on the nightstand told her that she'd overslept.

"Shit." She never slept past six, never. Jumping out of the bed, she found the attached bath where she put the extra toothbrush and washcloth to good use. Her clothes were yesterday's, but would have to do for now. A light knock sounded on the door.

"Megan, I heard you get up. I've got an extra t-shirt that would likely fit you. You're on your own for jeans, but this shirt is large on me so it might work for you." Bethany stuck her head around the bedroom door. "That didn't sound right… just try the shirt on; if it fits at least you'll feel better. I hate wearing the same clothes two days in a row." She confided tossing the shirt at Megan.

"Thanks." Catching the shirt, she laughed at Bethany's blush. "I know what you meant. No offense taken. I'm three inches taller and about fifty pounds heavier than you – I don't know why you think I can't wear the same petite size as you. How are you feeling?"

"Stiffer today than yesterday, but the swelling is going down and I should start applying heat this morning. Isn't it forty-eight hours before healing starts on muscles and bruises? Something like that. See you in the kitchen."

She backed out of the doorway, closing the door behind her.

Megan looked at the shirt. A bright orange; there was a dancing cow and horse along with a calf and colt on the front. "Bell Cow Boogie Endurance Ride, Chandler, OK." She smiled, another of Bethany's completion awards. Very cute, she thought putting on the shirt. It felt a little tight across her ample chest, but overall the fit seemed to work. Well, in this hunter orange shirt, she would definitely draw eyes. Using her hands on the inside of the fabric, she stretched it down the front so it wouldn't fit so snuggly. She smiled at her reflection, squared her shoulders and walked out of the room to face the day and the group gathered for breakfast.

Roger was talking when she entered the kitchen. "The construction crew that spent the night in the bunk house is going to use the road grader to plow us a way to the highway and a path around here. The snow's not that deep, but the drifts are impossible." He looked over the group and nodded at Megan's entrance. "Coffee's hot and there's still some bacon and eggs on the stove."

"Yes, Sir." Megan followed his suggestion and helped herself to the coffee and food before finding a seat at the table. "If they're plowing to the highway, that means the road past my place, too. Right? she asked.

Roger smiled. "Since I'm not planning on taking out any trees on the horse trail to the R-B, they'll have to plow past your place to get to the road before they can start plowing from the highway to the ranch yard. But, don't head out yet. It's going to take an hour or more and that's once the snow stops." He looked at Aaron, Shorty, Nick, John, and Mike, who supervised the construction crew. "Until the storm breaks, I need you to tend to regular chores as best you can. Be careful walking, but the stock need tending and we can shovel paths to the barns from the house, cabin, and the bunkhouse."

Each of the men nodded and the meeting broke up with them shuffling into warm jackets, gloves and hats before filing out the door to begin clearing paths around the property and tending stock.

"Mike, I need to ask you a couple of questions. You can tell your workers the plan when we're done talking." Mike followed Roger to his office where Roger closed the door. "Yesterday, we talked to your crew about Coup's theft. John forgot to take a count, but he didn't remember seeing you. What time did you leave the work site?"

"I left about noon. I needed to go to Montrose to check on a shipment of lumber. I've been having some trouble clarifying to the supplier that we need two different grades." John looked Roger in the eye and showed no hesitation in answering the question.

"Was there anyone else that either left early or didn't show up that you're aware of?"

"Jimmy showed up late, smelling like diesel from his truck breaking down, but other than him, everyone was working when I left. What are you getting at? Do you suspect one of my men of stealing that horse?" Mike glared at Roger.

"Well, we're looking at anyone who might have had access to the ranch. A person who would possibly know Coup and the fact he'd been up that trail; or just know he's the best mountain horse on the place. Since his tack is normally on the rack by his stall; anyone who grabbed him would be able to saddle and slip out without being in plain view of the hands." Roger remembered why he'd built that rack. Bethany had a long memory of her flight from Phil and wanted her saddle and bridle close to her horse in case it should ever happen again that she needed to escape danger. "So far, you and two others are lacking a good alibi about your location during the afternoon. Yours we can check out. I'm leaving the others to explain to the FBI when questioned. Stay close to the ranch. I expect to have either the agent up on the hill or one of his co-workers here this afternoon to investigate the attack." He ordered before opening the office door and leading Mike back into the great room. "Let your men know what's happening and get a volunteer to run that grader later." He stepped out of the way and allowed Mike to leave.

"Did he have any information?" Bethany asked.

"Says he went to Montrose about noon yesterday. Didn't say when he got back. I'll make certain they verify his information. Strange, I trust him, but I don't know him well enough not to suspect him or his crew. The other person I want checked completely is Red. He might work for me, but again, I don't know him well enough not to suspect him. He was off looking for dude stock yesterday." Roger scratched his head. "I really hate not being able to trust my own employees. But, somebody stole Coup and attacked Kam and the FBI agent."

"It's okay dear; the boys understand your dilemma. They know you want to have complete faith in them but they also know that someone knew where to find Coup and the fact that he was the best horse to take." Walking to him, Bethany put her arm around his waist. "We'll figure out what's happening. In the meantime, should we put locks on the stalls, or just on the tack room?"

"That's not a bad idea. I've got Coup's saddle in my barn office with the door locked. I'll have Aaron put a padlock on the tack room door. So long as each horse has a halter available next to the stall, locking up the tack shouldn't endanger any of them." Roger thought about the suspicious barn fire of two nights ago. Megan had freed the horses that night, without time to find halters. Walking over to the intercom, he paged Aaron. He heard horses stomping in the background when Aaron picked up. "While you're in the barn, find a padlock for the tack room and secure it for me. Bring the key to the house when you're finished."

"Yes boss."

"Well, if we can't keep eyes on everyone all the time, a few locks can go a long way to keeping things secure until we get to the bottom of this affair." Turning to his wife, his frown cleared when he looked down at her. "Your color is better today. Is the pain less or are you just getting used to moving carefully?"

"I'm still pretty stiff, but I've learned what movements I don't want to try. I was thinking about using the hot tub later this afternoon. The warm water should help reduce the pain and maybe help the swelling."

Roger smiled, his eyes glittering. "Well, I might join you, but I doubt my swelling will go down as easily." He muttered into her hair as he kissed the top of her head before moving away.

Megan turned away from the sight of them. Coughing politely to remind them of her presence, she inspected her coffee. "Did you notice the patrol car sitting in the pull off yesterday? Maybe the deputy manning the speed trap saw the rider on Coup crossing the highway? Might be worth checking into." She suggested to Roger. "I guess I'm stuck here until the roads are cleared. What do you want me to do, boss?"

"No, I didn't notice. I'll call the sheriff later and have him ask his deputy about it. There's not much for you to do at the moment. Why don't you keep Bethany occupied and out of mischief? No wait, that's what I asked you to do the day she got hurt. Hmmm." Roger scratched his chin and frowned at Megan then laughed at her expression. "I know, it's okay, you couldn't have controlled her actions and the fall was a fluke. Just keep her from overdoing today." He grabbed his hat, put on his coat and walked out the door without looking back at the glare his wife shot his direction.

"That man. He thinks he needs to find me a caretaker. Well, what mischief do you want to get into today? I'll bet we can find something to drive him nuts if we think hard enough." Bethany watched Megan's face fall and began to laugh. "You should see yourself. You look like a whipped hound. I'm just kidding. I wouldn't put you in the middle on purpose."

"I thought you liked me better than that; but you had me wondering what I did to make you want Roger to fire me." Megan shook a finger at her friend.

"The weather should clear in a couple of hours. We can either clean house, or we can play cards. What's your pleasure?" Bethany asked, walking toward the card caddy. She knew games would be first choice, because Megan knew Roger wanted her to rest.

"Poker, Black Jack, Cribbage? I'm a fair player of any of those. If you've got a scrabble board, I'm killer at that game." Megan warned her boss. "Just keep the Monopoly to yourself unless you want me to sleep."

"Roger doesn't play Cribbage, I'd love a game." She brought the board to the table. "Shorty, you don't mind us taking over the table do you? We won't be in your way?" She looked over at the man cleaning up the kitchen. Since her arrival, he had taken over making breakfast and lunch while she cooked dinner.

"No, Ma'am. The table's all yours." He watched the two women set up for the game. While he liked Bethany, he hardly could take his eyes off Megan. That shirt brought out features he hadn't noticed before and when she walked over to get a Pepsi those features were just about at eye level because of her height. Too bad Aaron had warned the men away from her just the other day. Course, she was half his age, but a man could really admire the view. Turning away, he smiled at the dishes he loaded into the washer, glad he had a reason to face the wall.

Megan and Bethany spent the morning playing cards and discussing the trail loop, the body, Kam and David Harrison. "You'd laugh if you caught the way he was looking at your new friend." Megan placed two cards facedown for Bethany's crib and waited for her to make a play.

"Sparks flying? That would be nice; maybe it'll lighten her life a bit. I wish I knew why she looks so sad." Bethany led with a seven. "Moving to a new place can be a factor, but when I met her she positively vibrated sadness. There has to be some cause; wonder why she moved out this direction?"

"I haven't really had a chance to get to know her; and I'm not certain she noticed the agent but some of the looks he sent her direction could warm a north wind." Megan laughed at her memory of intercepting one of those heated glances.

"Well, you know how men who live with danger are..." Bethany paused and made certain Shorty had left the area. "Passion and adrenaline are closely linked, hooked on one, hooked on the other." She nodded sagely.

"I think after my time in the military, I prefer my man to be less passionate, if it means he has a chance to live longer." Megan shook her head. "There's nothing wrong with defending yourself and your family; but there's no need to search out trouble just for excitement." She rubbed her shoulder, not realizing the movement drew

Bethany's eyes and sympathy.

"Does your shoulder hurt when the weather turns? Roger has an old wound that gives him fits if a cold front is headed this direction." She stood up and walked to the refrigerator. "I can get you something for it. A heating pad might take some of the ache out of the joint." She offered.

"No thanks, I'm just tired. The pain is only part of the problem." She gave Bethany a small smile. "I battle depression, and the other night when the barn burned; I had a mild meltdown. I'm embarrassed to say that Aaron gave me a shoulder to cry on; literally."

Smiling sadly at Megan, Bethany brought over a plate of brownies from last night. "You're allowed to melt down on occasion, and I can think of no nicer set of shoulders to cry on, except for maybe my husband's. I'd advise you to use Aaron, 'cause you don't want me to catch you using Roger." She smiled with the warning, but Megan caught a glint to her eyes.

"Yes Ma'am, got it, not Roger." Reaching for a brownie, she managed to laugh at Bethany. "Aaron was so sweet, but holding me on his lap caused something to 'come up' that embarrassed him. He kissed me because I laughed, said he wanted me to understand the chemistry." She fanned her suddenly warm red face. "Sparks were evident. Good thing Roger came in when he did."

"Well, Aaron's one of the best. He saved Roger's life at least once that I know of when they were Rangers. If you're interested, you could hardly do better." Bethany studied Megan while the woman studied her brownie, picking crumbs off the edges.

"That's just it. I think he's amazing, but my life is such a mess. Until I know what I want to do next; I'm just not ready to get involved. It wouldn't be fair to him." Her eyes shot to Bethany, pleading with her friend to understand.

Bethany sat down and covered Megan's hand with her own. "Don't you think he realizes all of that? Has he pushed you to make any decisions or jump into a relationship?"

"No, in fact he told me he would be waiting when I was ready. I feel guilty that he could be so supportive and get so little in return; but I don't have anything to give right now." Her eyes filled but she managed to breathe away the unwanted tears.

"Honey, you're so lucky. You have so many friends and now a man who thinks you're special. Don't be afraid and turn away from all of us; especially don't shut him down, if there's any chance at all you might want him in your life," she advised Megan.

Megan stood up and paced the kitchen, ending up at the sink where she ran water in her hands then passed them over her face. "Okay, you're right. I need to just calm down and not run scared from my life here. I'm so looking forward to growing with the R-B and making a permanent home in this area. Thank you for helping me see things more clearly. I've been needing the kind of friendship you've offered… more than you can imagine." When she turned back to the table, her eyes were clear and she managed a real smile at her friend.

The door opened without warning and the men entered. "It's cold out there. Any coffee left? What's for lunch?" The words flew around the room as they stomped feet, removing coats and hats before walking to the table.

"Sit. Shorty is busy, but he took out the chili knowing you'd need a hot lunch. Anyone want a hotdog to put under that chili?" Hungry men quickly surrounded the table. She eyeballed Megan to ascertain if she needed more time to collect herself but smiled when she saw Aaron had walked up to her friend and was talking quietly to her in a corner of the kitchen.

"Hey Megs, I didn't get a chance to talk to you this morning. Are you doing okay? Yesterday was a bit hectic, from the time of the fire until we got back here with Coup." He paused and brushed a lock of hair from the corner of her eye. "How are you holding up?"

"I'm fine. One small meltdown doesn't mean I'm falling apart." Megan stepped back a few inches from him. She wanted to move into his warm arms, but with all the hands not ten feet away, she thought it best to put a few inches between them. "How are Harley and Coup? Has the grader gotten here yet to plow us out?" She asked in a firmer voice.

"That's my girl," he murmured, brushing his lip to her temple before stepping away and smiling at her. "The horses are fine. Those two could go out again today without any problems. The grader has been working on the road and now is moving around the drive he should have all the drifts gone by two." He moved to the stove and grabbed the coffee pot to fill cups for the rest of the men. Shorty had left cups on the table along with the sugar and cream.

After a quick poll, Roger spoke for those gathered. "If the chili is hot and the dogs aren't, give us the chili."

Bethany grabbed down bowls and spoons while Megan filled them at the stove and Aaron passed them to the upraised hands. Soon everyone had steaming hot chili and spoons. All chatter ceased and the room was filled with the sounds of diners either blowing on the steaming liquid or slurping the chili.

"If the grader will be done by about two; I guess I should head back to my place. I need to feed the stock and Phil's cat. Though I swear that cat could live a week on body fat without any food." Megan smiled at the round of laughs at the table.

"That sounds okay. I'll tell the man driving the grader to clean out your yard on his way back to the construction site." Roger smiled at the relief showing on Megan's face.

The group slowly finished their lunch. The chili pot was empty before the last person pushed themselves away from the table. The weather and the possibilities of more snow were the major topics of conversation. The most recent report was for a south wind off the gulf to bring up more moisture, but also to bring up warmer temperatures causing it to rain on top of the snow.

"That's going to be a mess. I doubt we'll flood, we didn't get that much snow, but it's going to leave behind a lot of mud." Bethany frowned around the table. "I expect every one of you who come in my house to remove boots at the door. I'm not giving Shorty more work cleaning up after you." She shook her finger around the table. She'd noticed that none of them had removed their boots for lunch. "If you can't be bothered to remove your boots, then you can eat in the bunkhouse. I don't have to worry about how clean that space is or isn't."

Chapter Twelve

Walking out of the cabin, David stored his phone in the front of his jacket as he walked toward the arriving helicopter crew. "Hi, you guys can lighten our load; but we're riding out of here. Did you happen to bring any food?" his mouth watering at the thought of real food.

"We have two MRE, some candy bars, and bottled water." The lead person reached in his jacket and handed over the water while the person behind him took the MRE from a pack on the leaders back. "We're supposed to transport you back to Denver, Sir." He informed David. "Dick is a medic, and can bind your wound."

"I'm sorry, but I'm not going back to Denver just yet and I've had my own registered nurse so I've got a great field bandage on my arm. I'll be fine until we get to the clinic in Riverview. How're the roads? We have a trailer parked about a mile off the highway, think we'll be able to drive it out?"

"Well, Sir, if you insist, I can't force you into the chopper." The team leader shook his head and frowned at the FBI agent. "I don't think that you'll be able to drive out your rig. The drifts are over two feet in some places on side roads." He looked around, took in the horses and Kam standing up at the cabin. "Show us what you want us to take back. I expect you to tell your boss why you refused the ride back. I'm not getting in the middle of any battle." He continued to frown at David, but his eyes lingered on Kam and he felt he could understand the man wanting to stay in the area. He smiled at the nurse – not bad looking even after a night in the wilds.

"You can take anything from the packhorse. The corpse is well wrapped and protected, but there's a few bags of trace, soil, and boulders that will need to be handled carefully." David pointed to the packhorse, and gestured for Kam to lead the mare over to the team.

Walking the reluctant mare forward, the other two horses pulled back to the farthest end of their reins. None seemed pleased to approach the mechanical monster. "Here, David. Hold these two before they break free and head down the mountain without us." She handed David the reins of Radar and Lady Mica. She followed the rescue team back toward the helicopter. The mare only went about ten steps past David when she put on the breaks and refused to move any closer. "Sorry, but she's not going to get any closer for you and if she bolts, we could lose the very items you're here to rescue." Kam moved to the mare's face and stood rubbing and talking to the worried animal while the team unstrapped and unloaded the corpse and the bags of rocks and trace. Kam could see David munching on something and her stomach let out an unladylike rumble. "I hope you're not eating my food, David. Things could get ugly real fast." The team looked her over trying to assess the possible threat, noticed her grin and continued taking things to the helicopter.

Walking closer to her, David passed her an open candy bar followed by a bottle of water. By the time she finished the candy; the crew had loaded the helicopter and climbed back inside. The crew motioned them away, waited until they reached the cabin, and started the rotors. The backwash blew snow in the faces of horses and humans forcing them to turn toward the cabin and miss the sight of the majestic machine lifting out of the powdery snow and climbing into a bright blue sky.

"Here, this is for you, too." David passed Kam a MRE, smiling at the relief visible on her face.

"I thought maybe they only brought a snack for us. This is much more filling." Kam smiled around a mouthful of food. She managed to swallow and turned to watch the helicopter disappear over the ridge before she looked back to David. "Let's get going. Did they think the roads would be passable?"

"No, once down on the road, we're going to need transport. They said the drifts are deep on side roads. But, we'll know more as we get close to the rig." Mounting one handed, David patted Radar's neck for standing as still as statue.

Kam mounted Lady Mica with the lead for the packhorse in her right hand and they headed across the valley. Lady Mica pinned her ears and swished her tail only once to establish dominance over the packhorse. Once on the trail through the woods, Kam was relieved to find her deductions about its condition were correct. Much of the trail was clear and the rest had less than three inches of snow. The ribbons marking the trail were visible with the white background and other than a few spots where the trail dipped into gullies; they had no problems following the markings. Reaching the road in just under two hours, things got more difficult. The drifting snow at the bottom of the hills proved to be waist deep in one spot and the loose gravel under the snow made was treacherous.

From the woods, it took almost an hour to reach the trailer. With drifts in front of it, it was unmovable. Kam hoped Roger would be able to collect them at the highway. She remembered the way, but on horseback and through snow banks it would be a tiring ride.

Taking out her cell phone, she smiled at the two bars and hoped it would reach him. When Roger picked up on the second ring, his voice sounded relieved. "I'll get a trailer to you within the hour. Meet us where the BLM road meets Hwy 50" His voice comforted her and she heaved a huge sigh of relief at his words.

"I'm so glad to hear that you can get out and meet us on the highway. I think it's going to take us closer to an hour and a half to get that far. You may have to wait for us." Kam turned to David. "Roger'll meet us at the highway. We've only about a mile, I think. Are you feeling okay?"

"My shoulder's throbbing a little, but overall; I'm fine. How're you holding up?" He could see her face below her helmet and the smile seemed to be a little forced, but her color was good.

"Compared to an all day competition, this is a piece of cake. But then, if the weather were this cold, I doubt I'd be competing." She laughed.

"Let's get going. I don't want to keep our taxi waiting." He urged Radar into a faster walk as they headed up the snow covered gravel road toward the highway.

At the ranch...

Roger shot over to the phone when it's ringing interrupted Bethany's scolding. After speaking with the caller for a minute, he hung up and grinned over at his assembled hands and family. "That was Kam. She and the agent are at the rig and of course, it's buried in a snow bank. I told her we'd collect them at the highway. I'm taking Bethany's truck and trailer."

Aaron stood up at the same time as Megan. "I'll follow you with my truck to take care of the overload. Did you want to go with me, Megan?" He queried.

"No, I need to get my trailer out. Radar is going to

need a ride home and the Agent will need me to haul him to his car at my place."

"I forgot his car was there. Why don't I take his gear in my truck and just meet you at your place. I can spend a few minutes shoveling out your yard; what the grader can't get." He smiled at the thought. He wasn't going to let that agent have time to sweet talk her.

"Okay, let's get going. We have an hour for them to be at the highway, and I want to get there first. I don't want them to be targets, in case the shooter of yesterday wants a second chance at them." Roger walked over to the coat rack and grabbed his heavy jacket, hat, and gloves before turning to his wife. "Sorry, but you have to stay here. I don't want you to stress that bruise." He kissed her cheek, turned back to the door, and led everyone outside.

"Megan, grab some horse blankets from the tack room. I'll bring hay and feed in my truck." Aaron walked alongside Megan on the way out to the rigs. "Isn't there a half-assed storage shed about ten yards from the barn?"

"Yeah, it's kind of a three sided thing, holds a very small tractor and a riding mower. Why?"

"I was thinking until the barn is repaired, we can let the horses use it for shelter. All we have to do is take down the round corral panels and put them up from one edge of the building to the other. At least give the horses a wind block." Aaron smiled over at Roger who had paused to listen.

"Not a bad idea. Can you handle it without help? I hate to think of the horses standing out in the weather at this time of year. These wet fall storms are harder on them than the serious freezes of mid-winter." Roger nodded at Aaron in agreement with the plan.

"Hello… macho men. I can likely do that myself or at the very least assist Aaron." Megan waved her hand in front of the two men to remind them she was part of this crew.

Both men turned and laughed sheepishly. "You're right. We were ignoring the fact that you can handle most farm jobs without help. I'm sorry. I didn't mean to offend you." Roger had the grace to blush at his mistake.

Aaron laughed, blushing, but unrepentant. "I'll take the grain and hay over, and get started. You can help when you bring Radar home. How's that? Soothe your ego?" He smiled at the glare in Megan's eyes. She might be almost as tall as he was, but he still felt she was really cute when she got mad. He liked that fire in her eyes.

"Why, yes Sir, Mr. Aaron... us sweet, weak, feminine ladies always appreciate the help of you big, strong men." Megan batted her eyes and held her hands clasped beneath her chin in a "Scarlett O'Hara" type pose while she affected the southern drawl of a Georgia debutante. Ego, my ass; she thought.

"I love it when you talk Southern." Aaron laughed after her as she turned to walk to her trailer.

Roger shook his head and laughed at his foreman. "You've got it bad, don't you?"

"What? I enjoy teasing her and waiting to see how she'll respond. She's an easy mark with that temper of hers." Aaron managed to look innocently at his boss.

The group split up. Aaron threw three bales of hay and a full bag of grain into the truck for the horses. He also put in three feed pans in case there weren't any available. Without knowing exactly what burned in the fire, he could only take what he would need to set up feed and shelter for horses without any necessities available. Watching Roger leave with Bethany's truck and trailer, he jumped into his own truck and headed out to the highway. The agent's gear would have to fit in the back of the cab; the bed of the truck was full of supplies.

Megan finished cleaning the snow off her truck, went into the tack room in the barn, found horse blankets set out in stacks by size and took two for average size horses; Radar's was safe in her trailer, it hadn't been in the fire. She threw the blankets into the tack space in her trailer and returned to the barn to wait on Roger, Kam and David with her horse. She spent time grooming and petting both Harley and Coup before passing out treats to all the stock in the barn. Preparing the last two empty stalls in the barn for Lady Mica and the packhorse kept her busy for another half hour. Just finishing, she heard the sounds of a truck and trailer coming into the yard.

Roger brought the truck to a stop in front of the barn. "Taxi ride's over. There's a stalls in the barn for Lady Mica and the packhorse, should be set up with hay and water." Roger looked over at Kam. "Want me to take care of her in while you head to town? Or do you trust Doc Samuelson to care for David until you get there?"

"I'd appreciate you putting her up for me. I'll come back either later today or first thing in the morning to check on her. Thanks." Kam jumped out of the barely stopped truck and made a beeline to her own truck where it sat unhitched from her trailer.

Watching her hop into her truck, Roger chuckled. "You'd think it was spring by the number of relationships forming around here. Wait till I tell Bethany." He muttered to himself.

Megan joined Roger at the rear of the trailer just as he unlatched the door to release Radar. She caught her gelding as he stepped gingerly down from the back stall. "Where's she going so fast?" She pointed to the truck now driving out of the ranch yard.

"She thinks Doc Samuelson's going to need her to

stitch up that agent." Roger laughed over his shoulder while he unlatched the divider and let the packhorse back out. He handed the lead to Megan before going back into the trailer to unlatch the front divider and allow Lady Mica to back daintily out of the trailer. "I can take the mares; you load Radar and head home. I'm certain Aaron has the pen moved. He took the FBI agent with him."

"Crap, that guy's wounded. He won't be able to help." Megan shook her head as she led Radar to her trailer where he loaded easily. "See you later, I'll call if I think of anything else." She waved to Roger's back while she turned her trailer toward home.

Roger smiled after her. "Yep, you'd think it was April and not October. This news should cheer Bethany out of her 'sore butt blues'," he said to Lady Mica, as he led the mare toward the barn.

Chapter Thirteen

Gingerly climbing into Aaron's truck, David noticed the man narrowing his eyes. The look challenged him while taking his measure.

"No one ever took the time to introduce us. My name is Aaron and I'm foreman at the R-M. Served with Roger in the Rangers," he explained. "You going to be able to drive with that arm?"

"Nice to meet you. I'm Agent David Harrison, FBI." David turned his head to get a better look at the tall, broad shouldered man next to him. "I don't see why not, it's actually feeling quite good at the moment. Is Roger Meadows related to Richard Meadows?" David couldn't resist asking.

"Yeah, he was Roger's father. Why?" Aaron looked at the agent wondering where that question came from.

"So, Phil Dunkin is Roger's uncle?"

"Yeah, but Roger refuses to claim him after the man conspired to kill Richard and kidnap Bethany. Again, why do you ask?"

"We found some information in the cabin that leads me to wonder what Phil Dunkin knows about the time when Richard left the area."

"Hmmm, Roger will know more, but I remember last year that Phil said something about Richard running rather than staying to testify. We never found out what he could testify about. Phil is in prison for his part in Richard's death."

With that, silence reigned until Aaron pulled his

truck into the yard at Megan's place. The grader had pushed around snow, leaving a good-sized parking area and a clear path to the road. Except for a two-foot snowdrift blocking the front of David's car, Aaron shook his head. "Looks like we're going to be digging out your car. Grader operator did you a favor and left the front bumper – along with that snow bank." Aaron nodded to the banked snow in front of the parked car. "By the way, for your information and just between us… Megan doesn't need any 'help' from you so keep your paws off." His voice and manner had chilled with the statement.

David smiled then chuckled. "Damn man, you're brave…that woman scares me. Not my type at all. But, if we're speaking openly here – you keep your paws off Kam. I hope to see a lot more of her." He glared right back at Aaron after his laugh.

"Good to know. Glad we cleared the air, just don't let on to the women; they get a bit testy about men discussing them." Aaron's face split into a wide grin. "Welcome to Riverview." He put out his hand.

David turned around to face Aaron so he could reach the hand with his good left hand. "Thanks, seems like a right friendly place." He smiled back.

Exiting Aaron's truck, they walked around the car. Aaron looked at the pale face of the darker skinned man. "Why don't you sit on the porch, I'll dig out your car so you can get to town."

"Sorry to be such a wimp, but I think your idea might work the best at the moment. I owe you one." David managed to get to the porch and sit on the rocker. Hardly noticing the snow on the seat in his exhaustion.

Grabbing the shovel from the bed of his truck, Aaron began clearing the snow. "Toss me the keys, I'll start it for you and clean the windshield." He waited for David to find the keys in his pocket and pitch them with his left hand. They landed in the snow. "Okay, I'll start the car as soon as I find the keys." Aaron laughed.

"Sorry man, I'm right handed. I should have walked them down to you."

Removing his glove, Aaron found the spot where the keys entered the snow, dug straight down and managed to find them before his fingers froze. "Not a problem, here they are." He smiled, holding up his prize. Unlocking the driver's door, he wedged it open and slid in. With David being shorter, the fit into the driver's seat was tight. Starting the motor, he exited the car, picked up his shovel and began again to move the snow.

"Anything you want me to do that I can handle one handed?" David called as a truck and horse trailer pulled into the yard. He waved when Megan got out. She was quite a woman, tall, leggy and nicely shaped; just not the type that called to his protective nature. Silently he wished Aaron luck. As independent as she seemed, the man would need to handle her with finesse.

"Hi, I haven't gotten to the stock yet. Thought we should get the agent out so he can get to the clinic first. Want to help?" Aaron never paused from his shoveling duties while he spoke to the approaching woman.

"I'll get my shovel from the shed; we're going to need to move it anyway." She changed directions and walked over to the south facing three-sided shed, collected a wide flat shovel and came back to the car. "This Durango is all wheel drive so he should have good traction." She looked over the red Dodge and smiled, nodding her head in approval. No one in the backcountry had anything less than four wheel drive in this state.

Between the two of them, the car was ready to drive in minutes. Smiling, David came down the steps and managed to enter his car without hitting his wounded arm. "You two work good as a team. I'm impressed. Thanks, sorry I wasn't able to help." He touched the rim of his hat. "Megan, I'm going to need to question you, but it can wait a day or two. I'll find a place to stay in Riverview and set up a time. Maybe, speak with both you and Bethany to get the full story about how you found Caleb." Wincing, he put the SUV into drive, and let it slowly ease out of its parking spot before applying any pressure to the gas pedal to leave the yard.

Aaron stepped in closer to Megan as they waved goodbye to the departing agent. "Okay, how about some coffee before we set up the new pen? You grab Radar, and I'll throw the horses some hay, grain them and check their water. They can eat that while we have coffee and dig out the area around the shed."

Smiling back at him, Megan walked toward her trailer. "Sounds great. I'm certain Phil's horses are hungry and Radar never turns down food of any kind." She laughed while she opened the rear door of the trailer to let her gelding out. "Come on boy; let's get you into the pen. We'll get you a dry spot to rest before you know it." She murmured to the horse as she led him to the pipe corral.

Aaron had parked his truck close to the pen to ease feeding. Climbing into the bed of his truck, he cut open a bale of hay and threw flakes to all three horses. He paused to watch Megan walk up the steps and into the house. Damn, she had a fine pair of legs, not a bad ass either. Smiling to himself, he shook his head and continued with his self-appointed chores. He checked water, and then fixed a pan of grain for each horse. With the cold, the extra calories would help keep meat on their bones. Leaving the corral, he ran up the steps and into the house. "Damn, it's cold out there. The snow might be over, but it's not warming much."

"The coffee's just about done; go warm your hands around a mug." Megan directed.

"Ohhh, that's a great idea." Grabbing his index finger glove end with his teeth, Aaron pulled off one glove then the other as he walked over to the coffeepot, poured a mug and gratefully placed his cold hands around it to soak up the heat from the coffee. "Ahhh, pure Heaven."

Megan smiled at the tall man bending over a hot mug of coffee. Wow, he really did take up some space. Those broad shoulders set off his slender hips and long legs. Ummm, ummm! Too bad he thought of her as a mental case. She sighed at his back wondering what she could do to change his opinion.

Turning with his mug, Aaron caught the expression on Megan's face. He felt his body heat and his groin grow heavy, the expression showed an appreciation of his body before she had a chance to blush and turn away. Wondering if he should comment, he grabbed brought his mug to the table. She was blushing, now just what had she been thinking to make her blush like that? He smiled over at her, letting his eyes take in her body from her snug jeans up to that amazing tee shirt that left nothing to his imagination and finally to rest on her red cheeks. "The color in your cheeks is clashing with that shirt, but both are intriguing." He said, his voice sounding husky.

"Yeah well, maybe I need to find a shirt that fits, Bethany loaned this one to me and it's really not my size." Megan wished her mouth would get connected with her brain. He didn't need to know all that.

"Well, from this perspective, I think it fits just fine." Aaron teased, watching her nipples harden through the soft shirt under his gaze.

"Hey, my face is up here." Megan scolded him even

as her body heated from his inspection.

The electric coffeepot interrupted with its irritating "done" beeping. Both turned to look at it, looked back at each other and broke out laughing. Megan felt let down and elated at the same time. While he excited her and she wanted him closer; she wasn't ready for that yet so the interruption was perfect timing.

Aaron felt the tightness of his jeans loosen, making him glad he could walk and sorry that the moment had passed without any positive action on his part. He sat down to cover the softening lump in his jeans.

"Once we warm up, we can go out and on getting the horses moved. We'll need to move some snow to get the tractor and mower out of the shed. Do you want to do that while I find someplace to store the loose items in there?" Megan looked up from her close inspection of her coffee mug.

"Okay, I'll shovel then move the larger items. Once we get the shed cleared; we'll tie the horses to your trailer while we break down the pipe panels and move them over to the shed. Which side do you want that gate panel on?" He found himself admiring color of her eyes. Such a deep sapphire blue, his pants began to tighten again.

Megan took a long drink of her cooling coffee, set the mug aside and stood up. "Let's put it on the side toward the barn. I have to assume that Roger will rebuild it and if the gate faces it; it will be easier to bring feed out from the larger building." Walking to the coat rack, she put on her gloves, hat, and coat before opening the door. "Come on out when you're ready."

Watching her leave, he finished his coffee, visited the bathroom, and followed her outside. He grabbed the shovel and began working to clear space to move the riding lawn mower.

Time passed quickly while each worked at the agreed chores. Aaron paused now and then to admire the grace and speed of her movements and Megan watched his strength when he didn't notice. Both found themselves smiling while they worked and each felt their ears burning from the spreading warmth of their thoughts from time to time.

"Hey! Let's take a break," Megan called over to him. "I've got some cookies and can make hot chocolate. We need the calories."

"Well, we're almost done; but you're right about needing the calories." He followed her into the house. Both stopped just inside the door to shed coats, hats, and gloves. Aaron's elbow caught Megan in the back of the head as he shook himself loose from his coat. "Oww! I'm sorry!" He rubbed her head and pulled her into his body to massage her neck.

Megan hardly felt the hit, but the closeness and the massage of her neck and shoulders sent heat flowing down to her core, turning her nipples into hard peaks. "I'm okay, but you can keep the massage up, I didn't realize my shoulders were so stiff." She leaned back into his broad chest.

"If I keep up the massage, I'm afraid the stiffness of your shoulders will transfer to me and I won't be able to walk." He chuckled into her hair.

Megan jumped away from his hands, her face on fire as she walked over to put the kettle on high. "Oh, well, since you need to be able to walk, guess the massage is over. Thanks." With her back to him, she busied herself with taking down mugs, finding the cookies and the hot chocolate mix. "I've got extra mini-marshmallows if you like them." She offered, still not turning to face him.

Aaron smiled at her sudden nervous energy and the

red he could see on her ears. Yep, she wants me, now we just need to work out the where and when. His mind and body both found the thought enticing. Wondering if she realized his feelings and desires, he thought about dropping blatant hints. Maybe he'd dropped too many already, he didn't want to scare her off. Walking over to stand behind where she waited at the stove, he put his hands on her shoulders and turned her around. "Honey, I want you to know I'm very much interested in you. Not just for your hot body; I'm interested in you, the person. I know you think you have some issues to work out, but I think you're amazing the way you are." He softly ran a finger from her temple to her chin and raised her face so he could see her eyes. He felt her shiver under his touch and thought of a frightened filly. "Not only do I want to be here for you emotionally; but, when you're ready, I'll be waiting to have you in my bed. I'll never force or coerce you; but I'm not going to let you forget that I want you." He bent his head to lay his lips over hers, gently teasing them with his tongue until she opened to him.

    Megan froze at Aarons' touch. Since her injury, she hadn't let anyone close. His words sank in to her brain about the same moment he took possession of her lips. She melted against him, responding to his gentle passion with a building fire of her own. The kiss became a duel of tongues, they melded closer to each other; each responding to the heat. She felt his hands go from her hair down her back to her ass, pulling her closer to his hardening body. The feel of his arousal against her belly brought a hotter fire to her kiss and her tongue dove into his mouth. One hand then moved around her hip and up to cup her left breast, where it pressed into his chest. She froze. His hand only inches from her mangled shoulder, she immediately pulled herself free. "No, wait. I can't." She turned and ran for the bathroom where she locked the door before bursting into tears. Grabbing a towel to muffle her uncontrolled sobs, she flushed the john and ran water in the sink to cover the sound.

Totally confused, Aaron replayed the scene in his mind. When he got to the part where he fondled her breast, he re-examined her response. First hot and willing, then sheer panic. Why? Walking to the bathroom door, he knocked. "Megan, Honey. What's wrong? Can we talk about it?" He heard sounds that it took a second to identify as sobs. How had he made her cry, what had he done? "Honey, please, tell me what I did to make you cry? I'm confused. You know I'd never do anything to hurt you." He knocked again, heard the toilet flush and the water stop running. He hoped that meant she'd come out and talk to him.

"Aaron, it's not you and I don't mean that as a cliché. It honestly isn't you or anything you did." She leaned her head against her side of the door as she spoke softly to him.

"Can you come out and explain what just happened?" His voice gentle and the confusion of the moment audible.

Taking a deep breath, she forced herself to face her problem and try to explain it to him. "I'm not certain I can face you. I'm embarrassed. But, I'll try to tell you and then you can leave and let me get over this on my own." Megan spoke firmly still leaning against the door. She knew he was just on the other side.

"Well, if you're going to explain, you'll have to come out and face me. I'm going into the living room and will sit down to wait for you. No need to be embarrassed by anything you or I have done," he assured her.

Tears welling in her eyes once more, Megan lifted a

hand to the door as if to motion him back to her. She couldn't go out there and face him. She wasn't that brave right now and might not ever be. Listening, she heard the couch creak as his frame settled onto it. Now what? She busied herself in the bathroom, hanging up the towel, straightening the cosmetics on the back of the john, while her brain ran around the problem of Aaron. She knew he wasn't going to leave until she went out and talked to him and she couldn't spend the rest of the day hiding in the bathroom. Finally, she looked into the mirror, noting the red eyes and the pale cheeks. God, but tears made her ugly, and now he was going to see that, too. Then she remembered he'd already seen her after a cry. Great. The man was really going to think her a basket case. Twice in three days, she'd fallen apart on him. Shit. Gathering up what remained of her self-confidence, self-esteem, and courage, she took a calming breath and opened the door.

Aaron heard the door open, and the footsteps in the hall. He continued to read the horse magazine he'd picked up while waiting for her to collect herself. Listening, he heard her pause at the door to the living room and release a deep sigh. "Come on in and sit next to me. I promise I won't bite." He turned and patted the couch next to him, noting the traces of her tears. All he wanted to do was hold her and tell her she'd be okay.

Megan gave in to the need and found herself seated next to Aaron with his arm around her shoulders. Leaning the back of her head against him, she felt stronger, strong enough to explain this situation to him. "I don't know exactly how to explain this other than just telling you. You know I was wounded in Afghanistan on my last tour of duty. My shoulder was almost destroyed. It took four different surgeries over a six-month period to give me back movement and some muscle strength." She sighed, remembering the months of pain during the rebuilding of her damaged joint. "The doctors were amazing, but it will never be perfect. In fact, it's usable, but only under non-strenuous exercise." Her right hand went automatically to the damaged area to massage it. "The worst part is the scaring. It's ugly and almost scary in the lack of muscle tissue and the strange dips, hollows, and how they change when it moves. If I feel this way about it, and I see it every day..." She left off the sentence, unable to go on without choking up.

"Honey, you're worried about my reaction to your scar? Wait till you see the remnants of the hole in my right thigh." He found his hand resting against hers where it massaged the damaged shoulder. "You were a soldier. That wound is what you sacrificed for your country. It may not be beautiful in your eyes, but in mine, it's part of you and could never be repulsive." He kissed the top of her head where it rested against his shoulder. He felt her struggling to speak through the emotion that held her.

"But, it's so nasty. I'll never wear a regular swimsuit again. I won't subject anyone to seeing it. I swear, it would make a small child scream and run." She struggled to sit and turn her head to look at him.

"You have a very low opinion of small children, don't you? My nephews would want to touch it and feel it move while they held you down and either tickled you or fed you worms." He laughed, knowing the extreme curiosity of the twins. He continued smiling when he saw his words had brought a smile to her lips.

"Boys are the worst. They love nasty things, don't they?" Megan looked into his golden-flecked green eyes. "You're right, but their mother would haul them as far from me as possible with a look of horror on her face."

"Once you accept yourself, everyone around you will

accept you, too. I accept you, no matter what, but those who don't know you can only accept you by your actions," he told her. "When you decide to show me this horrible scar, I can guarantee that I'm going to be too involved with making love to you to notice it. Maybe afterward, I might notice it, but only to shower kisses over it while I learn your body with my lips." His voice had gone deep and husky while his mind played out a scene of lovemaking and tenderness. "You don't have to worry about me. There's no part of you that I won't want to worship because I think you are the hottest and bravest woman in the world." He really wanted to kiss her, but looking at her body language made him pause.

"Wow. I don't know how to respond to all that, but to say thank you. When the time comes, and I think it might, I think I'll be brave enough to let you see the scar. Right now, as much as we seem to want each other, I really feel the need to step back and grow accustomed to the idea." Putting her hand on his chest, she gently pushed him away.

"You're in charge, Honey. I've had all the time since you started working for the R-M to get accustomed to the idea that I not only want, but like you, so now it's your turn." Taking her hand, he stood and pulled her up beside him. "Just give me some kind of sign when you finish growing accustomed, okay?" He brushed her lips with his, turned and walked back to don his winter gear and return to work outside.

Megan watched him close the door before collapsing onto the couch. What was she getting into? He deserved so much more than a maimed lover. Aaron was all that was good, strong and true. Maybe she could find him a woman to match his great qualities, but she knew she wouldn't try and if one showed up, she'd likely shoot the bitch. He was her dream, the man she'd waited to show up in her life. He just deserved better than her. Rolling over onto her stomach, she screamed her frustration into the pillows. Why had she been wounded, why couldn't she be whole and strong? Damn, damn, damn! She pounded her clenched fist into the couch. Pushing herself back into a sitting position and shaking her head, she stood and walked back to the bathroom to splash cool water on her swollen eyes. Once her face was dry, she followed him out to finish setting up the pen for the horses.

Chapter Fourteen

Muttering several nasty words in English and their equivalent in his mother's language, David painfully and awkwardly maneuvered his Dodge Durango out of the ranch yard. His breathing heavy to counter the pain using his arm evoked, he wondered if he should turn around and head back. Aaron had offered to drive him to the clinic; maybe common sense would be best here. Then he remembered how Aaron looked at Megan and knew he couldn't do that to the man. If he had planned to spend an afternoon with Kam, he'd hate it if a new friend demanded assistance. Besides, turning around would be more painful than the simple drive to town. At least his Durango didn't have a manual transmission and most of the remainder of the drive could be done with his left arm; until he had to park. Gritting his teeth, he stopped at the highway and carefully turned right. Kam had given him directions to the clinic. It was a block off the highway two streets down from the Diner. All left turns from here; he could handle it.

Arriving at the clinic, Kam found Doc Samuelson had beaten her there, but David's red SUV was nowhere in sight. Worried, she parked on the south side, where the snow hadn't drifted, locked her truck and walked into the clinic. "Hi, George. I expected David to beat me here. I hope he's not having trouble driving." Her teeth chewed on her bottom lip while she peered out the window at the empty street.

"Don't worry, after the storm, they likely had to dig his car out of a snow drift. I had a good foot and a half blocking my drive." Dr. Samuelson attempted to ease her fears.

"Maybe. I'll get exam one ready. I wrapped his arm well yesterday, but didn't remove the dressing this morning. It's a through and through bullet wound and I don't think it nicked the bone at all. He got lucky." She walked past the doctor and into the exam room where she began to set out a trauma and suture tray, scissors, a set of scalpels to remove dead tissue if needed, and an injection of procaine to deaden the area. "I put out procaine; do you think you'll need any stronger painkiller? If so, you need to unlock the drug safe so I can prepare the needle and I'll need a dosage amount." She walked back into the lobby where the doctor was leaning against the counter.

"I'll need to see his overall condition before I decide on more than just a local. Were you able to clean the wound before binding it? Was any antibacterial ointment used when you bandaged the open wound?" He questioned his nurse about the conditions and original treatment.

"The cabin was horribly dusty, I tore up his shirt to make the bandage and other that free bleeding at the time, the most I could do was pour water over the site, use about half a tube of Neosporin on both holes and put a snug wrap around the wound." Kam described her original treatment.

"Sounds like you did the best you could do under the circumstances. I'm certain he'll be fine. Did he seem feverish this morning?"

"No, he's been eating and drinking, even using his arm to a small extent. I examined the bandage this morning and it looked dry with no heat or streaks above or below the wound. Look! That's his SUV." She watched the approaching vehicle slow and somewhat angle to the curb, hitting a low bank of snow before it came to a complete stop in front of the clinic. Shaking her head at the stubbornness of men in general, she grabbed her jacket and hit the door to assist him out of the car and into the clinic.

Waving his good arm at Kam and the man beside her as they approached, David struggled to unlatch his seatbelt with his left hand. Damn, you never realized how dependent you are on one arm until it refuses to work. His left hand just didn't have the same co-ordination or flexibility as his right.

"I can't believe you drove yourself. Let me get that." Kam was there, unlocking the seatbelt and putting his good arm around her shoulders to assist him to stand.

"I can walk, you know. It's my arm, not my leg." He smiled down into her worried eyes. "But, maybe you should stay this close. You're nice to hold on to."

Letting his arm go, Kam stepped back. "You're right, you should be able to walk. You're not dizzy are you?" As he stepped forward carefully on the ice, she took his elbow instead of putting his arm over her shoulder.

Dr. Samuelson stepped back to the clinic door and opened it for the couple. He chuckled as he followed them inside. Kam was mighty protective of this man. About time she found someone to take her mind off her own problems. "Hi son, I'm George Samuelson. You can call me either George, or Doc. I sometimes forget to answer to anything else." He extended his hand and noticed the agent clasped it with his left to shake rather than extend his wounded arm.

"Agent David Harrison, FBI. Thanks for meeting us here. The last thing I want is to get trapped at a hospital for this minor wound. For some reason they see a bullet and FBI as an automatic overnight stay in most places." David smiled at the friendly face of the doctor.

Kam frowned. "If you two are done with

introductions, Exam one is waiting. David, your face is kind of muddy looking. Did that drive take that much out of you?" She led the men to the room and patted the exam table for David to sit.

"Well, it wasn't a fun trip; but I survived it. No worse than riding a few hours." He rubbed his forehead and noticed his hand came back wet with sweat.

George watched him and noted the sweat along with the muddy look to his coloring. His experience told him that his patient was not only in pain, but might have the start to an infection. He stuck a thermometer into David's mouth while Kam put the blood pressure cup on his good arm. Once the thermometer beeped, he could see there was no temperature and Kam showed him the 115/75 blood pressure reading. "Kam, here's the keys to the drug safe. Bring me the morphine and a syringe. I think David will feel much better if we counter that pain. I expect trying to drive pulled at the wound, didn't it."

David smiled at the doctor and nodded. He wasn't stupid enough to deny that his arm hurt like a son of a bitch at the moment. "Yeah, I learned quickly not to use it; but not until I tried to turn the car around and pulled it putting the SUV back into drive." His breathing was beginning to even out, but from the look on Kam's face, George could tell his coloring still reflected his pain.

"Are you more comfortable sitting, or would you rather lie on you back while I work on this wound of yours? Either is fine with me, so long as you're not the fainting type. If you are, then lie back before you fall back and hurt yourself." George didn't think the agent had a fainting nature, but pain affected people in unexpected ways and he'd learned to let each person decide what would be best for themselves, up to a point.

Sitting on the table, David watched Kam re-enter the

room with a needle and a vile of medicine. He hated needles; maybe he'd be better off if he lay down and just looked the other way during this procedure. He had a hunch that more than one needle would be involved. "I don't think I'll faint, but laying down seems like a reasonable idea. That way, I can close my eyes and not see what you're doing. I hate needles," he confided.

Kam helped him stretch out on the table, extending it for his legs, and grabbing both a pillow and a blanket from the warmer. "There, now you can just close your eyes and sleep while George and I work on your arm. I'll wake you when we're done." She automatically pushed a few loose hairs back off his forehead.

Smiling up at her, he felt the morphine kick in and the office become hazy. Closing his eyes, his hearing became more acute and he listened to everything around him.

Cutting off the bandage, George examined the entrance and exit wounds on David's arm. Kam was right; it was a clean wound and didn't look like it had touched the bone. Careful application of the procaine to the surface and then the inner path of the wound allowed him to clean the area. Next, he removed some jagged skin, applied antibiotic powder into the wound, and sutured first the entry hole and then the exit wound. He smiled at the man whose face was turned, but whose color had improved remarkably. George knew if David had seen what he was doing, fainting was a distinct possibility; not many people could watch themselves be stitched.

Handing the doctor clean gauze squares to cover both wounds, Kam looked down at David. As if feeling her gaze, his eyes opened and he smiled up at her. "George is wrapping the arm, you're almost done. Feel better?"

"I think I'm flying. I'm a lightweight when it comes

to drugs and booze. Guess I should have mentioned that, eh Doc?" He chuckled, his good hand sketching vague circles in the air.

George taped the bandage and laughed down at his patient. "Well, now that I know, there's no way you're driving anywhere until you can feel your eyebrows move. That's the best test of the nervous system I've ever found. The first thing to go when you drink or take any drug is the feeling in your face. It's also the last thing to return. If you can't feel your eyebrows, you don't need to drive."

"Well, Honey, are you going to stay with me while I sleep this off? Does ole George have a bed for us?" David tried to leer up at Kam, but only managed to look confused.

Laughing, Kam rubbed his good shoulder. "It might be hard, but you can sleep here on this table for a while. I'll sit next to you to keep you from falling off."

"Bummer, I kind of fancied a bed after sleeping on that hard floor last night." He actually managed to pout at her.

"I'll be in my office when you two work out the sleeping arrangements." George chuckled on his way out of the exam room. Pausing at the door, he looked at Kam. "Nurse, I need to see you in my office as soon as he's settled. Bring the agent's credentials; I'll need them for the insurance forms." He paused, remembering he had news about her situation that she needed to know,, then waved and left.

"Yes, doctor. I'll be there shortly." Kam looked up from tucking the blanket over David's shoulder. She wondered why he needed her in his office. He was smiling, but that could mean anything. She hoped he wasn't angry about needing his services today. She moved to follow George, but David grabbed her hand, holding her back.

"You aren't going to leave me here alone, are you? I might need your tender care." He smiled sleepily up at her while pulling her down closer to him.

"Yeah, right. So long as you don't roll over, you'll be just fine." Kam said. If he would give in to the drug and fall asleep, she would be able to leave him for a few minutes; but he seemed to have permanent possession of her hand.

"I need you to stay with me and make certain I won't roll over." He ran his left hand up her arm while keeping possession of her fingers with his right hand. He began softly rubbing her palm with his thumb. "Besides, you should take a break; you work too hard." He murmured, still rubbing her palm while his fingers played with her upper arm. His knuckles brushed her left breast and she jumped. "Mmmm, soft but strong arms, I like that in my woman," his words fading.

Kam leaned a bit further away from him, so her breast would be safe unless he let go of her arm. "You've got strong hands, not soft and sweaty. I like that in a man." She whispered, she couldn't tell if he'd fallen asleep since he'd stopped stroking her palm. Then he smiled. Even with his eyes closed, her breath caught at his tender expression. She sat there watching him, letting him hold her hand while he fell into a deeper sleep. Slowly she began to work her fingers free. Freezing when his tightened, until his hand loosened again. Finally, she managed to get free. She looked down on him and smiled before searching his jacket for his credentials and heading to the doctor's office.

"Took you a while. Was he restless?" George took the proffered black credential wallet from her and motioned her to sit down.

"He's the possessive type. He wouldn't let go of my hand until he finally fell asleep. He should be out for a few hours." Kam smiled at her boss as she sat down in the chair facing his desk. "What's up?"

George set down the credentials and looked at his employee. Hoping that she would want to stay working in the clinic when he finished telling her the news. "You know that I run background checks on all job applicants. It's needed in this industry, a conviction or even an arrest can cause major problems for a clinic." He began.

Kam's heart fell. Damn, she had hoped Des Moines could be left in the past. She felt tears burning her throat, just when things were looking up with new friends and a place for Lady Mica. "It's okay, George; I understand. When do you want me to leave?"

"Not for twenty years or so if you can help it. You're jumping to conclusions. I have some good news for you." George stood up, grabbed the tissues from the table next to the door, and offered them to Kam. He'd seen that watery sparkle in eyes. "I don't know how much you've been following the Des Moines saga but you've been cleared completely. The clinic installed surveillance equipment everywhere, got enough on your favorite doctor to get a search warrant, then found hundreds of illegal child pornography files on his personal computer at his house." He found himself slapping her back when she looked up at him to see if he was pulling her leg. "He's been arrested; the charges he filed against you have been washed from the records, and you're not even needed to testify against him. He managed to hang himself on camera and on his computer. He'll never practice medicine again. At least not legally, and he's going to spend years behind bars. Congratulations! It took a lot of courage and cost you a great deal; but you managed to get him away from children."

"Thank God. That was my biggest worry; that I lost my creditability and the children would still be in danger from that man." Tears of joy began to flow down her cheeks. Grabbing a second tissue, she blotted her eyes and smiled hugely at George. "You have no idea how happy this news makes me. I don't want to return to the city, it would be too embarrassing to face my 'friends' who believed the charges against me. I understand why, but anyone who would believe without finding out the whole story isn't a friend and I'm done with that clinic." Looking down at her hands, she sighed before facing George. "Thank you for telling me all this and not jumping to conclusions when you found out my history," she jumped up and hugged him.

"Hey, wha'ss goin' on here? Doc get let go of my woman." A sleepy voice slurred from the open door. David leaned against the frame. It looked to be the only thing holding him up.

George set Kam away, met her eyes and both laughed. "It's okay, Son. I just gave the lady some good news and she gave me a hug. Don't tell my wife, okay? I promise there's nothing more." He laughed, almost choking, as he reassured the agent.

Laughing aloud herself, Kam stepped over to David's left side. "Come on, tough guy. You shouldn't be walking around yet. Did you need something?" Putting his good arm over her shoulder, she turned him around.

"Yeah, looking for the john. I need to pee. You going to help?" He perked up at the idea and tried to leer at her.

"Oh no, think I'll let George help you out." Kam passed him off to the doctor who'd walked up beside her. "I think we might as well pour him into his car and I'll get him a room at the motel to sleep this off. What do you think, George?"

"That might be the best idea. I'll call the motel so

Merle's son can help you get him into a room." George guided and assisted the agent toward the men's room while he spoke over his shoulder to Kam. "Do you want me to follow you to drive you back here for your truck?"

"No. I think it's best if he doesn't have access to his car until this wears off. I don't think he'll mind if I use it." Kam passed the men, collected the agent's jacket and keys, then grabbed her coat from the rack. Looking down at her shirt, she realized she hadn't been back to her room to change and looked nasty. Well, she'd stop at the boarding house and collect some clothes before taking David to the motel. She shrugged on her jacket, collected her purse and walked out to the agent's car. Pulling it up closer to the door of the clinic, she left it running to warm up before walking back into the clinic to help George get David into his coat. "There, all set. I'll help you get him out to the car." She pulled the door open to allow George to give David a shoulder to lean on as he stumbled toward the car at the curb.

"I'll call the motel and tell them you'll be there in half an hour, then I'll call Betty and have her put two hamburger baskets together for you so you can feed him dinner when he wakes. Sound about right?" George slid David in the car door held open by Kam.

"Thanks, that's a wonderful idea. I'd forgotten all about food. But now that you mention it… it's been a while since that chopper crew gave us snacks. I could eat a whole steer. Better add brownies to that order along with two sodas. I'll pay you on Monday." Kam laughed as she closed David's door and moved to open the driver's side.

"My treat. Call it a celebration dinner for your good news. Keep an eye on him for a few hours, by then he should be coherent enough to be left alone. See you on Monday." George turned from the car and walked back to the clinic. Once inside, he called Betty first to get the food started, then the Motel and finally the drugstore to see if he could con the druggist into delivering the antibiotic prescription to the motel so Kam didn't have to chase it down. Once everything was set, he locked up the clinic and headed home. Smiling to himself, he figured things might just work out for Kam. So long as she didn't decide to move to Denver with that agent. He'd felt a bit of chemistry between the pair and only hoped it would take the man a year or two to propose.

Taking the keys with her, Kam went to her room at the boarding house to collect a change of clothes. No sense giving him a chance to wake up and try to drive off. With her patient still dozing, she stopped at the diner for the food George had ordered. The food smells hit her at the door of the diner. She almost collapsed with hunger. God, how could she have forgotten she hadn't had a real meal in over twenty-four hours? "I need an extra brownie right now, or I'll not make it to the door." She told Betty.

Betty laughed, then grabbed a brownie and stuck it into Kam's mouth. "Lord, girl, I thought you were joking. You look about to faint. Sit a minute before you fall over." Betty steadied Kam and pushed her down on a seat at the counter.

"Until I smelled food, I was fine. Now, I'm shaking so bad I'm not certain I can stand." Kam said around the rich chocolate of the brownie. Quickly grabbing the water Betty handed her to wash down the mouthful. Taking another large bite, she moaned in almost erotic pleasure at the flavor and texture.

Betty laughed. "I can't remember when I've seen anyone enjoy food so much. Maybe I should grab my camera and get a photo to use in advertising this place." She laughed again at the glare Kam shot her.

"Don't you dare. It's not fair to laugh at a starving woman." Kam finished the brownie, washing it down with the remainder of the water. "How much do I owe you for that life saving treat?"

"Honey, it was my pleasure watching you enjoy it. That one was on the house, doc's paying for the two in the bag." Betty smiled. "Who's the hunk getting out of the car?"

"Oh shit! Got to run. Thanks Betty!" Taking the bags of food Kam ran out of the diner just in time to put David back into his SUV before he fell. "Where did you think you're going?"

"Smelled food. Hungry. Very hungry. What's in the bags?" David grabbed for the bags and Kam allowed him to help himself to fries while she drove to the motel.

"Don't eat everything. We'll get you into your room and have a real meal. How does that sound?" She pushed the bag closed around David's hand after he'd taken several handfuls of fries from one bag.

"Great. Soon. Starved." Remembering bits and pieces of the past day he grinned at her. "I know you, you're that nurse I'm going to marry." He smiled vacantly. "You're cute."

"Yeah, right. Marry… try remembering that tomorrow. You're cute too." She laughed at his nonsense. Arriving at the motel, she saw a teenager pointing to a room at the farthest end of the building and directing her into a parking space in front of the door.

"Ma'am, you're the one Doc called about; aren't you? Is this the FBI agent who got shot?" Intently the kid leaned over the passenger door, excited to meet a wounded FBI agent.

"Yes, watch out, he's not very coordinated at the moment. He's not making much sense either." She warned.

"Which room? Oh, I see, the one with the door open. I think I'm getting loopy too." Walking around the car, Kam grabbed the food from David's hands while the teenager took him by his good arm and began to propel David into the room. "Just get him to a bed, either one. He has to eat before he goes back to sleep and I've got the food. Thanks so much for your help. Do I need to check in at the office?"

"No ma'am, Doc gave dad all the particulars and everything is set. Here's the key." He handed Kam the key card for the room and left them, closing the door.

Looking around, Kam searched for a place to put the food. Seeing a coffee table in front of the small couch, she drug it across the carpet to set it in front of David where he sat with his feet hanging off the first bed. "Here, you ready to eat?" She began unloading the bags, and then slapped his hand when she felt it creeping over her butt when she bent over. "Quit that, you're not awake enough to get fresh." She slapped a burger into his hand while dumping the remaining fries onto the empty bag and ripping open a ketchup package. Watching him trying to peel the paper from around the sandwich reminded her of watching a two year old eating with a fork. Laughing, she took the burger, removed the wrapper and handed it back to him. "Here, now try not to get too messy." She chuckled; at least he managed to find his mouth with the food.

Sitting on the floor next to the table, she reached for her own hamburger, peeled the paper off and took a huge bite. When the telephone rang, she just looked at it in despair. Neither of them could talk at the moment, but she didn't want to miss a call. Crap, she hoped whoever was calling could understand a person talking around food.

"Eah?" Well, that should be a good enough greeting

she felt when she picked up the telephone. She continued chewing furiously, trying to empty her mouth.

"Is this David Harrison's room?" A firm male voice inquired, sounding confused.

"Es, ut, e ant talk. Eating." She managed to get two clear words out.

"Eating? Seriously? Tell him this is Jason Maddox, his partner. I need to speak with him." From the voice and the irritation, Kam thought it must be his senior partner.

"Drugged. Starving. He'll call soon." She hoped she was making sense. Swallowing the food in her mouth, she continued. "Doc gave him morphine. He's kind of loopy and needs sleep. You really don't need to talk at this specific moment do you?"

"Who the Hell are you? His personal secretary? I wouldn't have called if I didn't need to speak with him." The caller seemed to be losing patience with this conversation, or rather lack of conversation.

"I happen to be a registered nurse in Dr. Samuelson's clinic. I'm sorry I had a hard time answering the phone, but I had my mouth full." Kam sat up straighter as she took on her 'voice of authority' to this rude man. "Dr. Samuelson sent me with him to make certain the agent got a full meal before he passes out from the stress of the day along with the morphine. Would you like me to give you the doctor's home phone so you can call him to verify?" her voice dripping sweet common sense and sarcasm in equal measure.

"Oh, why didn't you say you're a nurse? What's his overall condition and how long before I can question him?" The voice reflected respect for her profession and concern for his partner.

"He's going to be fine. He spent almost a day without decent food and has a bullet hole through his arm.

No major damage done, but the doctor didn't know David was a lightweight and he gave him the normal dose of morphine for a man of his weight." She crisply gave Jason the status report on David. "If you know your partner, you know that was a heavy dose for him. Now, David's ready to sleep, but his body needs food; so I can't let him sleep until he eats.

"Babe! Who you talking to? I need more ketchup." David called over at Kam who had walked away from the table to speak on the room phone.

"Tell him it's me and tell him I'm heading to Riverview tomorrow." Jason told the nurse.

"Sir, your partner Jason wants me to tell you he's heading this direction tomorrow." Attempting to keep her voice professional, Kam explained the call to the drugged agent.

"Sweet! Gimme the phone. I need to talk to him." David fell backward on the bed when he reached for the phone. Kam choked on a laugh and began to cough. She passed the phone to David and continued coughing.

"Hey Jason! Just the person I wanted to talk to…Phil Dunkin's at the Colorado State Pen. Need you to find out why Richard Meadows ran from Riverview thirty years ago." David paused, his eyes clearing and his expression alert while he listened to his partner. Unfortunately, the effect was marred by the fact he was laying on his back holding the phone with the earpiece about mid cheek. "Talk louder, I can hardly hear you. You in the john or something?"

Kam reached over and pulled the earpiece up to David's ear while she doubled over laughing so hard she had tears on her cheeks.

"Man, you don't have to yell. I got shot, I didn't go deaf." David haughtily expressed to his frustrated partner.

"Here talk to Kam, maybe she can help." David held out the phone, which Kam took, hiccupping with laughter.

"I warned you. You should have seen how he was holding the phone." She chuckled, getting control of her giggles with difficulty. "I'm sorry sir, but patients on drugs are entertaining. He's going to be fine by the time you get here." She paused, waiting for Jason to get control of his irritation. "Yes sir, I know what he wants. It's common knowledge around here that Phil Dunkin, the brother-in-law of Richard Meadows is in prison at Canon City. Years ago, Richard ran from Riverview. The only person who might know why is Phil. If Phil can tell why, you may be able to arrest the man who not only forced Richard to run, but whose family stole a ranch by coercion. We think this man threatened Richard, forcing him to leave the area." She took a breath and listened again. "No sir, I know this because I've seen the primary evidence. If you can get Phil to tell the same story, then we have, or rather you have, Samuel Cole dead to rights for his crimes."

"Give me back to David." Jason sighed; he was getting more confused by the minute.

"Sorry, but David fell asleep just after he passed me the phone. Since he got a burger and fries down before he took the phone, I'd much rather let him sleep." Kam looked over at David who lay flat on his back, snoring softly. "Can he call you either later tonight or first thing tomorrow? Canon City is south of Denver; and Riverview is west. If you're headed for the prison, you can call him when you get there. He'll be able to cover what he needs to know from Phil." Kam softly argued with the agent, trying to get him to let David sleep.

"Okay, okay, I'll give him today. But, he better answer this phone first thing in the morning. I can't question the guy if I don't know the entire story." Jason hung up without any further discussion.

"Well, that was rude." Kam hung up the phone and picked up her lukewarm burger. Compared to last night's or this morning's fare; it was ambrosia. She managed to finish even the cold fries before she turned to look at David. Shaking her head, she knew she couldn't leave him like that, half on and half off the bed, still dressed with his shoes on and no blanket. What a mess. Standing up, she walked over and knelt to remove his shoes. Standing up again, she tried to pull him farther into the bed from the other side. She leaned over his head, grabbed his armpits, and began to pull him toward her body.

"Whoa, Babe. Nice, very nice." Feeling warm lips heating her cleavage through her clothes, she dropped him.

"You just keep those lips to yourself, Mister." She scolded but he'd already fallen back asleep. "Damn man. I can't even get mad at him without him falling asleep." Picking up his shoulders again, she pulled one more time and managed to get his legs and feet onto the bed. He filled it from one corner to the other, making her glad of the second bed in the room. She removed his lightweight jacket and his pants, so thankful that he was the sort who believed in underwear, not that she hadn't seen a naked man before, but she just knew David would tease the Hell out of her if he thought she'd stripped him to the buff.

Taking down the extra blanket, she covered him before she walked back out to his car to get her change of clothes and his suitcase. Dropping the suitcase inside the room she walked her things into the bathroom. Turning on the hot water, she breathed in steam while the tub filled. It curled around her and fogged the mirror but felt amazing. Without any further concern for her patient, she slid her tired body into the hot water. When the water finally cooled, she stepped out, dressed in clean underwear and climbed into the second bed, asleep within seconds of turning out the light.

Chapter Fifteen

Something tickled her ear; mosquito must have gotten in the holey screens. Kam frowned. Wait a minute, coming more awake from her deep sleep; she remembered she now lived at the Bailey sisters' boarding house. Their screens were fine. Her eyes popped open and she froze. She didn't recognize the room, and someone was curled into her body as she lay on her side. A low chuckle sounded in her ear and she felt lips nibbling on her neck. "Damn it, David. You scared the crap out of me. Why aren't you over in your own bed?"

"I got cold. I woke up alone, saw you over here, beautiful and sweet. You were snuggled down in the bedding and looked so warm that I couldn't resist the temptation to join you. I was right… you're toasty and this bed is a lot warmer than mine." His right hand had begun to move over her while he spoke and came to rest on her breast, fingers gently massaging the hardening peak. Obviously, his arm felt better.

Gasping at the sensations his hand caused, her body automatically snuggled into his when she discovered he had shed his underwear and only her underwear separated his skin from the building heat of her own. His right hand continued mapping her body, teasing and stroking sensitive spots as it worked from her tingling breast down. His lips began nipping and kissing her ear then moved down to her neck and shoulder. "Want me to stop?" His voice was soft and husky in her ear, sending chills and heat over her body and down to her core.

Trembling at the sensations he created throughout her body, Kam thought about the question only a second before rolling over in his arms to face him. "No. Kiss me." Lifting her chin to meet his lips as he lowered his head, their lips met. The kiss began softly, and then heated with the fire and sensations quickly filling both of them.

Reaching up to unfasten her bra, he managed to speak at the end of that amazing kiss. "You've got too many clothes on." Pulling the bra off and tossing it out of the bed, his hand worked its way down to her lacy bikini panties. His lips claimed hers in another mind bending, body heating, and passion arousing lip lock while his fingers tried to push down the edge of the irritating fabric that separated her heat from his need. After two failed attempts to get his hand under the clinging fabric he broke the kiss. "If you like this pair of underwear, you better get out of them before I find my pocket knife and remove 'em," he growled.

Laughing at his frustrated expression, Kam moved onto her back, slowly got both hands under the fabric at her hips and pushed the offending garment down, kicking out of it.

David's eyes never left her body, taking in her every movement and licking his suddenly dry lips. "Oh yeah, I knew you'd be beautiful. I like a woman with curves, full breasts, and soft skin." Leaning down, he kissed his way to her dusky areola; licking and nipping at her nipple before taking her breast into the heat of his mouth.

Arching her back, she gave him better access to her breast at the exact moment his hand moved between her thighs to stroke her core. The sensations brought a keening moan from her, her one hand stroked his head and neck as he suckled on her breast and the other hand grasping the bedding for an anchor. His stubble burned a trail over her sensitized skin when he moved from one breast to pay equal attention to the other while beginning to stroke her wet folds. She bucked into his hand when his fingers located the sensitive nubbin of passion and pressed against it. He timed the stroke with a nip and suckle on her swollen breast, causing her to almost jump off the bed. "Ahhh, please, ohhh please, please…"

"Please what? You want me to stop?" he teased, bringing his lips back to her mouth.

"I need you in me, please… ahhhh, that's it. Oohhh, ahhhh." Kam lost words as her world came apart under his skilled fingers. Her body shuddered in its release and bucked up in an effort to take more of his hand as he dipped his fingers into her heated wet sheath.

He stroked her through her climax, extending her pleasure with pressure against her bud while pushing his fingers in and out, building a fast rhythm that brought on a second, hard climax. She bucked against his hand, pounding the sheets and spreading her legs apart to give him more access. His mouth covering her moans, he slid over her body and into her sheath before the waves of sensation finished. Her sheath pulled him into her, still convulsing with pleasure. He began moving, rotating his hips with each thrust to put pressure on her bud, not allowing her relief from the pleasure. "That's it, Baby. Move with me. Yeah. Let go and ride the pleasure." His voice breathy, his movements hard and fast, he watched the expressions roll over her face. Her eyes opened, dazed but searching his face as he pumped and ground into her body; building up the heat and yearning yet again. Sweat dripped off his body, hers was slippery where his hands stroked and pinched her nipples. Together they moved, each climbing to ecstasy, they both screamed as they reached the pinnacle of pleasure.

David collapsed, rolling to his side to save Kam from the pressure of his larger body. In so doing, his body left hers and she moaned, rolling to snuggle against him. Without words, he kissed her ear and she kissed his arm while he drew the blankets back up to cover their naked bodies.

Later, they made love again. This time it was a tender and calculated giving of pleasure between them. They were passionate, and bold, but without the wild desperation of their first experience. Exhausted, they slept the remainder of the night in each other's arms.

"What the Hell?" David rolled over, stretching to reach the ringing telephone on the nightstand. Fumbling, he managed to pick up the receiver without dropping it and get it to his ear. "Who is this? What the hell time is it? Where am I?" He grumbled into the receiver.

"Well, sir, I'm very sorry to bother you; but I just came on duty and there's a package for you from the drug store up here at the check in desk." A small apologetic voice responded to his gruff questioning. "It's eight in the morning on a beautiful Sunday here at the Riverview Gorgeview Inn."

"It's Sunday? How did I get here? I don't remember checking in." David rubbed the stubble on his chin and looked around the room. He noticed he was naked and a warm body snuggled next to him. The memories of their lovemaking came flooding back. "Did Dr. Samuelson handle my check in? Does he use this place for patients who need overnight care?" He whispered.

"According to the records, Doc did call in your information so we could bill the government; sir. I hope that's okay with you." Again, the voice sounded uncertain and timid.

"Yeah, it's fine. I'll be down in a bit to collect the package. Thank you for letting me know it's there. Sorry to be so nasty when I answered the phone. I need coffee."

"Well, sir, we offer a breakfast in the lobby until ten. Just doughnuts, sweet rolls, muffins and fresh fruit; but the coffee is hot and wonderful." The clerk bragged on the Inn's breakfast amenities.

"In that case, I'll be down in ten or fifteen minutes." Smiling, he hung up the phone. He stood, swayed and sat back down. Wow, either he was weak or the drugs were still in his system. Since his stomach was protesting lack of food, maybe his blood sugar was low. He grabbed for the half empty watered down drink sitting on the coffee table to wet his dry throat. Either tea or Pepsi, half water and not much flavor, but wet. This time when he stood, he could walk without feeling weak in the knees. Finding his suitcase was on the luggage stand; he grabbed clothing and his shaving kit before heading to the bathroom and turning on the shower.

Kam felt like she was swimming through a dense fog as she slowly became aware of the sounds of movement in the motel room. Damn, she'd wanted to be up before David so that she could monitor his condition. Listening, she heard the sounds of water running and possibly a toothbrush on teeth. Lifting the blanket she remembered her nudity, she looked around the room trying to remember where she'd put her clean clothes. The events of the night came crashing back to her. Smiling at the soreness between her legs, she sat up holding the cover to her chest. She visually searched the room for any of her clothes. Then, she remembered. Shit, she'd left both clean and dirty clothing piled next to the bathtub when she'd slid into that amazing hot water last night. "Excuse me, David. Could you, would you please pass me my clothes?" Happy that her voice didn't sound too desperate, she frowned when he stuck his head and shoulders out of the bathroom holding out her clothing in his good hand.

"You mean these? Why don't you come get them? The shower is hot and I'll wash your back." His voice was husky and teasing but his eyes were simply hot.

Kam felt her face turning red at both his question and his heated gaze. "I don't think it's safe to let you do that; we might never get out of the shower."

Laughing at her blush, David tossed the clothing toward the bed, and then closed the bathroom door to allow her to dress. Later, he could coax her into bed again, now he needed to eat breakfast.

Looking through the strung out pile of clothing that hit the bed, Kam managed to sort out the clean shirt and pants. The remainder she folded into a pile to take back to her room at the boarding house. Finding her underwear on the floor proved more difficult. Seems her panties had managed to end up under the other bed.

"Oh baby, don't give me that view at this time of day." Walking out of the bathroom, the sight of Kam's naked butt in the air while she fished for her panties gave him an instant erection.

"Behave yourself. I wouldn't be in this position if there hadn't been such a rush to get these off without ripping them." She scolded, sitting back on her knees to protect her ass. "By the way, do you remember talking to your partner just before you fell asleep yesterday?"

"The last clear memory I have before our lovemaking is being at the clinic and the doc mixing up a pain shot for me. Everything from then on is a blur; at least until I woke up and moved in with you." He wiggled his eyebrows at her. "Do I owe any apologies for actions or words?"

"None to me that I want to remind you about, but your partner might be a different matter. You ordered him to go question Phil Dunkin about what happened with his brother-in-law thirty years ago. It was funny. One second you were 'hey dude' happy and the next you were ordering the man about. Are you his boss?" Naked, Kam strolled into the bathroom before David could answer and began running the water to brush her teeth.

"Naw, we're equal partners; but in this case I'd take the lead because I'm here first and involved." David spoke loudly at the bathroom door. "How did he respond?"

"Well, he's headed that direction but he's going to call you this morning before he gets there to find out exactly what he has to know to question this guy. The man was seriously pissed that you passed out before he could question you further. By the way, he thinks I'm your nurse. Which I am, but he doesn't know I was with you on Friday as well as Saturday." Kam walked out of the bathroom; clothed with her black curls shining and her cheeks rosy from scrubbing. "Now, did I hear you say something about coffee on the phone? If so, where?"

Taking her hand, David grabbed the door key card from the nightstand and led her out of the room. The bright daylight reflected off the melting snow blinding him before he got fully out the door. "Damn, I forgot how bright snow can be." He shaded his squinting eyes. "Which way to the lobby, do you know?"

Squinting against the glare, Kam looked both directions, trying to remember their arrival the day before. "Yeah, okay, since this is the end of the building, the lobby should be that direction. What do you think?"

"Right sounds like a good direction to head. Also it put's that rude glaring sun behind us so we can see where we're going." Keeping her hand in his, David strolled along the walkway that led to the right. At the other end of the building, they found a smaller building that faced the road. A large sign in front proclaimed "Gorgeview Inn" with a smaller sign below "Registration" along with an arrow pointing to the front door. "I like your powers of deduction; maybe you've missed your calling." He smiled at her, still holding her hand.

"No way, you're the FBI agent, I'm a nurse and happy to be one. I'm not in love with delving into things that could get me shot." Kam slipped her hand free when he opened the door for her and preceded him into the lobby where the aroma of dark, rich coffee hit them. "Ahhh, I think we found the coffee. What's there to eat?"

David walked to the counter. "Hi, you called my room. I'm Agent David Harrison; I understand you have a bag for me from the pharmacy." He smiled warmly at the young clerk behind the counter.

"May I see your ID sir, sorry to ask, but this could be a controlled substance so I need to be certain you are the person who is supposed to have it. Also, I need your ID for the registration form and a signature if you don't mind, sir." She smiled at him politely, timidly extending her hand to take and examine his credentials. "Thank you, Sir. Please sign here." She pushed a form to him and handed back his creds wallet.

"Very professional, you handle your position very well. I'd have been worried if you hadn't asked to see my ID." David assured her, signing the registration. Passing it back to her, he kept his hand out until she passed him the bag from the pharmacy. "Thank you, Miss."

The young clerk blushed and looked down, fumbling with the pen he handed back. "I hope you enjoy your stay. Let me know if I can help you in any way, sir."

Chuckling, David walked over to the coffeepot. He

poured a cup of the "Columbian" before taking it over to the pyramid of muffins and helping himself to a plate and adding two. Smiling over at Kam, he paused at the fruit bowl and took a pear and an apple before walking to her table.

She looked over his plate and the full cup of black coffee, shuddering, "That coffee will curl even your hair. I took the milder roast coffee and it's quite strong. I'm surprised yours isn't eating through the cup." She smiled at him as he sat down next to her, putting her on his left side. Her plate held half a doughnut, a muffin, and an orange. Next to her coffee cup was a small glass of orange juice.

"I love a woman who's not afraid to eat. These chicks who constantly diet just irritate me. Life's too short for that kind of shit." He took a large bite of the muffin before sipping his coffee.

"Well considering what we had to eat yesterday, I think I've dieted my share for a few days." Kam began peeling her orange after finishing her doughnut. "How are you feeling? Your color is good. Let me see the bag, George said he'd call in a prescription and get the pharmacist to deliver it." She extended her hand for the bag.

They finished eating and enjoying their coffee while Kam read the instructions and handed him a large white tablet. "Here you go. Take one every twelve hours. So take this now, and then one again at nine tonight."

Surprising himself, David took the pill without any argument. "So, Jason knows you were spending the night? He won't let that slip by without some sort of comment. Especially once he gets a good look at you." David watched her color change while he took another sip of coffee.

"Maybe I should be gone before he arrives."

"Oh, no you don't. We have evidence to go over and

when he gets here, we'll know more about what's happening. I need to speak with the local sheriff. He might be able to fill us in on local gossip and lore about the original murder victim and about who might not want the story to come out, besides Samuel Cole." He spoke softly but noticed that the lobby was very quiet when he finished. "We need to take a cup of coffee back to our room and discuss this." He stood up, ready to take Kam's arm.

"I can walk by myself, and I want to refill my coffee." She stepped away from him, not exactly certain why she felt the need for space after the night before. "Why don't you head back to *your* room, and I'll get the items in question from your car. Sometime today, you'll have to take me back to my truck." Turning her back, she refilled her coffee and headed out the door.

David followed, watching the movement of her hips and the roundness of her butt while she walked ahead of him. For a short chick, she had long legs with a very nice, graceful and subtle swing. He chuckled softly, aware that most men would enjoy this view. She stopped at his car, unlocked it and bent over the back seat to pull out the tin box and her laptop. The sight of her sweetly rounded ass in the air brought him to an abrupt halt, unable and unwilling to take his eyes away until she stood up and frowned at him.

"You checking out my ass?" she accused.

Turning to unlock the door, David mumbled his guilt.

"Keep your eyes where they belong. It's not polite to ogle a woman; didn't your momma teach you manners?" Scolding him, she walked past where he stood holding the door for her, his hand automatically pinched her butt gently.

"Yeah, momma taught me better; but my hormones

control my eyes. I try to be good, but you can't wear those jeans without expecting me to watch." He smiled again at her butt as he followed her into the room.

"Well, from now on, you can lead and I'll ogle your ass. See how you like it."

"Changing the subject, let's get the coffee table cleared off and set out the evidence there." He pointed to the table, set down his coffee and began to gather up the papers and wrappings of their late dinner. One bag had some weight and inside he discovered two brownies. "I can't believe we missed these. Here, one for you and one for me." He handed one to Kam who had just set the tin box in the middle of the table.

"Thanks, I forgot they were in there." Taking a bite of brownie, she took her laptop over to the desk and found the Wi-Fi information to connect to the internet. "I'll Google as much history of the area as I can find before we get into the tin box. We need some background on the Hendrix ranch, and the Cole ranch of that era along with the current Cole ranch and Meadows family." Kam paused and cussed under her breath. "We need to get Megan here to represent the R-M; she likely can give us data on Richard Meadows."

"Great idea. I'll call her. According to her file, she's got top level skills in computer data mining. She may have already checked out some of these people, so hold off on your digging until she gets here." David dialed Megan's number as he spoke.

Jumping at the ringing of her phone, Megan ran to get it from her computer table. At least this time it was close by. "Hello, Megan here. How are you feeling, David?" She recognized the caller ID.

"I'm fine. Kam and I are getting ready to go through the evidence we brought back from the cabin and thought you might want to be part of the investigation. Can you come over to the Gorgeview Inn, room 128? Have you done any research on Caleb Preston or Sheriff Tucker?" David listened, motioning Kam to get him a pen. "Wow, that's a lot of data. Bring it with you and we've got another name or two to add to the research." Changing his mind, he waved Kam off when she offered paper and pen. "See you in half an hour. Bye."

Looking at her watch, Megan decided to call the R-M in case Bethany wanted to join the party. On the third ring, a familiar voice picked up the phone. "Hi, Megan. Roger took Bethany to church, so I stayed behind to man the home front. What do you need?" Megan smiled at the question, several things came to mind but she behaved when she answered Aaron. "I'm headed for the Gorgeview to look over some things found in the cabin. I thought maybe Bethany would want to see and maybe have answers to the Agent's questions."

"Hmmm. She'll be sorry she missed out, but this is her first outing since the fall and I know Roger will be standing over her shoulder every second. I doubt he'd want her to go anywhere after church but back to bed." He smiled; remembering the care Roger showed when he put his wife into the car. "Do you want me to join you? I might have answers to questions or know who to ask for the hard ones." He offered.

"Why not, you've been around Riverview a lot longer than I have; even if I did spend a summer or two here with my Aunt Marge as a kid."

"I'll be by to pick you up in ten minutes; that work for you?" Aaron looked at his watch, thinking that Roger and Bethany should be back from town within an hour. He'd tell Shorty to be on the lookout; since that fire, they were keeping a sharp eye for strangers.

"Fine, see you then." Hanging up the phone, Megan looked at her clothes and decided she wanted to change. Aaron had only ever seen her in jeans. She ran up to her room and sorted through her closet looking for just the right thing to wear. Nothing flashy or too sexy, it wasn't a date; but something different from jeans. She found her favorite floral print v-neck form hugging knit top and a pair of solid leggings. The top came down below her butt and the leggings would help her legs look long and amazing. She added her half boots to the outfit and smiled at the reflection just as she heard his knock at her door. "Coming!"

Aaron's attention focused on the leggy blonde creature who answered the door. Wow! Her height had always appealed to him, but in that outfit, he felt his pants tightening. "Lord, woman, where have you been hiding this outfit? Nice, very nice." He stepped in to aide her in putting on her winter jacket, getting a nice view of cleavage from over her shoulder. He stepped quickly back.

Laughing at his expression and comment, Megan let him hold her jacket while she slipped her arms into it. "You like it? I felt like wearing something other than jeans and a work shirt. I don't look too dressy do I?" Suddenly less certain of her appearance, she ducked her head and looked away; picking up her laptop.

"I love the look. It suits you. Casual and natural." He liked that she neglected makeup and brushed back her thick shoulder-length curls before gathering them at the nape of her neck. A few had already worked loose and framed her face. "Yeah, a very good look for you." Taking her elbow, he steered her out the door; locking it behind them.

Megan found herself smiling all the way into town. Glancing sideways at him, she caught his eyes a few times and blushed at the heat she saw there. Her only problem was that while she enjoyed his interest, she wasn't certain she was ready for it. The past few days had proven to her that she still needed time to heal and get beyond the mental and emotional injuries that accompanied her physical wounds. Well, he'd said he'd wait. She only hoped he could be as patient as she was going to need. "There's the Gorgeview. David said room 128."

Driving around the Inn, Aaron spotted the room number and parked a couple of spaces past it. "Here we are." Jumping from the truck, he got to her door before she opened it.

Collecting her laptop Megan turned to find Aaron opening her door and extending a hand to assist her down from the high cab. Her expression clearly showed her surprise, most men she knew expected her to be "one of the guys" and having doors held and offers of assistance didn't fit that picture. "Thanks." Allowing him to take her arm, she stepped out of the truck with more grace than her usual athletic speed allowed.

Aaron couldn't suppress a smile at her expression. They had been working side by side for over a month, and this was his first time treating her as anything other than one of the ranch hands. "My pleasure." He followed her to the door where she knocked and waited for an answer. Keeping himself at her elbow, he was prepared to move in front of her if needed. Realizing his sudden protective urge, he paused to wonder where it had come from.

David swung the door wide and stepped back to allow the couple entrance. He hid his surprise that Megan had brought Aaron, and then reasoned that Aaron would be a perfect person to grill on the area. He'd have access to all of the local gossip.

"Welcome, come on in and find a spot to sit. It's a bit crowded, but at least this is a double room and not a single." He grinned as he pointed toward the beds, couch, and the chair in front of the small desk. He and Kam had straightened the beds and aired the room while they waited.

Once everyone found a seat, David positioned himself in front of the coffee table. It held a notepad, Kam's laptop, and the tin box of evidence. "Megan, would you like to start with the data you have on Caleb, Tuck, and Riverview of 1933?"

Kam and David both took notes while Megan relayed the ancestry she'd found on both Caleb Preston and the Tucker family. While she spoke, David made notes next to names. "Aaron, you work for the Meadows ranch. What can you tell us about Richard Meadows? What have you heard about his disappearance in 1983?"

"How'd that get into this investigation? It was almost fifty years past the Preston murder." Aaron looked at David.

"We found a note from Richard dated 1983 in which he explained he was going to try a possibly dangerous confrontation and if it failed, he might be in trouble."

"Wow, Roger will want to know about this. As far as I know, Roger has never understood his father's disappearance and until Bethany witnessed Richard's murder last year, Roger had no clue where his father was living." Aaron reached for his cell phone to call his boss.

"Wait a moment. Bethany witnessed the murder of Richard Meadows – *last year*? I figured he had likely been killed back in '83. I know from his note he thought it was a possibility. Did they find the killer?" Both David and Kam listened intently as Aaron answered the questions; explaining about the plot to steal the R-M from Richard and Roger that went awry when Richard tried to escape his kidnappers. After his death, the kidnappers – under orders from Phil Dunkin, went after both Bethany and the deed to the ranch that Richard had hidden. Phil's identity had remained a secret until he made a final desperate attempt to get the papers by attacking Bethany at the R-M and chasing her to Riverview.

"Whoa, that's quite a story. So, Phil Dunkin masterminded the kidnapping, murder, and attempts against Bethany? Is that why he's in the state pen?" David made notes. Needing to talk with his partner, he was reaching for his phone when it sounded with the distinct ring tone David assigned to Jason. "Hi, Partner. I was just going to call you. I have some data for your interview with Dunkin." Pausing he listened to Jason for a moment. "I'm fine, my arm is sore, but it's doing fine too. Now listen, here's what you need to know...." He explained the situation about Meadows and Dunkin before telling Jason to question Dunkin about anything he knew on the disappearance of Meadows in '83. "Let me know what you find out as soon as you're done with the interview. If it plays out like I want, we could be making a collar on blackmail and possible extortion charges against a local rancher."

Fidgeting as she listened to the story and the telephone call, Megan really wanted to see what was in the box. Would he ever get to opening the darn thing? "Kam, why don't we begin going through the tin box while the men are covering the old news about Meadows and Dunkin?"

"Nice try, but no cigar. We need to go through things in some sort of sequence or we might miss valuable information. Why don't you look up the Hendrix family, Jacob and Michelle who lived on a farm or ranch near here in the early 1930's? We need to find any descendents of the couple. They owned the H/J up until 1933." Kam knew the chore would take care of Megan's fidgets for a spell and allow Aaron to finish his explanation of Richard's death.

David hung up from speaking with Jason and turned back to Aaron. "So, it never came out in Phil's trial what caused Richard to run all those years ago?"

"No, but Roger told me at the time Phil was arrested he said something about Richard running instead of testifying about someone or something. I just figured we'd never know and let it go. Roger was so involved with Bethany that he dropped any questioning about his father."

"Ah ha! Found the Hendrix clan." Megan chortled, looking up from her laptop. "Jacob and Michelle moved to Montrose in 1933 to take over running the local hotel. There's a Chamber of Commerce type announcement in the Montrose Gazette. Says the family had run a ranch until Jacob was injured and lost the use of an arm earlier that year. The Chamber welcomes the family and extends best wishes in their new endeavor. Another entry a few years later proclaims that Jacob and Michelle bought the Montrose Manor from their retiring boss and will continue running the hotel and restaurant. I love old newspaper articles. They're like little gossip columns." She looked around, pleased that she had everyone's attention.

"Did they have kids? Is the hotel still in the family?" Kam asked.

"Well, there's a photo when they bought the place and it shows a man and woman and three boys. The caption names them and Nathaniel, William, and Jacob, Jr. That was in 1940. Now, so long as the boys made it through WWII and Korea, there should be Hendrix family that we can trace. I'll continue checking and see if I can come up with any clear descendents." Her fingers flying across the keypad, Megan once more became immersed in data mining.

"Good job. Kam, why don't you do some checking

on the sheriff who took Tuck's job? Let's see what happened to him and if he has any descendants who could tell us more about him." David reached for the tin box. "Aaron and I will go through both Tuck's journal and Caleb's to see what we can find out about the motive for Caleb's murder. Who knows, maybe we can find some reason why we were attacked on Friday." Rubbing his sore arm gently, he untied the string on the tin. Before opening the box, he found two pair of latex gloves, one for himself and one for Aaron. "Here, put these on. I don't think there are any prints, but we want to keep the evidence as clean as possible."

Aaron took the gloves and watched David pry open the tin. Next, he pulled out the two journals, one large and one small with reverence and care. "These are amazing. It's like they're new, even the covers don't look aged." Aaron extended a hand to take the small journal that David offered.

"You've got Caleb's book. Take notes on any data that might incriminate or otherwise point at possible criminals and crimes. Something in there got the poor man shot. I'll work on Tuck's book that details his time in office and see if it names the local bad guys or offers any clue as to what got him murdered." David pulled out and carefully opened the larger book.

Each man set their respective journals on the coffee table and began to read while the women searched online for data surrounding the families and their descendants.

Chapter Sixteen

Loud knocking startled the intent group, making them all jump. "Sheriff Bill Casey. Anyone home?" sounded through the door before David had managed to pull his pistol. Relaxing, he opened the door.

"Hi, Sheriff. We needed to talk with you. Glad you saved us a trip to your office. Come on in and join the party." David extended his hand to the portly sheriff, noticing that the man was slow to shake hands. Then he stepped back to let him enter. "Sorry we don't have a chair to offer you. Have you learned anything about the person who shot at us up in the woods?"

"No, nothing other than the fact it looks like he might of stole a horse to get up there. Thought I'd ask you some questions." Using his left hand, the sheriff awkwardly pulled out a notebook while looking at the assembled group. As his eyes landed on Kam, he glared at her. Seeing the tin box and the journals on the coffee table, his eyes lit up. "What's all this?" He stepped closer to get a better look, but Aaron and David both closed their books before he could read anything.

"Why don't you pull off your coat and stay a while Bill?" Aaron watched the heavy man step back at his suggestion and frowned.

"No, don't have time. Is that all evidence? Were you able to identify the body? Do you have any suspects or person of interest yet on the body?"

Having caught the look of almost hatred the sheriff shot Kam, David wondered to himself what she'd done to anger the officer. "Well, it's all pretty cold, but we're checking data we found in that old cabin to identify the victim. Also, we're looking into families who lived around here back then to see if we can locate any relations to the possible victim. What do you know about Riverview history? Who was sheriff in 1933, and in 1983 for that matter?" David watched Bill scratch his head with his left hand.

"Hmmm, well old Sheriff Miller held the office for about fifty years. I think he was short only a couple of months from that record."

Grabbing a notepad, Megan asked, "What was his first name? Do you know if his family still lives in the area?"

"Everyone knew old Bob Miller. I doubt there's an adult living here today that wouldn't have some sort of family story to tell about him. Both good and bad. But, the man never married or had kids that I can think of." Sheriff Casey explained. He noticed Megan writing down the name then opening her laptop. "From what I've learned about the office, after Sheriff Tucker was shot by supposed horse thieves about the middle of 1933. Miller took over the job. I think he was just about twenty, but the town was a quiet place and he'd been deputy for about a year. Next election, he won the office fair and square. He kept it until about May of 1983. I think he retired because his health was giving out. I can check for you," he offered.

"Thanks, I'll see what I can find online. Sheriff, do you know who was manning the speed trap on Friday? Excuse me, I mean the speed control check point. I saw the patrol car parked in the pull out when I came across the highway. He was still sitting there when we brought Coup back to the ranch. Maybe, he saw whoever rode Coup across the highway. It's a long shot, but who knows?"

Megan continued watching her screen. She missed his quickly hidden look of surprise.

David made a note of it. "Yeah, maybe we can speak with that officer, you know, jog his memory."

Sheriff Casey unconsciously backed toward the door a step. "Let me get back to you on that. I'll have to check to see who worked that route on Friday."

"Sheriff, your family's been in this area quite a while, haven't they? Ever heard of the H/J ranch? We know it failed in the thirties, but the owners may play a role in the murder." Aaron watched the sheriff. The man knew something; but what and about which incident, he wondered.

"No, I don't recall ever hearing about what closed the H/J. It failed before my family became shopkeepers in Riverview in the mid '30s. Well, I'd love to stay and chat, but I've got things to take care of and if you don't have anymore questions; neither do I." Wincing, he put the notebook in his shirt pocket and turned for the door. "I'll call you as soon as I get a chance to question the deputy working that highway on Friday. If any of you hear anything about the theft of that horse. Call me. The cabin is on Federal Lands, you FBI types can handle that investigation." Waving over his shoulder, he walked out.

"Did anyone notice the look he shot Kam? Honey, what did you do to piss off the sheriff? Stick him with a needle? I don't like shots, but I seldom despise the person giving it." David looked over at Kam who raised her head at his question and observation.

"Well, he was in for his physical about a week ago. But Doc did all the nasty stuff; I just took his blood pressure." Looking confused, she went back to her research.

Looking at Aaron over the bent heads of the

women, David dropped his voice. "Did you notice how he kept edging toward the door when we began to question him?" The women were back at work on their computers and oblivious to the undercurrents.

"Yeah, I wonder what he knows. Let's give him time to stew on what's got him worried. The longer he worries, the more likely he'll let something slip the next time we see him." Aaron picked up Caleb's journal. "So far, this is pretty dry reading. He's quit his job at the Cole Ranch and moved up to the cabin. It's July and hot. He says that Tuck was investigating a bootlegging operation along with a moonshine still in the area. No names as yet."

Silence interrupted only by the sounds of key strokes and mouse clicks settled over the room once more. Each person deep in thought as they followed clues and leads both online and in the journals. Time ticked by, unnoticed until a distinct loud rumbling came from David's stomach. The first was politely ignored; but when a second followed almost immediately David found three sets of laughing eyes and smiling faces looking his direction.

"Okay, I think my stomach feels we should take a break. Let's find a meal and compare notes. Where do you go to eat in Riverview?" He grinned back at the group unashamedly.

"Well, the diner is the best place to eat; but I'm not certain we want to hold any discussion there unless we want the whole town involved." Aaron offered.

"Yeah, Betty does love to talk and be involved. But, if you need any current history, she's the one to ask." Megan added.

"The Burger Barn has the best to-go food selection, but, I think at least partially involving Betty might be a wise move. Besides, I like to be comfortable when I eat and Betty has a good Sunday Special and comfortable booths.

Who's driving?" Kam stood up. "My truck's at the clinic so after lunch you can drop me off there and I'll bring it back here. David, I think your Durango will hold us all easier than Aaron's pick-up. I can drive it to the diner and Aaron can drive it back so you don't need to stress that arm." She grabbed hers and David's coats from the closet before heading to the door.

****

The watcher sat in his car, unbuttoning his jacket for more comfort. Sitting in his sedan in the lot across from the Inn, he patiently waited for the Durango to disappear down the road. He knew he'd been very lucky that the rifle bullet had only managed to graze his arm, he massaged it gently. If he had been standing up full, it would have hit his chest. He frowned at the memory of the botched attempt to scare the agent off from the body so he could destroy it. At least he'd been able to doctor the wound himself, though sewing it up had been a nasty experience he didn't ever want to go through again. The tissue had been sliced by the bullet rather than torn by it when it passed across his arm as he ducked behind the tree. His anger boiled at the thought of that woman shooting him, especially a woman of mixed blood.

Damn woman. He knew it was the nurse who'd fired. That agent had been bent over double when he stumbled into the cabin. No way could he have managed to get a shot off that soon after the door closed. Had to have been her, half-breed bitch.

The watcher knew he should have gone up the mountain, found the corpse, and destroyed it years ago, after his uncle told him the story in his demented ramblings before his death. Luckily, the staff of the nursing home never gave any credence to the old man's tales. Most dementia patients connect past memories with current events and even TV shows until they tell stories of unreal nature with clear eyes and earnest honesty. The staff members just smile, agree and let them ramble. There's no sense distressing the patients by forcing them to face reality. Memories, even false ones are much easier for them. Bob spent his last few years enjoying fellow seniors whose memories were likely as false as his own.

Now, the shit could hit the fan and his family be disgraced by the actions of his great-uncle in years gone by. The watcher benefited from Bob. Scratching his rounded belly through the straining buttons of his shirt, he remembered the old man had even paid for his college. He and his mother knew, but never mentioned, the fact that the Cole Ranch employed Sheriff Bob Miller and paid him handsomely for "extra" services over the fifty years he served as sheriff.

Sheriff Miller had supported Marie, his sister, after her husband died in WWII. Marie took a job as the housekeeper at the Cole Ranch, serving old Samuel in whatever manner he needed. Her daughter was born only nine months after she began the job, her pay increased accordingly. When young Samuel married Jessica Tucker and brought her home to the spread, Marie moved on to greener pastures, marrying a traveling preacher at the age of forty-five. Even without any DNA testing, the watcher knew he was related to Samuel Cole in one way or another.

Samuel was only ten years older than Marie's daughter, Sophia. Jacob Cole's wife had never known, or at least never acknowledged, that her husband was bedding the housekeeper. Receiving a handsome dowry from an unknown source Sophia married well. She and husband James set up a small store and prospered. The watcher had been born in the home they made over the store. When the big chains had come to Montrose and Gunnison and the small store died, they had moved on, but the watcher stayed behind with his great-uncle.

All this was ancient history, and should be of no interest to anyone. If only Robert Miller hadn't shot Caleb Preston. Now he was stuck cleaning up details of crimes over seventy years in the past. Damn him anyway.

Plotting his revenge against the nurse, he smiled evilly. She'd be begging him before he was through to end her life. She'd know her place by the time he was done. Dragging his mind from that plan, he forced himself to focus on how to stop the group from finding out about his great-uncle and his grandfather's involvement in the deaths of Caleb Preston and Sheriff Tucker as well as the other illegal deeds of both men over the span of their association. He needed to get that evidence they had in that box and those books.

That's it! His face lit up. Without the evidence, they had no proof of anything. He just needed to destroy the evidence. Another fire might work, the one at Megan's barn had gotten him the GPS but that hadn't kept them from finding the body as he expected. This time, he had to make certain to get it all without them knowing he had it. Maybe an explosion at the motel, followed by a hot fire. Hmmm, that might do it.

Driving to his house, just outside of town, he collected a can of gasoline and the large propane tank from his grill. This should do it. Parking around back of the Inn he casually walked up to the door of room 128 and picked the lock. Entering, he found the journals out on the table where they'd been left. Collecting them, he reached for the old tin box, and set everything by the door. Then he poured some of the gasoline on the beds and table to help spread the fire around the room. Next, after putting the box and journals in his car, he took the propane tank and set it up in the bathroom of room 127. He made a simple igniter from a book of matches and turned the tank on full before leaving the room. Throwing another lit book of matches into room 128 as he left, he could see the blaze taking hold. Soon the explosion in 127 would cover the cause of the fire as well as the fact that 128 had been his real target. He managed to waddle around the corner before the blast that shook the building.

****

"What the Hell?!" David jumped up from his seat at the sound of an explosion. Overturning his meal that had just been set on the table, he ignored the mess as he ran out of the Diner.

"Look, to the south, there's smoke!" Aaron joined him in the parking lot, pointing toward the highway junction. "Shit. The Gorgeview is that way. I'm driving!"

Rushing to David's Dodge Durango, they climbed in. Aaron started the engine just as Megan and Kam ran out of the restaurant. Managing to get the back door open, the girls jumped in before SUV lunged forward; spewing gravel when he jammed it into drive. "Buckle up!" Aaron advised his passengers.

Megan and Kam righted themselves in the back seat, each reaching to buckle up while managing not to slide into one another as Aaron took a corner too fast. "Where're we going?" "Was that an explosion?" They spoke at the same time.

"Sounded like one. It also looks like there's a fire over toward the highway junction where our motel is located." David explained. The Durango accelerated through town and out the other side while he spoke. "Easy cowboy, you don't want to kill anyone, or us. We'll get there, just be careful."

Sirens sounded both in front and behind them. A fire truck appeared in his rearview and Aaron pulled over to let it by, and then jammed his foot on the gas pedal to follow it. Collectively, their hearts fell when they saw it turn into the Gorgeview parking lot and continue down the building before stopping in front of David's room.

"Damn it! The journals!" David jumped out of the SUV before it came to a full stop. Running to the door of the room, a strong arm grabbed his belt before he could get close enough to enter.

"Easy, Mister. Stay back. There could be another explosion. Let us get this under control. Someone in there?" A deep voice asked as the hand on his belt pulled him back further from the door to 128.

"Not a person, just evidence and computers." David reached for his credentials wallet. "David Harrison, FBI" He flipped it open for the man who now blocked his progress.

"Daniel Wheeler, Riverview Volunteer Fire Department. Nice to meet you. Sorry about whatever you had in that room." The man extended his hand to David.

"What's going on Dan?" Aaron walked up with Megan and Kam in tow.

"Hey, Aaron. Don't know yet, I got here a minute ahead of the truck. Two rooms fully involved. Room 127 exploded and took the fire into room 128 as far as we can tell at this moment. Good thing neither was occupied and the upstairs rooms were vacant too." He smiled at the thought of no casualties. Any fire without injuries was a good thing.

"Chief, we're going back to the Diner and let you

work. Could you join us there when you're done here? I need to know any thoughts you can come up with about this fire." David turned on his heel and walked disgustedly back to his car. The others followed and silence reigned on the much slower drive back to Betty's.

Betty had left their meals sitting on the table waiting for their return. "I was wondering if ya'all were going to come back. Want me to heat up those plates for ya?" She asked as they filed in and returned to their seats.

"Thanks, Betty. That's a great idea." Aaron smiled over at her.

David pulled his ever-present notepad from his shirt pocket. He passed each a sheet of paper. "Can you find us some pens?" He asked Betty as she collected the plates of food.

She nodded, took the plates back to the kitchen, and brought back four pens. "Here you go. Anything else you need?"

"Thanks. That should do it. Appreciate your help." David smiled up at her when he took the pens and passed them to the others. Turning back to them his eyes were thoughtful. "I need each of you to write down everything you have found out so far. Aaron, write down what you've read and ladies, what you found online." He looked at each before he turned to his own paper.

Betty returned with their food and found each industrially writing. "Would you like me to put the meals on the table behind you so you can finish; or can you make some space for them where you're sitting?"

Each person hardly looked up at her, but instead moved their paper to the side so she had room to set the food. "Stomachs always win." She muttered, putting down the plates and heading back to the kitchen.

Setting down their pens, Kam and Megan turned to

the Sunday Special of ham, yams and green beans. "This smells amazing. How can you guys keep writing with this food within reach?" Megan teased the men who both continued to fill paper with data.

Cutting off a bite of ham, Kam shrugged at Megan. "I guess our data is retrievable but theirs will be lost if they don't write it down." Then she frowned. Her laptop was only a year old and contained all of her contact data for family along with her resume and personal records. Since she'd depleted her savings during her battle with the doctor, she'd be lucky to be able to replace the hardware, much less the variety of software the machine housed. "Shit." She grumped.

"What?" Megan asked around a mouthful of food.

"You do realize our computers are toast; literally, Right?" A wry smile showed around her lips while her eyes expressed the depth of her loss. "I don't know what you had on yours, but mine had everything and all my apps for day-to-day chores. So... Shit. I'm going to miss that damn thing."

"Crap. You're right. I hadn't thought beyond the loss of the evidence box. I'm going to miss that machine. I've got a desk computer back at the ranch, so my data and apps aren't all lost." She admitted.

"Lucky you. That laptop was my only computer. Wonder if the motel has insurance that will get me a new one?"

Looking up at the women, David smiled. "I'll see that your computers are replaced. After all, you were assisting in the investigation and neither machine would have been in that room if you weren't."

"That's sweet of you. And the FBI, of course." Megan smiled at him.

Still not too happy Kam muttered. "If I get my own,

will they reimburse me? I don't have weeks to wait for a new laptop."

Raising his head from his writing, David smiled at her, trying to coax a return smile. "We could go to Montrose or Gunnison and get you both computers today. I'll put them on my government card and then battle my bosses about the expense later. How does that sound?"

Kam looked at his smile and her lips turned up involuntarily. Her heart quickened and her temperature went up. Damn, all he had to do was look at her and her body responded. How could an offer to buy her a laptop make her think of steamy nights and warm kisses? Oh boy, she was in so much trouble with this man. "I think we need to work on salvaging what the fire burnt. I can give you model and maker for you to shop while I'm working tomorrow."

"Now that the room is toast, where are we going to set up for a private, gossip-proof, session?" David looked at all of them in question.

"The ranch I'm renting has a large great room where we could set up. It also has four bedrooms so you could move in there if you wanted." Megan offered the agent. She missed the evil eye that Aaron cast her direction as well as Kam's glare.

Even admitting she was right about the space, Aaron didn't want a strange man living in the same house as Megan. "I know. We could work over there today and see where we are at the end of the day. David, there's always space in the bunkhouse at the R-M too." Aaron suggested, mentally patting himself on the back for diverting the possible disaster of Megan and David sharing the house.

"I'll call my partner to let him know where we've moved. He should be here by dinner." David sent a text to Jason giving the details and location of the group.

Pushing back from the table, David looked at his fellow diners. "Think that fireman will be here soon, or should we stop back up at the Inn on our way out of town?"

"Well, speak of the devil, here he comes. Betty, find out what Dan wants and set him up here with us." Aaron moved around the bench, squeezing closer to Megan, while waving to the Fire Chief.

The odor of smoke following him, Dan sat on the corner of the seat, as far from Aaron as he could get. "Hi, glad you're still here. Betty, I want a coffee and a tall ice water. My throat is like the Mohave desert, from all that smoke."

"I take it the fire's out?" David asked the obvious.

"Cold ash and soaked carpet. No more explosions, thank goodness. What were you doing in that room that would make someone want to torch it?" Dan turned his narrowed eyes at David.

"I take it that arson was involved, not a gas leak?"

"It was a gas leak all right. Some yoyo set a propane tank next to the wall to your room and caused the explosion. But, before he did, he used a can of gasoline in your room and then set it ablaze just to make certain the fire would get there." Frowning, Dan looked around the diner.

"We found a propane tank, or what was left of it, and the odor of gasoline just about gagged my men when they finally got into your room. Didn't need the 'sniffer' to confirm it was arson." He noticed the women looked worried and the men looked pissed. "What was going on in there, can you give me a clue?"

Sighing, David looked at the group before turning his attention to the Fire Chief. He waited for Betty to place the coffee and water on the table before he responded. "It's all concerning the body that Bethany and Megan found in the woods on Friday. Since then, a fire at Megan's place took out her GPS unit, then someone fired on Kam and I, and now this. Even though this crime is about eighty years in the past, it's obvious that someone is concerned with keeping it in the past. Seriously concerned. We found a box containing two journals and some other evidence about the original crime, along with evidence of a different crime in 1983 located in the cabin where Kam and I sat out the storm. That's what this fire and explosion was about. Did you find a metal box anywhere in the rubble? It should have been on the coffee table closest to the door."

"You can look for yourself, but all we found was a couple of pretty melted laptop computers and a set of leather saddlebags on the couch. I've got those in my truck, you can have them. It's possible the force of the water we used to douse the fire pushed anything light under the bed. But no box, metal or otherwise was anywhere in sight." Dan explained.

"Well, sir; I expect that if you saw the computers and didn't see the box then whoever set the fire took it. Likely has destroyed everything by now and we're screwed in solving the crimes. But, maybe, just maybe there's another way. If we can track who this person is; we'll be able to get justice for his current crimes. The other crimes might be beyond prosecuting; but attacking an agent, destroying evidence, and arson are crimes in themselves. The FBI doesn't condone having agents ambushed. The lab is processing the corpse and trace found with it right now. We may well yet be able to find this criminal. But, please, keep this investigation under your hat." David stood and extended his hand to Dan and led his group out of the café, stopping to pay for the meals as they left. Dan followed them and handed David the saddlebags and the warped laptop computers.

"Do you want to take a quick look at the Inn? I have to collect my truck if the fire engine has unblocked it. I hope it was far enough from the explosion to escape damage." Aaron started David's SUV and waited to see which direction David wanted to go. Right to the ranch or left to the Inn.

"Might as well visit the Inn, check out of the room and collect your truck. You can look around the room while I take care of details." David frowned out the window as Aaron headed for the Inn.

Once there, while David was in the office, Aaron and the women carefully poked around the remains of the room where they had been working so diligently not two hours earlier. Nothing was salvageable and Aaron lifted the bed frames to check for the tin box but found it suspiciously missing.

Walking to the hole where the door had been David looked at the group goose-stepping through the debris. "Anything of interest still useable?"

"No, not that I can see," Kam and Aaron spoke at the same time. Megan just shook her head with a sigh. "Either nothing survived, or it was taken out before the fire was set." Aaron confirmed to David, stepping out of the room into the bright afternoon sun.

"Well, let's head for Megan's place. Kam, would you like to ride with me? Or maybe, drive me since my arm doesn't need the exercise?" David smiled over at Kam, wiggling his brows at her.

"Looks like my truck isn't damaged. I'll drive Megan. Come on, Honey." Aaron possessively put his hand on Megan's arm to assist her into his truck. He pointedly looked over at David, once more stating his claim to this woman without voicing it.

Kam took David's keys from Aaron and stepped into the Durango. "Let's get going, David. There's nothing here to salvage." Starting the engine, she waited for him to climb into the front seat next to her before putting the vehicle in gear and heading out, following Aaron.

Chapter Seventeen

Megan and Aaron beat David and Kam to the ranch; and then wondered what the other couple was doing. "I know they were behind us as we left the Inn." Aaron scratched his head and looked out toward the highway, listening for the sounds of an approaching truck.

"They might have stopped for something. David knows how to get here and Kam rode over with me from the R-M on Friday, so they shouldn't be lost." Megan assured him, leading the way up the steps to the front door. "Would you shovel and salt the steps? I don't want anyone hurt. I'm going to put on a pot of coffee." She passed him the shovel and deicer.

Laughing, Aaron took the shovel. "You know, all you have to do is ask; I'll do just about *any*thing you want." His eyes twinkled at her when he stressed anything.

Megan blushed and continued walking into the house muttering something about "in your dreams, cowboy" under her breath.

"I heard that." Aaron called.

After working on the steps about fifteen minutes, Aaron heard then saw the approaching Durango. It pulled into the ranch yard and parked behind Aaron's truck, the engine so quiet he could hardly tell when it stopped.

The darkened windows protecting them from prying eyes, David reached over, laid his hand at the nape of Kam's neck and pulled her in for a long, hot kiss. "I've wanted to do that since we left the room this morning. Too bad, we don't have a private place any longer. We'll have to go necking sometime. I could make the back of this thing more comfortable." His eyes burning hotly over her face as he released her.

"Now, you're trying to make me feel like a teenager again." She laughed at him while she opened her door. Reaching in the back of the SUV, she grabbed the case of beer that caused their late arrival. "Hi, Aaron; sorry we're late. Hope you like Miller Lite. Couldn't find any wine in the grocery store." She waved and called to Aaron as David caught up with her and took the keys to his vehicle. He tried to take the beer, but she refused to let his bad arm take it from her. "No! I won't have you hurting yourself. For crying out loud... I can handle the beer. Honest."

"Here, let me take it if you two are going to argue over it. I don't want it all shaken up from pulling back and forth." Aaron stepped between them, deftly snagging the container from Kam's hand in a smooth move that would make any fraternity brother proud.

David stepped closer to Kam and ran his good arm around her waist while Aaron walked past them into the house with his prize. Whispering into her ear, "That's how you get someone to take a load from you" and smiling when she laughed aloud as his comment.

"You're so bad, but then again, most men wouldn't want to see the beer out of their control, so maybe you aren't that bad after all." She laughed up at the change in his expression as it dawned on him that he had just trusted another man with the beer. She planted a kiss on his cheek in consolation for his loss.

David turned at the feel of her lips and managed to brush his lips over hers before she could withdraw. "Got'cha."

Huffing in exasperation, Kam turned a shoulder to him and continued up the steps and into the house;

ignoring both his action and his words. "Hi, Megan. Sorry we took so long but thought a beer run on the way here might be a good idea."

Megan returned her smile while she cleared off her dining table to create a workspace for the group. Her desktop computer in front of her chair waited for her to plant herself behind it.

"Hey, thanks for thinking of beer. I've got tea and diet sodas but my beer supply was two cans." Megan waved at the arrivals and turned back to her task. "There's glasses in the cupboard for the sweet tea, and cups for the coffee; if you want beer or diet soda those are in the fridge. Help yourself." She directed her guests while finding note pads and pens for everyone.

Carrying their drink of choice, each person selected a preferred seat at the dining table. "Why don't we start with the 'who' aspect of all this. Ladies, what did you find out about the people from both 1933 and 1983? Who is related to anyone currently in the area?" David directed his question to Kam and Megan.

Reaching for her notes, Megan looked at the group and began with the data she'd collected on Friday. "Well according to the 1930 Census, there was a Caleb Preston working at the Cole Ranch in Gunnison County. Also, from the same source, there was a Michael Tucker living in Riverview with his wife, Angelica. Shows his occupation as deputy, not as sheriff. The next census shows a Michael Tucker, Jr., age six, living with his mother, Angelica McMillan, and half-sister, Susan, but there's no record of Caleb in the 1940 census." Looking up from her notes, she paused before continuing. "I found an article in the Riverview paper from May of 1933 that tells of Michael Tucker, Sheriff, being shot by person or persons unknown during a robbery attempt at the Riverview Livery during the night of May 4th. It notes his funeral and the fact that his wife Angelica survives him. Michael Jr. lived in the area until his death in 1999. I found his son James shown as a teacher in Gunnison at the time of Michael's death. The Obituary names a daughter Jessica Cole, wife of Samuel Cole. This is a small world around here. Wonder if she ever figured out that her father-in-law had a hand in the death of her grandfather?" Megan mused.

"Well, I found that after Michael's death, his position was taken by his young deputy until an election could be held to replace the sheriff. Robert Miller is shown as age 20. The article explains that he had a full year of experience in the position and knew all the routines. His family ran the dry goods store owned by the Cole family. When I looked up Robert Miller in the 1940 census, it shows him as sheriff of Riverview and living with his widowed sister and her daughter." Kam looked around then directly at Megan. "I was interrupted by lunch at that point and then our computers burned. Would you check on the sister and niece of Robert Miller? We need to follow that family tree. Between the Cole family and the Miller family we could have our "person or people of interest" in the arson fires and the attack on David and I."

"Sure. Let me access Ancestry.com for data on Robert Miller of Riverview, CO. If he was 20 in 1933, he would have been born in 1913; right?" Megan's fingers flew with the mouse then across the keyboard as she began to search.

"Okay, while Megan is searching, Aaron, what did you find in the journal you were reading?" David looked over at Aaron then jumped when a knock sounded at the front door. "Damn. This house is pretty sound proof. I didn't hear a car drive up." Pushing back from the table, he stood and walked to the door. "Jason, about time you got here. Come on in and meet the group. Need anything to drink?" He motioned a tall, thin man with kind eyes and a balding head into the room. David pointed around the table to each person as he named them. "Megan, Aaron, Kam; this is my partner at the FBI, Special Agent Jason Wunderlich." He pointed to a chair in the corner. "Pull that over to the table. What did you want to drink? Tea, diet soda, or beer?"

"After the drive, I'll take a beer." Walking over to the chair, he pulled it up to a space made for him by Megan who scooted closer to Aaron with her computer. He sat and pulled out his laptop from his satchel. "What happened at the Inn? I thought this was a 'cold case' but seems to me that things are pretty active." He looked around the group with his eyes coming to rest on his partner.

"It appears that someone doesn't want the original crime solved or maybe they don't want the secondary crime committed by the Cole family to come out. What did you find out from Phil Dunkin?" Aaron passed Jason a beer with a glass then sat back down next to Kam.

"Well, it seems like this place was a hotbed of illegal activity back in prohibition and the same people ran things all the way through about 2000." Jason pulled out his notebook and set it next to his laptop. "Phil didn't have proof, but he knew that Richard had some sort of evidence against the Cole Ranch. He knew Richard was going to face down the old man. Phil also said that Sheriff Miller didn't retire until mid year and even at seventy-something he was a bastard who followed any orders given by Cole." He glanced at his notes then continued. "Phil himself is a piece of work. He still feels that the Meadows ranch should be his and has no qualms over the fact that Richard died and he almost killed a woman who had very little to do with anything other than being in the wrong place at the wrong time."

"So Dunkin fingered the Cole family as responsible for Richard leaving the area?" Aaron asked.

"Cole and his buddy, Sheriff Robert Miller. According to Phil, Cole would direct and Miller would carry out the dirty work. Around the time that Richard left, there had been two nasty brush fires close to the R-M ranch house. Phil remembered his sister being scared that the ranch house would burn next. Everything quieted once Richard was gone. No more fires, no more accidents or stampedes; just quiet ranch life. Phil says he saw the sheriff's cruiser on a back road while he was creating a firebreak with the tractor during the second fire. His thoughts were that Miller had set the fire; but he had no proof." Looking up from his written notes, he noticed that everyone watched and listened to his report.

"Roger will want to know all this. He was only about ten when his dad left, so he never knew anything about what made him run. Think Cole threatened Richard to leave or lose his family and ranch?" Aaron again asked the question.

"From what Phil said, I would gather that was the actual reason Richard left his family. To protect them from the trouble he stirred up with Cole and Sheriff Miller." Jason nodded at Aaron.

"Okay, now the question is: who wants all this information to disappear and everything to go back to 'status quo' in Riverview? We need to know who in the Cole family was giving orders in 1983. If it was Samuel, then he could go down for blackmail. If it was his father, then we have no culprits to charge in the older crimes. We need to find a plausible suspect for the arsons and the attack on Kam and me." David looked at Megan. "Did you find anything about Robert Miller?"

"Yep. I was able to find his parents, siblings and decedents. The good sheriff never married, but his sister did. She had one daughter who married William Casey. They have one son, William Casey, Jr." She paused for effect. "Sheriff William Casey, Jr. to be exact." She grinned at the group. "I'm still checking on a brother listed in the family; but the boy only showed up until the 1930 census; then there's nothing. Strange not to find a death certificate, but in those days it wasn't uncommon for a man to go somewhere and start fresh by taking on a new name and identity. I'll search the papers to see if he was involved with anything unsavory." She offered and turned back to her computer.

Smiling at the top of Megan's bent head, David turned to look at Aaron. "What do you have down that you read in the small Journal? Did Caleb have any evidence about Tucker's murder? How far had you gotten before we broke for lunch?"

"Other than those two photos that Cole used against Hendrix to get the H/J ranch, there was no hard evidence. Caleb knew that his friend was going to face Cole about the crime and he said something about the photo with the petroglyphs in the background put that moonshine still on Cole Ranch property, not on the H/J. The date on the back of the photo was two months after Tucker was killed." Aaron recounted what he'd written in the diner.

"Well, I read that Michael Tucker took office in 1931 and from the start he was approached by a representative of the Cole family to become a 'valued member of the industries that support Riverview and the surrounding ranches'." David looked up from his notes and found all but Megan were watching and making notes on his statement. "I only got about six months into his term as Sheriff of Riverview, but that was far enough for him to know that the ranches in this area were dirt poor and those that looked to be prosperous actually were producing more than beef. Keep in mind that Prohibition was in full swing until late in 1933."

"You know, people survived any way they could, especially after the crash in 1929. Bootlegging and making moonshine seemed to be better than letting your family starve or losing your home. Unfortunately, there were those whose ambition was to get rich, 'no matter what it took'; and those are the people who murdered and stole from the people around them who had so little to lose." Jason mused about the era when Tucker lost his life and the Hendrix family lost their ranch to the local "crime baron". "So this Cole fella, he had a ranch as well as running booze?"

"Actually, over the fifty years between the death of Sheriff Tucker and the disappearance of Richard Meadows, several of the Cole family ran the ranch and the county. Three brothers started the Cole ranch, 3CS, at the turn of the 20th century. Two of them died, each leaving his share to be split by remaining siblings until only one lived and owned the entire spread in 1925." Megan explained what she had found in earlier research. "The surviving brother was named Samuel; the same as the current head of household. The original Samuel left the ranch to his son, Jacob Randolph Cole, in 1945 who, in turn, passed away in 1980, leaving the spread to the Samuel Cole who owns it today. I can't find anything about his wife Jessica or his daughter Angelica. I found birth notice in 1990 for the baby, then nothing. No death notice or divorce papers; just a blank. Maybe the FBI can follow them, but without hacking into sealed data, I can't." Megan looked from one agent to the other; hoping one would volunteer to search further on decedents of the Cole family.

"So we would have to guess that the original Samuel was responsible for the death of Sheriff Tucker and Caleb Preston. Since Samuel Cole of today was in charge when Richard Meadows wrote the letter we found in the box, he was responsible for Richard's disappearance in 1983." David had been writing down dates and comparing transitions to crimes while Megan spoke. He detailed who caused which grief.

"Only Samuel would be open for prosecution, and then it would be questionable as to the exact crime the man committed. We no longer have proof as to why Richard ran, and the old Sheriff Miller is long since buried. It looks like we could be stuck in not seeing anyone pay for these old crimes." David scratched his head and looked around the room for suggestions. "We can pass the data about how the 3CS ranch acquired the H/J to the Hendrix family; they might want to sue for the property to be returned. If only we had the old photos. Kam, you and I saw them and need to find the spot on the 3CS where the photo of the illegal still was taken. If we can find it, then with our testimony; the family might be able to get back the ranch or restitution from the 3CS for the loss of it."

"That's a great idea about helping the Hendrix family. They deserve some sort of restitution even if they don't want the land to be returned." Kam agreed. Getting up from the table, she walked to the refrigerator pulled out a beer and looked at the others still seated at the table. "Anyone else think it's 'Miller Time'?"

Those without a beer all agreed that a cold brew would taste great. Megan got up and found glasses for herself and Aaron, Kam and David declined the offer, preferring to drink from the cold bottles.

"Hey, I'll take another." Jason chimed in before Kam made it to the table, gladly taking the one she had for herself.

Opening the fridge for a second time, Kam paused, taking out one more beer. "Anyone need anything else before I close this and get half-way to the table?" Her voice revealed the tiredness of her body and spirit. It had been a long day after an eventful night. She realized that all she wanted was a warm bed and sleep. Damn, her truck was *still* parked behind the clinic. Crap, she couldn't even go to bed without asking someone for a ride home. She looked the group over, trying to figure out who would be the most likely candidate to take a drive back to town. "You know, I'm not certain about David; but I'm beat. I haven't had a chance for a good night's sleep since Thursday. I'm about ready to call it a day."

"I know what you mean, honey. My last full night of sleep was Thursday, too. Would you like a ride into town? I can drop you by the clinic after we grab a bite to eat. It's after seven already." David looked at his watch after taking a long pull on his beer.

Smirking, Jason looked over at his partner. Honey? Really? Then he remembered the telephone conversation of the night before. Kam had been at the motel, but David had been drugged. Nah, nothing could have happened between them; at least until the drugs wore off. But, what happened in the cabin on Friday night? Something was happening between those two, the air was tight with sexual tension. Damn it all. He frowned. Maybe some day it would be his turn, he sighed to himself.

"I could bring a bag of burgers back here after dropping her off if you guys could wait that long." David offered Aaron, Megan, and Jason.

"Well, if we're about done here for the night; why don't we all head into the Burger Barn for dinner? Take two vehicles, my truck and David's SUV. That way, after dinner, I'll head back to the ranch and David can drop Kam off at her truck. You agents are spending the night in Megan's guest room; aren't you?" Aaron looked around the room. He hated leaving Megan with two men but two was safer than one – so long as the men shared a room.

"Yeah, we're about done here. Let's make some plans for tomorrow and we can meet at the Diner for either lunch or dinner and discuss what we've found by then." David picked up his notepad and reviewed it. "Megan, continue searching and investigating the Millers online or in the library. Aaron, talk to your boss and see what you can find out about his father. Jason, see what you can find out about the Cole family and the petroglyphs and I'll chase down the sheriff to see what he found out from the officer manning the speed trap. That is, after I visit Gunnison to get two new laptop computers to replace the fried ones. Ladies, write down what you had and I'll see if I can match it or go to a more current model."

"That sounds good to me. Let's exchange cell numbers so we can figure a meeting time once we have more information. I'll question my boss about local gossip and families to see what I can glean about the Cole and Hendrix families. He may not know the Hendrix family if they moved to Montrose in the 30's but he'll know all about the Coles. He might be able to fill in what happened to Jessica and Angelica Cole." Kam smiled at David, happy to be able to offer assistance to the group, even without a computer and while she was working.

Finishing their beers, the group pushed back from the table, stood and walked to the coat rack to retrieve coats and hats before venturing out into the cold night. Melting snow had frozen hard with the setting sun, making the steps and the walk to the vehicles hazardous and slow. The women clung to the arms of their respective men and each performed a penguin slide/walk down the small rise from the house to the ranch yard.

"Well, one thing's certain: if you can walk on this crap, you're not too drunk to drive." Laughed Jason watching the unstable group ahead. Once beyond the light from the house, they became shadows alternating with silvered slices of bodies. They slid in and out of moonlit shadows cast by each other and surrounding trees.

Chapter Eighteen

Awaking to a chirping sound, Kam rolled over and stared at her bird alarm clock. Crap, it was seven on Monday morning. Glad and yet sad, she realized that for the first time in the past three days, she woke up alone in her own bed, after a good night of sleep. Smiling she recalled how the evening before had ended. The burgers had been excellent while the group hashed out a few more details before they broke up with Aaron taking his truck and heading for the ranch.

Using David's Durango, Jason drove Kam to her truck. David walked her to it before kissing her goodnight to the hoots of his partner and Megan. She felt her face flush at the memory. A simple kiss goodbye seemed so lame after the night before. Feeling her body heat, she rolled over on her back, reliving the feel of his hands memorizing every curve and sensitive spot. Damn, she had better get up or she'd be calling him for phone sex.

Thirty minutes later, showered and in her nicest set of scrubs, she headed for the diner to grab a bite before going to work. Something sweet to give an extra sugar rush to the caffeine she knocked down in the Bailey sister's kitchen. After the danish, she drove to the clinic with brownies in a bag on the seat next to her. Everyone could operate on sugar today. Chocolate makes Mondays survivable.

Finding the door unlocked she entered and spoke with the receptionist, Barb, handing her a brownie. "Keep this at your desk; once George sees the bag, you know he'll finish off the rest." She laughed. She put her purse and coat in her locker, adding a brownie to the top shelf before she took the other two and set them on the table in the break room. Pouring herself a cup of coffee, she turned at the arrival of her boss. "Good morning. Did you have a good weekend?"

"Fine, how did our patient fare on Saturday night?" Seeing Kam blush, George figured the man likely recovered just fine.

"Oh, he fell deeply asleep once I got some food into him. He weighs a ton, but I managed to get him into bed. I crashed in the other bed in case he needed anything during the night." Her face got redder as she recalled what he needed during the night. "Sunday he woke without a fever and his arm is only minimally sore. Megan, Aaron, David and I worked at the motel room until after one when we broke for lunch. While we were gone, someone caused an explosion and our room burned. I lost my computer but more importantly, all the evidence went up in flames." She related the story, then asked "What do you know about the Cole family and the 3CS ranch? They're part of all this and we trying to figure out how much of a part."

"Well, a lot of what I know about Samuel and his father is under patient confidentially and I can't tell you. However, there's lots of common knowledge about the family. Where do you want me to start? Our first patient is only a half hour away." George spied the brownies on the table, snagged one with a napkin and began to devour it. "Damn, Betty makes the best brownies."

"Back in Prohibition, the 3CS acquired the H/J ranch. From what we saw in the stuff that burned, there was coercion used to get the family to sell. Who was the patriarch during that era? In 1983, it's very likely that the Cole family used coercion to get Richard Meadows to leave his home and family. Who was in charge then? Also, what do you know about Jessica and Angelica Cole?"

"Well, since I delivered Angelica, I can tell you she was born healthy and both parents welcomed her arrival. Jessica wasn't happy about something just before she left. She and Sam were seen arguing in town a couple of times and the last time she was at the Burger Barn with a loaded car. A doctor in Tallahassee, FL sent for their records about two weeks later. That's the last I've heard about or from her. You might want to ask James Tucker in Gunnison about his sister." He took another bite of brownie, finishing the treat. "In Prohibition times old man Samuel led the ranch; and the county for that matter. His son took over the reins during the Korean War era, don't recall what year and young Samuel began running the ranch sometime after he got back from Viet Nam. That change was very gradual, with Sam doing more and more until no one would approach his dad about anything. So, I guess he would have been in charge of the 3CS at the time of Richard Meadows disappearance. What makes you think he had anything to do with that?"

"Richard left a letter in with the evidence we found saying he was going to see 'Cole' about how the ranch obtained the H/J in hopes to get some restitution for the Hendrix family. At the same time, Phil Dunkin knew his uncle had some sort of proof against a powerful man in the county; and then Richard was gone. Phil had planned to point the finger of guilt at Cole for Richard's death; but he never got the chance since he was caught chasing and shooting at Bethany." Kam drank her coffee and watched her boss study his. "What do you know about Robert Miller?"

"He was sheriff while I was growing up. You didn't want him mad at you. All the parents used him as the boogey man to keep us on the straight and narrow" He smiled at the memory of the threats his mother used to make. "As I grew older, the tales became more detailed and the word was that the old man had a pit someplace where his and Cole's enemies were buried." He shuddered at the memory. "All the way up to his retirement in 1983, he was a scary man."

"Do you remember anything about his family? Did he have a wife at any time?"

"As an adult, I heard folks say he was gay – but no one ever proved that rumor and if he was, he took the knowledge to the grave. He lived with and took care of his younger sister who returned to town with a child after WWII. That girl married William Casey and their son is our current sheriff." Looking at his watch, he stood up. "That's about all the local gossip we have time for. Why don't you check with Barb and see who's waiting?" He walked back to his office to clear his desk for the day.

Picking up her cell phone, Kam speed dialed David. He was going to Gunnison this morning. "Hi, have you gotten to Gunnison yet?" She asked without preamble.

"Hi, Sweetness. Yeah, I'm just paying for the computers. Do you want the service contract?" Handing the clerk his government credit card he shook his head at the offered service contracts.

"No, I can handle the computer and they seldom go bad after the first 30 days. Before you leave Gunnison, you might want to contact James Tucker about Jessica. Dr. Samuelson says he got a request from a clinic in Florida for their records. James might be able to give you more exact contact data."

"I'll do that. Want to meet for lunch at one? Betty's might be quieter then than during the noon hour." David made the date with her and ended the call. Putting the laptop computers into his Durango, he used his tablet to pull up data on James Tucker and headed for the man's house. According to the files, Tucker had retired last year. Before getting out of his SUV at the Tucker residence, he called Aaron; arranging to meet with him and Megan at the Diner at one.

A man was pulling plants from a brown garden as David walked up to the gate. "Hi. Are you James Tucker?"

"Who else would be tending a worthless garden at this time of year at the Tucker house?" Snapping, the man watched the approach of the FBI agent.

"My name is David Harrison. I'm with the FBI." He extended his credentials to the man now leaning on a hoe. James looked ready to use the hoe in defense if needed.

"What can I do for you?"

"Well, we're looking into your brother-in-law, Samuel Cole. What can you tell me about him? Also, do you have a current address on your sister Jessica?" David watched the disgust play across the face of the man when he asked about Cole.

"Don't tell me that the law is finally catching up with that bastard." An evil smile touched James lips, but failed to reach his eyes. "We found out his grand pappy was responsible for our grandfather's death back in prohibition and he just laughed at Jessica when she told him she knew. Son of a bitch was proud of his family, said, 'They did what was needed to grow the ranch and survive'. Then when Richard Meadows came around telling Jessica he had proof about the death and about how the 3CS acquired the H/J. Sam bragged about chasing the man from the county." James sadly shook his head. "He told Jess that he had Robert Miller pull Richard over and tell him that if he wanted his family to live; he would keep his mouth shut and leave town. The next day there was a fire close to the

R-M ranch house and the day after, Richard was gone." He looked at David. "No way to prove any of this, of course. Just what he bragged to his wife. Jess packed up and left him. Went to Florida for a few years, then moved to Dallas for a job at a publishing company. Still works for them. I'll get you her address." Letting the hoe fall, James walked toward the house pausing to wave David along with him.

David waited while James copied the contact information onto a clean sheet of notepaper. "We may be able to put Samuel Cole and Robert Miller at both the death of your grandfather and the threats to Richard Meadows. If we can, we'll need testimony from Jessica to cinch the deal. Think she would do it?"

"Well, she never divorced him because of Angelica; but she hates all that he stands for, so she just might." Shaking the agent's hand, James handed him the paper.

"Thanks, we'll contact her if we have any chance at all in prosecuting her husband. You've been a great help."

Walking back to his Durango, David waved to the man who watched him leave from the front porch of the old house. Smiling, David headed back to Riverview. So far, the morning had been very productive. Turning on his radio, he let his mind wander to Kam. How was he going to get her to move to Denver? What if she wanted to stay in Riverview? Maybe they could meet at his cousin's Dude Ranch every weekend… it was about halfway between his post in Denver and her job in Riverview. Sighing, he knew that would be nice, but not a long-term solution to a long distance relationship. Just how badly did he want to keep her in his life? Frowning, he admitted to himself that he wanted her not only in his life but also in his home as well as his bed. He couldn't remember wanting anything more.

At the clinic, Kam's mind had been thinking over the same problems with fewer possible solutions. While she worked with patients, setting up exam rooms, taking temperatures and blood pressure readings for the doctor, her mind wasn't really on her job. Showing Mrs. Peters into exam room one and prepping her for her annual visit with the doctor, Kam was surprised to hear that Sheriff Casey was here to see her.

"Hi, Sheriff. What can I do for you?" Smiling she approached the man waiting at the reception desk, extending her hand in welcome.

"I need to speak with you in private. Do you have an office, or would you like to step outside?" Frowning at her, the sheriff ignored Kam's extended hand.

Looking around the empty waiting area, Kam looked over at Barb. "Would you mind assisting George with Mrs. Peters? I'm going to take my break. We'll be in the break room if you need me." She led the sheriff back to the break room and shut the door. "Okay Sheriff; what's this all about?"

"You may not realize it, in fact it's obvious you don't, but our office runs background checks on new residents, especially those who take up sensitive positions within our community." He scowled at her. "Yours has brought to light several facts that would not only embarrass Dr. Samuelson, if they came out, but would cause him to lose patients. If his patients knew that the new nurse had a sordid past and Doc hired her and let her associate with innocent patients, they would take their business to Montrose or Gunnison, not to mention Mrs. Samuelson might take action against her husband. She sure as Hell wouldn't trust him to work with a nurse accused of seducing a doctor in the clinic where she worked in Des Moines." He leered with the final statement; his eyes traveling from her face to her chest where they rested an uncomfortable amount of time before returning to her face.

"I beg your pardon, but the doctor knows about my past and I have to assume that his wife does as well. Not only that… all charges against me were dropped." Kam's back had stiffened at his perusal and her face reddened at his words.

"Are you certain she knows? Obviously, the rest of the town doesn't… yet," his threat as obvious as his salacious look at her chest. "Just how badly do you want to stay here? Badly enough to risk the happiness and livelihood of the man who's given you a job and entrance to the community? *If* you have any self-respect left, you should leave this town and find a job in a city where no one will care about your past. I suggest you leave as quickly as you can unless you want the gossip to start and the scandal to become known." He stepped in and ran a hand up and down her arm. "Unless you want to set up housekeeping with me, and I'll keep you safe from wagging tongues."

Jerking back from his touch, Kam shuddered, unable to hide her disgust at his touch quickly enough. "I'll think about it. When do you expect this gossip to become known to the town?" She spit the question while watching him through narrowed eyes.

"I get off at four, after that; I don't think I'll be able to keep the gossip from spreading." He leered again but kept his hands to himself. "I'll be on patrol until then, you can call if you decide to accept my offer of 'protection'." His wording was careful, but the thought plain. He'd know if she stayed or left town.

Walking to the breakroom door, Kam swung it open and motioned him to leave. She jerked back when he attempted to brush her breasts with his elbow when he moved past her out the door. Frowning after his departing back, she returned to the break room, sat at the table and began to cry. Was her past ever going to stay there? Would worms like him bring it up whenever they wanted to control her? Sighing she realized he was right. A big city would give her anonymity. In a large hospital, she would be just another nurse. Maybe she should head for Denver. After a few years, the dust would settle and the charges in Des Moines would be so far in the past that she might be able to move out to a smaller town and settle with her horse at a smaller clinic.

Standing up, she dried her eyes. She had no choice; she couldn't let Dr. Samuelson suffer because he'd been good to her and kept her working even after he discovered her past. If she left now, it wouldn't cause the same scandal as it would if she left after the sheriff spread the gossip. Once she was gone, there would be no gossip because there'd be no victim.

Her feet dragging, she walked out the breakroom door and almost collided with Dr. Samuelson. "George, I'm sorry, but I have to quit. You've been so great and I appreciate everything you've done for me; but I can't stay and cause you both embarrassment and loss of patients. Sorry to leave you in the lurch, but I have to go. I wish all the best for you and I won't expect a letter of reference since I'm not giving proper notice. Thanks again and I'm so sorry." Turning on her heel, she grabbed her purse from her locker and made it out the door before her tears started.

Watching her go, George scratched his head. Totally confused, he walked up to the reception desk. "Barb, what's happening with Kam?"

"I'm not certain, but she had a visit from Sheriff Casey. She seemed upset when she ran past my desk a second ago." Barb noticed the concern and confusion on the face of her boss. "When the sheriff got here, he was grim and when he left, he had an evil look to his face. Kind of smug, self satisfied, and almost happy, all at once." She shuddered, remembering the evil gleam.

"Damn. See if you can reach him. I want to know what's going on." George turned and headed for his desk to call his wife. She would have to go back to work until either Kam returned or he found a replacement.

Hardly able to see through her tears, Kam made it back to the Bailey's rooming house and ran up to her rooms to pack. Throwing clothing in her suitcase and the boxes still stored under her bed, she had all of her things collected in less than an hour. Blowing her nose for the fifth or sixth time, she looked at her watch and noticed it was almost noon. She would miss her lunch date with David, Megan and Aaron. No way would she risk waiting to leave town. She had to do it before she lost her nerve. Taking two trips up and down the stairs out to her truck, she soon had her belongings stowed and was ready to leave. Spotting Idamae, she took the house and room keys from her key ring and handed them to her. "I'm sorry not to give you more notice; but I'm leaving town. I didn't get a chance to clean the rooms, but you know they're not a mess. Thank you for your hospitality. I'll miss both you and your sister. Goodbye." She hugged the surprised old lady before turning back to her truck, starting it and pulling away from the beautiful old Victorian structure.

Tears continued to flow as she headed her truck out to the R-M to collect Lady Mica and her trailer. About three miles out of town, a siren sounded and she saw the whirling lights of a patrol car. Automatically checking her speed, she pulled over and rolled down her window. "How can I help you, officer? I wasn't speeding, was I?"

"Well, I figured when I missed you at the boarding house that you'd be heading to collect that horse of yours.

You need to come with me. David's been shot and he's asking for you." Sheriff Casey pulled open her door and reached into the truck to help her out. Hardly waiting for her to unfasten her seat belt, he pulled her along to his vehicle.

"Wait! My purse." Kam tried to turn back to her truck, but the sheriff kept a tight hold on her arm.

"No time. We have to get there before the ambulance takes him off." Arriving at his cruiser, he pushed her in the back seat and closed the door.

Using her key, Kam remotely locked her truck as the sheriff drove past it. "Where is he?" Her heart racing in fear that David had been so seriously hurt that the sheriff felt they had to break laws to reach him. Then she heard the ominous click as the door beside her locked. Trying to calm herself, she reasoned that all car doors lock once the vehicle begins to move. "Sheriff, where are we going?" Her nerves began to jangle when he still didn't respond.

"Don't you worry Miss, we'll be there soon. He's out at the old H/J ranch house." Bill saw no reason to lie about where they were headed. She didn't have her purse, so she didn't have her phone. He snorted; damn women were so predictable; he smiled.

Chapter Nineteen

While driving back to Riverview, David's mind ran over all the known facts of this case. Caleb Preston was most likely killed by Sheriff Robert Miller, as was Sheriff Tucker. Miller worked for the Cole family while holding the position of Sheriff of Riverview, about 50 or so years taking payments from them for side jobs. Robert Miller passed away several years ago, but Samuel Cole is still alive. Could they tag Cole with running Richard Meadows out of town? Miller was related to Bill Casey, the current Sheriff of Riverview. How much does he know about Robert's extra-circular activities? Is he on the Cole Family payroll? Doing what? Who wants to stop the investigation enough to cause an explosion at the Gorgeview after taking potshots at an FBI agent? Why risk Federal charges?

Half waving at the Riverview patrol car that past him heading east before scratching his head, his thoughts whirling around all the unanswered questions. Must be time to interview the sheriff. Maybe he had talked to the officer manning the western speed trap on Friday. He drove to the sheriff's office only to find that Sheriff Casey was out patrolling. Might even have been him that David had seen on the highway.

"Would you like to leave a message or can I help you?" The young, blonde receptionist pulled a sheet of paper out and pushed it to him on the counter.

"I'll leave my number for him. By the way, who was working the 'highway speed regulation' unit on Friday, out west of town?" David wrote his number and attached a card to the sheet of paper before pushing it toward her.

"Let me see... Friday, hmmm. We had a sick call on Friday so Sheriff Casey was the only person working out of the office." She answered.

"You're certain of that? Friday, three days ago?" He questioned.

"Yeah, the other officer's wife went into labor. She had a lovely girl at 5:35 on Friday afternoon. They were just happy that they made it to the hospital before the storm hit. You want to see the picture he sent me on my iphone?" She offered, finding it and showing it to him.

"Sweet. Thanks for the information. If you speak with the sheriff, just tell him I need to interview him." Looking at all the electronic equipment on her desk, something occurred to him. "Can you tell where he is; maybe I can meet him out on the highway."

"Sure, our cars have GPS locators so we can find and send the closest unit when needed." She looked at a screen and tapped a few keys, shook her head and did the same again. "That's strange; it looks like he's in the middle of the Cole ranch. He's supposed to be watching for speeders out on the highway." Her brow furrowed and she had a cute, confused expression.

"Is there a road to his location, maybe I'll head that way?"

Tapping more keys, she brought up a map showing not only the location of the cruiser; but the road it was traversing. "Looks like it's the old road to the abandoned H/J ranch. Wonder what he's doing heading that direction? Maybe I can reach him on the radio, but coverage is kind of sporadic in those hills."

"No, don't bother; and that's an order from the FBI. My partner and I will head that direction. Give me the GPS co-ordinates for both his location and the ranch house."

David waited impatiently as she wrote down the information. "There's a specific reason why I don't want you to try and reach him. I'll know if you do and charges will be filed." With that, David turned and walked quickly out to his car where he called Jason to meet him at the Diner since the 3CS was east of town and Megan's place was west. Sitting at the counter in the Diner, he'd just ordered his coffee when Jason arrived.

"Hey, doesn't Kam have a Chevy Silverado, kind of a light blue or blue/gray?" Jason asked, sitting down.

"From what I remember, I think she does. I know it's a Silverado, but color I'm not certain about since I've only ever seen it once."

"Well, there's one sitting on the side of the highway about three miles from town. I stopped, looked inside and there's a purse on the seat with bags packed in the back. No sign of engine trouble or a flat. Wonder if it's hers, where would she go without her purse?" Jason scratched his head and took a sip of his coffee. "Was she planning a trip?"

"Not that I know of. She's due here for a lunch meeting in about an hour. Let me call her." David frowned, dialing her cell. Then he tried dialing the clinic from the card Dr. Samuelson had given him. "Hi, this is Agent Harrison. I need to speak to nurse Kam Marjani please. Official business." He listened to the response. "What do you mean she's no longer with the clinic? When did this happen?" He demanded. "Let me speak with the doctor." He looked over at Jason while the receptionist put him through to the doctor. "According to the receptionist, Kam quit her job this morning." A voice could be heard on his phone so he turned his attention back to the conversation. "Dr. Samuelson, what's this I hear about Kam quitting? What happened?"

"Well, David, we don't really know. The sheriff stopped by here and had a private conversation with her and ten minutes later, she had quit and left the clinic. I tried to find out what had upset her so, but she just clammed up and walked out the door. Damnedest thing I ever had happen."

"Shit! If you see Sheriff Casey before I do, stall him and call me. I think he's at the bottom of everything. Kam's truck is sitting on the highway with her purse and she's missing." He hung up the phone and turned to Jason. "Son of a bitch! I knew the other day that the sheriff was hiding something. We're out of here. Come on!" Grabbing Jason's wrist, he pulled the man from the counter and started out the door. Jason managed to throw a five on the counter for their coffees.

Slamming the door on his Durango did nothing to alleviate any of David's fears, but the sound made him feel better. Jason closed his door more gently and barely managed to get his seat belt fastened when his partner slammed the vehicle in reverse before standing on the gas and spinning gravel into the air as he turned East on the highway.

"Easy there. Do you know where you're headed?" Jason watched David and the speedometer.

"I programmed the navigation system while I waited for you. Start the damn thing; would you?" David scowled at the slow moving pick up that dared to be ahead of him on the highway. Waiting for a clear view, he gunned the Durango so heavy it "walked" around the truck.

"Crap! You just passed on a double yellow. *Are you crazy?*" Jason glared at his partner.

"Kam may be in trouble. I could see that I had room. Just hang on." David listened for the Nav system to give directions, as he watched his speedometer climb.

****

While the sheriff's patrol cruiser bounced along the washboard dirt road, Kam couldn't help but wonder what David had been doing out here. In addition, she noticed the road didn't look like any vehicle had traveled it for years. "What happened exactly?" she questioned. The silence lengthened, so she asked again, more loudly. "Sheriff, what exactly happened and what was David doing out here? Was Jason with him?" Moving to get a view of the sheriff's face in the rearview mirror, she realized from his expression that he had no intention of talking and was enjoying her increasing fear. It began to dawn on her that maybe she needed to be plotting on a way to escape rather than worrying about David. "We're not going to rescue or see David, are we? He's not shot, is he?" She questioned while watching the mirrored face of the man driving her toward an abandoned ranch.

"Well, you do catch on. A little too slow to save yourself, but I'll give you credit for figuring it out before we can see the ranch." He smiled an evil smile into the rearview mirror. "I have some questions for you. Answer them and you won't feel a thing. Refuse and you'll beg me to end your pain before we're through."

Knowing that he intended to kill her either way, Kam kept her mouth shut and began trying to figure how she was going to get away from this car once it stopped. She might have a chance when he opened the car door. If she hit it hard enough to knock him over, she might have ten to fifteen seconds to run. She'd read once that a pistol isn't very accurate unless the shooter is very skilled. Many shooters only thought they were skilled with a pistol. She had no other choice. She knew David wouldn't miss her until she didn't show up at the one o'clock meeting at the diner. He'd never figure out where she was in time to rescue her, she was on her own. Shit.

"Let's get started. I saw the four of you pouring over stuff at the motel. How many others saw the evidence that puts my great uncle at the scene of Caleb Preston's murder? Did the body hold any sign of what happened?" He watched her, willing her to answer his question, his face turning red with anger at her silence.

Debating on lying or just keeping quiet, she had no illusions about his intentions; he was going to kill her. Maybe she could keep him off guard if she seemed to cooperate. Hmmm. "Well besides us, the evidence was seen by Jason and the body is at the FBI lab in Denver. Everyone knows about it and the results should be done by next week."

You're lying to me, bitch. I know Jason didn't get there until after the explosion. I saw him drive into town, then followed him out to Phil's ranch. For that lie, you're gonna suffer and I'm going to enjoy that luscious body. Don't lie again. How many people saw that evidence?" He scowled at her reflection in the mirror.

"Sorry, I forgot. You're right. Jason did meet us at the ranch." Kam quickly tried to regroup. Knowing that she could endanger anyone she named, but wanting to make him think the evidence was seen by others, she thought about her next lie more carefully. "Lots of people saw the evidence. There were two agents that flew food in to the cabin; they saw everything. I don't know their names but they work in the Denver office." She hoped he would believe this lie since there was no way he could know how blatant it was.

The washed out road took all of his attention for a few moments, the steering wheel jumping in his pudgy fingers from the potholes. Topping a low ridge, he could see the old homestead below them, now he just had to make it down there. Navigating the half-washed out road took his attention away from asking more questions. In some spots, half the road was gone, falling away into the valley. The cruiser crawled, hugging the uphill side as it worked its way down the zigzag track. "I don't believe you, but we'll get this sorted out once I get you in the house. Nothing like pain to clear your memory and bring back details," he snickered.

Looking down at the overgrown abandoned ranch, Kam noted the brush and trees that had grown close during the 80 years the ranch had been empty. Cover, she just might be able to get away with that kind of cover. It wasn't dense… nothing in this arid land grew dense, but some of the brush looked to be over her head and the trees would give more solid cover. They were planted at intervals around the house, shading it and protecting it from harsh weather. All she needed to do was get one between her and the sheriff and she might have a chance. Her spirits began to climb as she prayed she could move fast enough to get beyond his reach. While the cruiser crawled, she plotted a path away from the house. If she could make the valley she saw just beyond it, she might have a chance to evade him long enough for help to arrive. Maybe someone would see her truck abandoned along the highway. Then she fought the despair of knowing that it would take a miracle for David or anyone to know the sheriff had kidnapped her and more of a miracle for him to know where the man was taking her. Still, buying time would keep her alive and she wasn't going to give up hope. "You know, if you turn me loose now, you're only in for kidnapping and shooting at a federal agent. It was you who shot at us on the hillside, wasn't it?" Kam hoped to keep him talking about his exploits would keep him distracted from questioning her.

"Should have managed to kill you both up there. That damned rifle hadn't been sighted in for years." He snorted in disgust. "Everything would have been so much simpler. But, I only managed to wing the fed and then you shot me and it began to snow. I owe you for that too. Yeah, you're going to pay; bitch." He sneered, remembering his intention of hurting her for having the nerve to shoot him.

"How did you get Coup saddled and off the ranch without being seen?" Playing to his vanity, she kept her voice even and managed to sound amazed at his feat.

"All the hands were off working; I just walked up and grabbed him. Once I got him out of the barn, I kept the barn between the house and me until we made it to the tree line. Piece of cake" He boasted.

"Wow that was so clever to take the horse who knew the trail." Again, she kept her voice mild and avoided the sarcasm that welled up. "You even managed to avoid the construction crew. All they could say was that they saw 'a rider', but not able to say if it was a man or woman. Clever"

"If it weren't for that damn storm, you never would have gotten out of that cabin and all rest of this wouldn't have happened." He pulled the cruiser next to the dilapidated structure, parked and turned it off before looking at her. "Now, here we are. Are you ready? You and I are going to have fun, at least I will." His smile turned evil when he saw the fear in her eyes. Yeah, this was going to be fun; even if she never told him anything. He chuckled.

With the sound of his chuckle turning her blood cold and knowing she was in deep shit, Kam struggled to not fall apart. Thankful that the man appeared more flab and gut than muscle, she prayed that she could outrun him.

A bullet in the back was preferable to having him touch her in any fashion.

She quietly gathered herself while he left the vehicle, walked to the passenger side, and put his hand on the door handle. One hand rested on his holstered gun, but he didn't take it out or unsnap the leather keeper. Listening carefully until she heard the click of the door latch; she launched herself into the door, shoulder first. She barely glimpsed the surprise on the sheriffs' face as the door pushed him off balance before he disappeared from sight. Hearing him land on his ass with a grunt, she was on her feet and running for the line of trees.

"Get your ass back here, you bitch!"

Running, Kam didn't look back; three more strides and she'd be out of the open driveway and into the trees and brush. She heard the shot and felt the bullet hit at the same time. The pain blinded her, but didn't stop her. Breathing hurt and each step was excruciating but knowing her life was on the line she kept running, swallowing the pain. A second shot zipped past her head. Great, he was no longer looking to slow her but to kill her. Blood seemed to pour from the exit wound on her right side. Hoping the bullet had done no major damage, she applied pressure to the wound with her arm as she ran. The first tree loomed in front of her and she thankfully ducked around it, putting it between her and her assailant.

Cussing, Sheriff Casey began to run after the wounded woman. Knowing that he'd hit her by the blood he could see on her shirt, he only had to follow her; she wouldn't be able to run for long. He just hated having to chase her, damn bitch. She better be alive when he found her; he'd make her sorry for running. He smiled evilly at the thought of his revenge, yeah he'd kill her but not until he heard her scream. He thought about how long he would keep her alive before he gave in to her pleas and let her die. The more she made him run, the longer he would hurt her. His brain plotted special ways to make her scream while he followed her blood trail. Tracking caused him to slow but he'd been slowing anyway; guess he'd had one too many burgers at the Burger Barn lately.

Knowing that trying to double back to the cruiser would put her in plain view of the sheriff, Kam continued through the brush. She recalled the sound of crossing a short bridge before they had topped the hill that looked down on the ranch. She prayed she could make it all the way to the highway, but didn't think she would be able to continue that far. Weakened by the blood loss, she kept moving at a steady pace. Thanking God every step for her time spent both riding and on her feet at work that gave her enough energy to continue. Behind she could hear the heavier man scrambling through the brush. His pace sounded slower than hers, thank God. Time seemed to go on forever. One foot ahead of the other, around this boulder, that tree, she kept moving, listening, and praying.

Swearing, Sheriff Casey realized he hadn't seen any blood for several yards. He retraced his steps to the last blood, scanned the area and found a footprint leading to the right of where he had been, around a large boulder. He followed it, paused and listened for sounds of her breathing or moans of pain. She had to be hurting. Gunshot wounds hurt, didn't they? He'd never been shot but all the movies showed people dropping when shot. Why didn't she? How could she be so quiet? Maybe he'd find her, dead from loss of blood, just around the next tree or boulder.

Pausing for breath and to listen, Kam saw ahead where the creek in the wash went into a culvert and under the road to the ranch. In the distance, she thought she heard the sound of a car. She moved forward again, with more hope than she'd had. If it was the highway, help was close enough to hear; all she had to do was avoid flying bullets and keep moving.

The sounds of a struggling, winded, Sheriff Casey were behind her; he had yet to see the culvert or road. He wouldn't know she had gotten her second wind and was traveling faster. He might not even hear the approaching car over the sounds of his own breathing.

Climbing up to the dirt road, she looked over her shoulder but Casey wasn't in sight. The sound of a car seemed closer; she decided to risk being seen and stay on the road. The lack of cover could be fatal, but she hoped Casey's aim would be off due to his heavy breathing and exhaustion. If Casey caught her, he'd kill her; but shooting her on the run would be almost impossible after running and scrambling through the brush as far as they'd come. Bent double in pain, Kam began what she thought was a jog, but was more of a stagger, down the dusty road toward the highway, thankful again for years of distance training.

Breaking clear of the brush, Sheriff Casey saw the culvert and caught a glimpse of his quarry, bent double, and staggering down the dirt road. All he had to do was get up there and she'd be an easy shot. He smiled through his panting then cussed the stubborn woman for being able to climb up to the road. With the last of his strength, he climbed up the small embankment, his feet slipping in the loose dirt around the boulders. Making it to the road, he collapsed onto a handy boulder to regain his breath. His heart pounded at an alarming rate, he cussed the fact he had let his physical condition get this bad. Then he heard it: an approaching vehicle. More quickly than he thought he could, he began to jog after Kam. He had to catch her before the car saw her; he had to shut her up.

Keeping up as fast a pace as she could, Kam finally

got a view of the oncoming vehicle. David, Thank God. Tears flowed down her dirty, bloody cheeks in relief as the SUV approached. Moving became more difficult, but Kam kept putting one foot ahead of the other, she heard the cussing of the sheriff behind her. She needed to warn David that Casey shot her and still had his gun. "David! Sheriff Casey shot me!" Crying now because her voice was only a whisper and David couldn't hear, she approached him as he jumped from his SUV and ran toward her.

Beyond sense or sanity, Casey stopped and raised his gun at Kam's head. He couldn't let her live for what she'd done to him. First she shot him then she'd run from him, bitch didn't deserve to live. Using his left arm to stabilize his right he sighted on her, his finger tightened and he pulled the trigger over and over.

Without any hesitation, Jason yelled "FBI!" before firing repeatedly at the man shooting at his partner and Kam.

David lunged at Kam when he saw the sheriff bring up his gun. The first bullet zinged past them as he tackled her to the ground, trying to reach his own gun. Then he heard shots from Jason to counter those from the sheriff before the sound of the heavy man falling over in the dirt. He heard the sound of Jason running toward the sheriff. "Did you kill the bastard?" He asked, moving from his protective position over Kam and pulling her gently into his arms.

"Unfortunately, no. He'll spend some time in the hospital, but from what I can tell, he should live. Damn it." Kicking the gun away from the fallen man, Jason pulled the sheriff's arms behind his back, smiling when the man screeched in pain. "I got him in one arm and the torso, but not the chest. I think his arm's broken." Still grinning, he pulled his prisoner to his feet. "How's she doing?"

Holding the unconscious woman in his arms, David looked up at his partner. "She's lost a lot of blood. Call this in and get a chopper out here. Tell them we have two patients, but she goes first. As far as I'm concerned that asshole can bleed to death."

Jason reached for his cell, found no reception and headed up the hill at a trot until he had three bars showing. Dialing 911, he explained their location and the situation. Once finished, he worked his way down the hill to the scene below. By now the sheriff had managed to stumble to the SUV and was leaning, and bleeding, against the passenger door on the driver's side.

Controlling his anger, David opened the back of the Durango and placed Kam inside so he could use the first aid kit he carried to work on her wound. At this moment, he could have gladly shot the fat man for what he'd done to his woman. Instead, he gently rolled her to her left side, moved her shirt up, and exposed the entrance and exit wounds on her right side; glad she was unconscious so his actions caused no pain.

"Damn, that looks nasty." Jason commented, seeing the wounds over David's shoulder as he walked up.

"Yeah, she won't be riding for a while; but unless she's bled too much or had an organ hit, she should live." David said a prayer that all he was seeing was blood and not organs or intestines. It only smelled like blood. Taking two large gauze pads from the kit, he used the ace bandage to hold one in place on the front and one in place on her back while applying pressure to reduce the bleeding. He checked her pulse, heartened by the fact that it seemed stronger, but worried it seemed faster.

"Hey, I'm bleeding over here and I can't feel my arm below the bullet hole. One of you yahoos want to work on me?" Sheriff Casey asked the wrong question.

"Until we get Kam taken care of, you better keep your mouth shut. It wouldn't take much for me to turn you over, put one in your back and claim you tried to escape… don't even tempt me." Jason glared at their prisoner who suddenly quieted.

In the distance, David heard the sound of at least one helicopter. Thank God. Off in the distance, he could hear sirens, as the Highway Patrol and possibly the second cruiser from Riverview headed toward the crime scene. Suddenly, his knees became too weak to hold him and he sat on the bumper next to where Kam lay.

With pain surrounding and beating through her body, Kam struggled to open her eyes. "David, Sheriff Casey shot me." Her voice croaked, causing David to bend over her.

"Shhh, it's okay, Honey. We've got him. You just don't move. Rest. The chopper is almost here." He rubbed her arm gently, feeling the need to touch and comfort her.

Looking up he spotted the helicopter as it landed on the top of the hill. Two paramedics jumped out, one carrying the rescue stretcher while the other had the medical kit. The men scrambled quickly down the hill. Seeing the sheriff, they approached him, but Jason pointed toward the back of the vehicle. "This yahoo can wait; the woman in the back is in worse shape."

One paramedic stayed with the sheriff while the man with the med kit walked to the back of the vehicle to attend Kam. Within minutes a second chopper arrived, the first paramedics loaded Kam into their helicopter; allowing David in the chopper only because of his FBI status. As it lifted off, David saw the other paramedics tending to the sheriff. There were two different law enforcement vehicles pulling in behind his SUV.

Chapter Twenty

Steady beeping sounded around her, aching in her side, something nasty across her nose and her left hand couldn't move, Kam moaned. Struggling again to bring her hand to her nose, but someone pressed it back down.

"Easy, you've got to quit trying to remove the oxygen from your nose, honey." David gently held Kam's hand to the bed and brushed a curl from her face. "Kam, honey, do you know where you are? You're safe. I'm here with you." His voice went from firm to get her attention to soft as he tried to reassure her.

Laying there in the sterile bed, Kam forced her eyes to open. She shifted them around the room; taking in David, hanging bags and beeping monitors. "Hospital." She squeezed David's hand where it held hers. "Intensive care?" She asked.

"No, surgical recovery room. As soon as you're awake, they will take you down to a private room." Again, he reassured her. "You're going to be just fine; but you lost a lot of blood and nicked your small intestines. You were in surgery almost two hours. Just rest, sweetheart, you need it. I'll contact your family." David walked to the station to let the nurses know she was awake and mostly coherent.

Kam dozed, in and out of a dream that included David, her brother and the spirits of her mother and grandmother. The fabric of time seemed to thin and she dreamt of her childhood, then of her nursing school, then of the ride back to the skeleton and suddenly all seemed to combine into a nightmare that woke her with a moan.

Trying to sit up, she gazed around the darkened room. She looked and her left arm was still attached to tubes and IV bags but at least the nasty oxygen tube was gone from her nose. In the shadows, she saw the outline of someone sleeping in the padded chair with a hospital blanket over him. David. She smiled, lay back and let sleep claim her again; secure with his presence and knowing her nightmare wouldn't return.

Noise filtering in from the hall brought David awake with a start. His eyes flew to the bed where he found Kam safely sleeping. He pushed off the blanket the nurses had given him and stood up, quietly moving across the room to the attached bathroom. He washed his face and hands with cold water before returning to check on her. Unable to resist picking up her pale, fragile looking hand; his soft touch woke her. "Hey gorgeous. How are you feeling?"

Focusing on David wasn't easy, but Kam forced her mind to deal with the background sounds, the light pain in her side, and the man standing beside her. "I feel like I've been shot. How long have I been out?"

"Well, you were shot, spent almost two hours in surgery, and have been sleeping under the drugs for almost a whole 24hrs. Welcome back to the land of the living." He smiled down at her before pulling the chair close to the bed and sitting down, once more taking her good hand. "By the way, I called the contact numbers we retrieved from your purse. I've kept your brother up to date and he thinks he can take some time off from college. He'll be here soon and is willing to take care of you until you're stronger." Pausing he watched her face, encouraged by her frown he continued. "I mentioned to him that you could use my place to recover in Denver. I'd be willing to take care of you until you can take care of yourself. That way he wouldn't lose a whole semester of school."

Kam felt her face flush at his offer. "Did he say anything to that?"

Looking down, David mumbled something Kam didn't catch.

"What? Don't mumble. What did he say?" Kam pressed, knowing full well what her brother was very likely to say.

Lifting his head, David once more looked her in the eyes, sighed and answered her question. "He wanted to know a few things. About my family, job, career, and when we were planning the wedding." His face turned as red as his heritage allowed and Kam laughed at his expression but it turned to a grimace at the pain using those muscles caused.

"Well, the wedding part doesn't count; we haven't gotten that far yet. Was he pleased with your background and other answers?" She teased.

"I gave him my family's contact information so he could check me out to set his mind at ease. I told him no wedding contract had been negotiated but my family had many horses to trade." He laughed at her expression. "If you have any older male relatives, one should contact my grandfather to negotiate something." He teased her back, referring to his culture's tradition of the groom paying the family of the bride for her release into his care.

"I'll bet that got him going!" Kam grabbed her side as her laugh turned to a cough at the thought of the conversation between her brother and David.

"Easy, honey. I didn't mean to get you laughing so hard. Actually, your brother seems very nice. I did mean what I said about you moving in to convalesce; both you and your brother. I have a three bedroom place with lots of room, and you'd be close to Denver for any physical therapy or medical attention you need." He tried to make the argument so logical that Kam would sound silly if she refused. "My cousin is about a fifty miles outside of Denver and he can keep Lady Mica for you until you're strong enough to move back on your own." If he had his way, she wouldn't want to move out.

Watching his face Kam squeezed his hand to get his attention so she could talk. "Okay, okay. If my brother hasn't made plans, we'll move in with you until I'm stronger. I can't stay here in the hospital, costs too much and there are so many things you can catch." She found her voice was failing along with her strength. "Could you hold the water so I can get a sip; then I'm going back to sleep, I can hardly focus. Pain meds are a bitch but I don't feel much pain." Her voice trailed off as David put the straw to her lips.

He watched her take a long drink of the water, put the glass back on her table, and returned to sitting beside the bed holding her hand.

Kirabo Otieno **Marjani** entered the room quietly. His name meaning "gift of the night" described his stealth to perfection. At 19, he was slender to the point of painfully thin, but his wide shoulders showed the promise of filling out as he matured. His wide set eyes took in the sight of his sister laying in the hospital bed, with an IV and a single monitor connected to her fragile arm while her other hand was encompassed by the large hand of the man seated next to her. In silence, he observed David watching over his sister, concern and affection plainly shown on his face. He watched when David gave Kam's hand a gentle squeeze and the fingers in his grasp fluttered in response. He smiled at the wordless communication evident between them. The man was Native American; that was evident from his appearance, if not from his name. This must be Agent David Harrison, FBI, who called him yesterday with the news of Kam's injury. From his tone, he had known David cared, but he was immensely pleased to discover his sister cared too. Maybe the plan David proposed wasn't so impossible after all. It would save funds, and would give the couple a chance to realize and acknowledge the feelings he saw so plainly. "Excuse me, Agent Harrison; I'm Kirabo **Marjani**, Kam's brother." He stepped further into the room and extended his hand to the man.

"Kirabo, I didn't expect you for another few hours. I was going to arrange for someone to collect you at the airport." Looking confused, David consulted his watch.

"Well, I managed to con my way onto an earlier flight and rented a car. Thanks anyway." He smiled at David's consternation. "We'll be needing transportation while Kam recovers and her pick-up just won't work." He explained further. "I wanted to tell you, unless my sister has other plans, we'll take you up on your offer."

"Those were Kam's words exactly." Releasing Kam's hand he moved over to where Kirabo stood then led him out of the room so they could talk. "The doctors think she's out of the woods, but they want to monitor for any infection caused by the nicked intestine. Her blood loss might just have helped her there, washing out the cavity as she bled. They've given her whole blood, plasma, and are dripping saline to help her recover the lost fluids. She's also on morphine, which makes her loopy and drowsy. Sleeping through the recovery is a good idea for now. For the most part, she's been quiet once she realized she was hooked up."

"Well, I can take over holding her hand if you would like to find a bath and some sleep. You look worn out." Kirabo patted his arm. He wanted the man to know that he accepted David's involvement in his sister's life.

"To be honest, I haven't left here since we brought

her in." Looking down at his scrubs, he frowned. The nurses had kindly provided them so he could shed his blood soaked clothing. "I could use a shower and some sleep. Here comes Diane, the day nurse for this room. If you need anything there's a button next to Kam, press it and Diane will come to help." He smiled at the approaching nurse who carried a fresh IV bag. "Diane, this is Kirabo Marjani, Kam's brother. He's taking over while I go get cleaned up." David made the introductions.

"Nice to meet you, I'm certain you've been giving my sister the best of care." Kirabo shook the free hand of the older woman.

"I'm glad Kam has a second person to sit with her. He keeps sending nurses and visitors away. One more hour and we would need to roll a second bed into the room when he collapsed." Diane smiled at Kirabo while rolling her eyes at David.

"Okay, okay, I'm out of here. I'll be back in a few hours. I need to know what hotel has a good rep and where's the nearest Wal-Mart." He asked thinking about his burnt suitcase from the Gorgeview with a sigh. Jason had brought his Durango to Gunnison and given him the keys, so transportation wasn't a problem. But he needed clothes and a place to sleep.

"There's a Wal-Mart about half a mile up Main St. on your right as you go north, then the Comfort Inn entrance is across the street from the Wal-Mart parking lot." Diane offered.

"Thanks Diane. Want me to make a reservation for you Kirabo?" David offered, knowing they would be in town until the doctors released Kam.

"I'd appreciate that. If needed, have them call me and I'll give them my credit card data. Just a single queen bed is fine for me. Any student discount would be appreciated." He smiled and waved David on his way. "I'll tell Kam that you'll be back soon."

Pulling out his cell phone before he got to the elevator, David dialed Jason. "Hey partner, what's the status on our case against Sheriff Casey and Cole? Did the sheriff survive?"

"He spent almost four hours in surgery, but they think he'll make it. He's been awake enough to give a statement… not all of which is coherent, but it does tell us more than we knew." Jason proceeded to tell David what Casey had said and what investigating officers had found at his home and in his car. "Seems like our boy kept the tin evidence box from the motel, that's why you didn't find it. Guess he wanted a trophy. The tin was under the passenger seat of his cruiser." David smiled at this revelation. They would need that evidence to convict Cole of coercion. "At his house were a journal written by old Sheriff Robert Miller, detailing all of his 'side jobs' for the 3CS over the years; and a wealth of photos of Casey and Miller from the time he was a kid. It explains why he was willing to kill to protect the memory of the man who raised him, but really, this guy is a nut job." Jason wondered how the man ever got elected. "How's Kam doing? Will she be okay?"

"Kam pulled through surgery well, she's been sleeping but when she wakes she seems coherent. Her brother just got here." David said.

"Seems we were the only ones who didn't know that Casey and Miller were related. Damn small towns." Jason huffed in exasperation as he continued his part of the story. "All the data has been turned over to the Gunnison County District Attorney, and Samuel Cole has been arrested on charges of coercion. The federal DA has been given the information about Casey's actions, and since some of the action occurred on federal lands they are working up charges as I speak. Likely, the county DA will get involved in the arson at Megan's place and the Gorgeview. Looks like the man won't be turned loose for quite a while. You and Kam are needed to give statements to both DA's, when Kam is up to it." Looking out the window of his government issued sedan he continued. "I'm heading back to Denver, when can I expect to see your grimy face?"

"I'm here until Kam is released. She and her brother will move in to my place while she convalesces. Wipe that smirk off your mug, Jason. They need a place until Kam can handle living alone again. My cousin is heading out to the R-M to collect her horse, truck and trailer. We're just being neighborly." He listened to the rude comment made by Jason after the hoot of laughter. "Keep a civil tongue in your mouth. You're talking about someone I like." Like was a mild word for his current feelings. "Hey, I just pulled up at Wal-Mart so I'll talk to you later. I've cleared with the boss taking a week off. Since I worked my three day weekend he approved the time off." David made his goodbyes and returned his phone to his pocket as he left the car and headed into the store to get some clothes.

Meanwhile, Kirabo sat at Kam's side, holding her hand while she slept. Almost asleep, he started when the door to the room opened and a couple entered. Wearing a cowboy hat, the man was tall and broad shouldered with a neat curly beard. The woman was shorter, but still tall and carried herself gracefully but with a tense athleticism that belied her soft smile. The man set down the suitcase in his hands and smiled before extending his hand.

"You must be Kam's brother, the resemblance is there, but her hairs' curly. I'm Aaron Grant and this is Megan Holloway. We're friends with your sister, her truck, trailer and horse are at the R-M where I work." He watched the slender man rise and walk over, shaking his extended hand.

"I'm Kirabo Marjani. Friends of my sister are family members to me. Welcome and thank you for seeing to her possessions." He stepped back and watched the couple. The man was flustered and the woman amused at her companion's confusion.

"Thanks, you're too kind. I only wish that I'd been with her when the Sheriff kidnapped her on the highway. It pisses me off that Jason shot the rat bastard before I got to him." Megan said.

Kirabo took a better look at the woman. It wasn't often that he heard such threats of violence from a woman. "I'm sorry that you weren't allowed the chance to protect my sister." His assessment of Megan changed as he watched the expressions cross her face. This was a woman fierce in her passions and loyal to those around her. He took Megan's hand and held it between his own, his eyes clouding for a few seconds before continuing. "You should seek work in law or law enforcement. Your nature is that of a warrior and protector of the innocent." His eyes cleared and he smiled again at Megan.

Disconcerted by Kirabo's words and actions, Megan found her instinct to step closer to Aaron irresistible. His arm went around her waist, settling her sudden nerves. "What an interesting comment." Was all she could think to reply.

"We brought her suitcase, but the rest of her things are still loaded in her truck. We put the truck in one of the barns." Aaron explained.

"I'm certain Kam will appreciate having clean clothes when she leaves and clean sleepwear as soon as they let her dress in anything other than the hospital gown." Smiling, he waved the couple next to the bed, moving his chair out of their way. "She's in and out of sleep, but she can hear you if you speak to her."

Megan approached the bed cautiously, worried about her friend. With Aaron by her side, she took Kam's exposed hand. "Hi Kam. We were so shocked when the news came in that Casey kidnapped you. Then we heard he shot you. I'm glad you're going to be okay. I know it hurts like a bitch, but keep your chin up and work to get out of here. We miss you." She turned to Kam's brother who smiled and nodded at what she said.

"Yeah doll, you know if Megan's not happy, I'm not happy. So get well soon and make my woman smile, will ya?" Aaron kept his arm around Megan as his deep voice filled the room.

Kam's eyes opened. "I thought I'd never see you guys again. I'm glad you came in together. That's nice." She said while her eyes closed and a smile touched her mouth. A noise in the back of the room brought her eyes back open. "Bethany, Roger, looks like everyone is here except David. Where's he?" Kam frowned.

"I sent him to get some rest and food. He's been with you non-stop since you were shot." Kirabo stepped into view from behind Megan and Aaron.

"Kir! I dreamt I heard your voice. How long have you been here?"

Kam's smile of recognition warmed her brother as nothing else had done. While his sister had been fading in and out of sleep, this was the first moment that she acknowledged his presence. "Only a few hours, honey. I haven't even seen your doctor yet. I told David that we would take him up on his offer once they let you out of here." He patted Kam's foot, needing to touch his sister and feel the life in her. Behind him, he listened to the greetings exchanged with the latest arrivals.

"Kirabo Marjani, I'd like you to meet two more of

Kam's friends. This is Bethany and Roger Meadows. They own the R-M Ranch where Lady Mica is boarded and Kam's truck and trailer are located. Roger, Bethany, this is Kam's brother Kirabo." Aaron made the formal introductions then stood back and watched the man hug each of his employers, chuckling at their surprised looks.

"Thank you so much for the kindness you've shown my sister. Perhaps we should all step out of the room and you can tell me exactly how this all happened." His smile didn't slip, but a tone in his voice added steel to the quiet request.

"Yes sir. We'll be back in a while Kam. You just rest." Bethany smiled at her friend before the group opened the door and moved out to the hallway. "Well, I'm not certain where to start and we don't have all the details of what happened after Casey kidnapped her; but this is what we know and have learned." Bethany took over telling the tale of the skeleton along the trail, the blizzard, the theft of her horse and attack on Kam, their night in the woods and rescue the following day. "Are you with me so far?" She had taken Kirabo's hand as she spoke, knowing that parts of the story would be upsetting. Seeing the expression in Kirabo's eyes looked strong and still curious, Bethany looked at Megan. "Why don't you take it from here, you saw quite a bit of it."

"Well, once David had been treated by Dr. Samuelson for his gunshot wound, Kam nursed him through the night and Aaron and I were called in the next day." Taking a deep breath, she continued with how the group was examining the evidence when Casey dropped by to ask questions. When they broke for lunch, the hotel was bombed and burned, with all the evidence still out on the table. They adjourned to Megan's ranch where they continued to work on the case. Kam went home because she had to work the next day. "This is where we need Kam to fill in details. The last thing that we spoke of Sunday evening was that we would all meet at one for lunch at Betty's Diner on Monday. None of us knows what happened, why Kam was driving west out of town with all her stuff when the Sheriff managed to grab her. Was she leaving town?"

"I think I can fill in that information." A firm voice behind them offered.

The group turned as one to face the newcomers. Dr. George Samuelson walked up with David at his side. "Found him downstairs in the gift shop looking lost, figured he needed to be up here with Kam." He said before he began the part of the story he had deduced from Kam's actions. "I think that Casey convinced Kam that her presence in my clinic would damage the business. While she and I had discussed her situation completely, he still managed to coerce her into quitting and leaving town. I think he just wanted to get her alone so he could find out what you knew and silence her."

"Well, that explains the truck and belongings." David put in. He went on to explain the final situation to Kirabo. "Kam and I still need to give statements, but Sheriff Casey has been charged and is currently downstairs in a secure room. A psychologist will evaluate him. We know he's out of touch with reality but we need to know if he was aware of the crimes he committed. All in the name of saving the memory of Sheriff Robert Miller. Really doesn't make sense, but nut jobs don't need to make sense – they're nut jobs." He sighed.

"Well thank you all for the information. Now, where's her doctor? We need to find out when we can take her home to your house, David." Kirabo looked around as though he expected the doctor to be standing behind one of the group facing him.

Epilogue:

Denver, Colorado – 3 weeks later

David's home had never been so lively. Laughter bubbled, conversations flowed, and the sound of champagne corks added punctuation. Everyone was there. Bethany, Roger, Megan, Aaron, Kirabo, Kam, his partner Jason, even John Hendrix who took over the H/J.

Today had been the first and last day of testimony in the U. S. vs. William Casey. Indicted for kidnapping, assault on a federal agent, and obstruction of justice; he'd sat doodling while David and Kam testified to his involvement in the crimes. Without a single witness or person able to deny the charges, the closing arguments were heard only two hours after the opening arguments. The group understood the verdicts should be rendered quickly, tomorrow at the latest.

Once the federal court was completed and sentencing handed down; then it would be the state's turn. Arson, coercion, obstruction of justice and attempted murder charges were pending on that level. Yeah, the man wouldn't see the outside world for a long time except through prison bars.

Arrested for his part in the coercion of Richard Meadows back in 1983, Samuel Cole suffered a massive stroke within hours his arrest. His sudden death unfortunately saddened very few, since his behavior over the years had alienated most of Riverview. His daughter, Angelica, and her mother Jessica inherited the 3CS as his only surviving relations. Fate works in strange ways. Tucker blood would control the massive 3CS Ranch.

The Hendrix family negotiated with Angelica and she conceded the property without any fuss. The original H/J belonged to John Hendrix who began working on restoring the old farmhouse and barns. Hendrix and Cole would be neighbors without any animosity or guilt for crimes committed in the past. 3CS hands were even helping with the reconstruction at Angelicas suggestion.

Standing, David surveyed the group in his living room. His eyes returned to Kam. With her brother leaving tomorrow, she consented to remain with him and find a new job in Denver while they looked to purchase a home with a few acres to move Lady Mica closer. Life was good.

"Friends, let's toast our victories. Today we've seen some justice for the deaths of Robert Tucker and Caleb Preston. May they both rest in peace now that their story is known." David raised his glass in silence to the memory of the men that brought all these people together. "Each of you played a part in solving the mystery. Without you, it might never have been revealed; thank you for your persistence and courage." He looked at Bethany, Megan, and Kam in that order. His eyes not leaving Kam he continued. "I'm grateful that I was able to meet all of you and become part of your lives. It's an honor I hope to deserve." Again, he silently raised his glass with the group.

"Don't spread it too thick, David. We all realize you mean Kam." Jason called from the back of the group, drawing laugher and smiles while David felt his face flush.

"Okay, okay, I'll admit the best thing about this case was meeting Kam. But the rest of you were integral in solving the crimes and have become friends along the way too." He argued. "But I still think that naming the trail the Skeleton Trail Loop was the only reason Bethany made the discovery." David teased Bethany who had the grace to blush to the hoots and laughter from the group as David took his seat.

"Well, sooner or later, someone in the woods would have discovered him; but I'm just happy it was us. I only wish it hadn't been so painful." She rubbed her butt to the polite laughter of her friends.

Waiting for the laugher to die, Megan stood to face her boss. Aaron sat behind her and watched fondly. "I have an announcement to make. I hope to have all of your support, but I've decided to run for the position of Sheriff in Riverview. I've decided that law enforcement is what I want to do with my life. Sorry boss." She watched her words sink in to the group before everyone began to clap. Roger and Bethany were the first to stand, followed by Aaron, Kirabo, Kam and the others.

"That's a great idea! I'll recommend you to the council to take over until the election." Roger offered.

Her heart overflowed with the support of her friends, Megan wiped happy tears from her face. "Thanks, I'd love that. You guys are great. I've even found a property. The State is putting Casey's 10 acre property up for auction. I plan on being the successful bidder." She sat down next to Aaron and felt his arm surround her waist.

"It's about time you decided what to do with your life. I'm proud of you." He whispered in her ear.

Around the room conversations flowed again, while the group discussed Megan's idea and the upcoming changes in Riverview.

Who would have guessed that a descendant of Sheriff Tucker, murdered by order of the original Samuel Cole, would someday own the 3CS. Old man Cole, the original Samuel, must have been rolling in his grave while Robert Tucker, next to his friend Caleb Preston smiled down from Heaven.

The End

I hope you have enjoyed this story and I want to thank you for your support.

You may not realize, but book sales today are driven by reader reviews, your opinion counts. Please leave a review at this link:
http://www.amazon.com/dp/B00MTUQLH0

The market place used to be driven by the reviews of major publications, but today it is the opinion of every reader who leaves a review that makes a difference. I read all reviews and hope to improve my writing by understanding what the public wants. My writing is for the public and I want to know what was liked about the story, and what can be improved.

ABOUT THE AUTHOR

With over twenty years of horse ownership and Endurance riding to her credit, Kasey Riley (Kim) brings a wealth of knowledge to her novels. Her love of the trail, outdoors, and rural living give color and vibrancy to her books. This realism has drawn many readers to her novels. She strives to make readers see through the eyes of her characters and imagine themselves enmeshed in the plot along with them.

The fictional town of Riverview, Colorado is the setting for her stories. The town is full of characters, each with a story to tell or who may become either victim or villain. Small town, rural living brings them together and the rugged Colorado countryside creates the backdrop for the action.

Her first two novels are mysteries with romances building around them and the third is a romance, which uses suspense to draw the couple together as they strive to stay alive. She plans on each book being a stand-alone novel that can be read in any sequence without the reader missing details of the story. Her mind sees every news article as a possible story plot for the people in Riverview to endure and every trail ride as a possible setting for the next crime or mystery. Needless to say, she loves the alone time on the trail to work her way through the next plot and create new characters. When not writing or riding, she enjoys reading a wide variety of genre novels and sounding out new plots on her husband of 40+ years. Together, they care for a large assortment of animals on their 13 acre hobby farm in Southeastern Oklahoma.

Made in the USA
Columbia, SC
13 July 2022